To Marghe[rita]

REAP THE WIND

Lovely to meet you!

JOEL BURCAT

an imprint of Sunbury Press, Inc.
Mechanicsburg, PA USA

MILFORD HOUSE

an imprint of Sunbury Press, Inc.
Mechanicsburg, PA USA

NOTE: This is a work of fiction. Names, characters, places, and incidents either are the product of the author's imagination or are used fictitiously. While, as in all fiction, the literary perceptions and insights are shaped by experiences, any resemblance to actual persons, living or dead, events, or locales is entirely coincidental.

Copyright © 2024 by Joel Burcat.
Cover Copyright © 2024 by Sunbury Press, Inc.

Sunbury Press supports copyright. Copyright fuels creativity, encourages diverse voices, promotes free speech, and creates a vibrant culture. Thank you for buying an authorized edition of this book and for complying with copyright laws. Except for the quotation of short passages for the purpose of criticism and review, no part of this publication may be reproduced, scanned, or distributed in any form without permission. You are supporting writers and allowing Sunbury Press to continue to publish books for every reader. For information contact Sunbury Press, Inc., Subsidiary Rights Dept., PO Box 548, Boiling Springs, PA 17007 USA or legal@sunburypress.com.

For information about special discounts for bulk purchases, please contact Sunbury Press Orders Dept. at (855) 338-8359 or orders@sunburypress.com.

To request one of our authors for speaking engagements or book signings, please contact Sunbury Press Publicity Dept. at publicity@sunburypress.com.

FIRST MILFORD HOUSE PRESS EDITION: February 2024

Set in Adobe Garamond Pro | Interior design by Crystal Devine | Cover by Lawrence Knorr | Edited by Taylor Berger-Knorr.

Publisher's Cataloging-in-Publication Data
Names: Burcat, Joel, author.
Title: Reap the wind / Joel Burcat.
Description: First trade paperback edition. | Mechanicsburg, PA : Milford House Press, 2024.
Summary: REAP THE WIND is an action/adventure thriller in which three lawyers set out from Houston heading to Cincinnati in a rented Lincoln Town Car. They must drive across Texas and he Midwest in the midst of the worst hurricane of the century so Josh Goldberg can be with his girlfriend who is giving birth to their baby. They have to survive a hurricane, tornado, hailstorm, driving rain, and each other to get there.
Identifiers: ISBN : 978-1-934597-93-4 (paperback).
Subjects: FICTION / Action & Adventure | FICTION / Disaster | FICTION / Thrillers / Suspense | FICTION / Romance / Action & Adventure.

Product of the United States of America
0 1 1 2 3 5 8 13 21 34 55

For the Love of Books!

For Gail
The wind beneath my wings

BOOKS BY JOEL BURCAT

FICTION

Drink to Every Beast
(Mike Jacobs Environmental Legal Thriller, Book 1, 2019)

Amid Rage
(Mike Jacob Environmental Legal Thriller, Book 2, 2021)

Strange Fire
(Mike Jacobs Environmental Legal Thriller, Book 3, 2022)

NON-FICTION

Pennsylvania Environmental Law and Practice
(Pennsylvania Bar Institute Press, Co-Editor, 7 editions)

The Law of Oil and Gas in Pennsylvania
(Pennsylvania Bar Institute Press, Co-Editor, 2 editions)

"For they sow the wind and they reap the whirlwind. The standing grain has no seeds; It yields no grain. Should it yield, strangers would swallow it up."

—Hosea 8:7

"Everyone has a plan until they get punched in the mouth."

—Mike Tyson

Human-induced climate change is already affecting many weather and climate extremes in every region across the globe. Evidence of observed changes in extremes such as heatwaves, heavy precipitation, droughts, and tropical cyclones, and, in particular, their attribution to human influence, has strengthened since 2014.

—Climate Change 2021: The Physical Science Basis, Summary for Policymakers, Intergovernmental Panel on Climate Change (August 19, 2021)

PROLOGUE

MAJOR LOGAN

The rain rat-a-tat-tatted against the fuselage of the Weatherbird aircraft and sounded like an old World War II movie soundtrack the moment before the plane was shot from the sky. Major Stacy "Windy" Logan white knuckled the yoke of the Lockheed WC-130J Weatherbird to make sure it continued on course as they flew through the violent hurricane. She decelerated to 240 knots to reduce the furious shaking as the Hurricane Hunter made its way toward the eye of Tropical Depression 39, in the Eastern Atlantic Ocean, about five hundred miles west of the Cape Verde Islands. This was supposed to be a relatively small storm, odd for late November, but it was weirdly intense and had grown a lot larger since the briefing back at Lakeland.

Windy and her crew were dispatched on this mission because it was unusual for a tropical storm to be located this far east and so late in the hurricane season. The Weatherbird bounced through furious downdrafts. She took deep, cleansing breaths to maintain her calm demeanor, like she'd done fifteen years earlier when she gave birth to her only child, Maddy. That helped. A little.

The clouds were a malevolent mix of gray and black, punctuated with flashes of lightning. Rain fell up and sideways, pelting the fuselage like machine gun fire. The windshield wipers were useless. Visibility was negligible, from cloud to cloud; it was never better than five hundred feet. Thankfully, they were flying at 10,000 feet over the Atlantic. No one else was insane enough to be anywhere near them and nothing was rising up out of the ocean to bump into. Windy flew on instruments and guts. Her slim body was electrified; she lived for this.

Just a few minutes earlier, as they approached the storm, Windy chatted with her co-pilot, First Lieutenant Jasmine "Jazzy" Turner. "You know, I had the sex talk with Maddy a couple of years ago and we both hated every moment of it."

"You a brave woman." Jazzy smiled at her.

"The thing is, she had her first period last year and I noticed her body's been developing some curves, so just last week I had the birth control talk with her."

Jazzy shook her head. "Oh, boy. How'd that go?"

"After some eye-rolling, Maddy seemed unusually interested in what I was saying. She even agreed to an exam with a gynecologist." Both women shook their heads. "You know, I miss the Mommy's home! phase . . ."

An unexpected drop of fifty feet snapped them back to reality.

Windy glanced at her co-pilot. Jazzy was busy checking dials, gauges, and monitors on the instrument panel. The two women were alike in many respects, the most important being they loved flying into hurricanes. A small gold pendant around Jazzy's neck—two interlocking hearts—glinted in a flash of lightning. Jazzy's wife wore an identical one. Windy and her husband were among a small handful of guests when Jazzy married the love of her life. Jazzy felt it was best to keep the wedding low-key; prejudices ran deep among the older officers. She wanted to be in the left-hand seat one day.

Windy wiggled her eyebrows up and down at her co-pilot. "Pretty crazy flying today. Not too bad for an all-girl team. No?" She held out her fist and Jazzy bumped it, top down, then bottom up.

Before Jazzy could say anything, a bolt of lightning flashed about 2,500 feet starboard at one o'clock. The aircraft shook violently from the shock wave.

"Crap," Windy said. She spoke into her headset. "Thor, did that lightning do anything to our equipment?"

"Checking, Major."

While she awaited a reply from Master Sergeant Theodore "Thor" Johansen, who was stationed in the cargo compartment behind her, Windy did a quick check of the engines. Four Rolls-Royce turboprops. They were all good. She breathed a sigh of relief.

"We're okay, Major," said the sergeant. "Several monitors automatically reset, and one breaker flipped. Jackson brought it all back online in about five seconds. We're good to go."

Windy knew the sergeant well enough to know that, like all of them, he craved the adrenaline rush of flying into hurricanes. When he wasn't on a mission, the thunder-god spent all of his down-time running from one of his four kids' sports events to another.

"What's the barometric pressure?"

Thor didn't pause. "Nine hundred seventy-nine millibars."

Jazzy looked at Windy and raised her eyebrows. "That's right between a cat one and cat two 'cane," Jazzy said. "Right?"

"Yes, Lieutenant," said the sergeant.

"Have you ever seen any readings like that this far east? In November?"

"No, but let me get Mr. Spock on that." There was a moment of static.

Second Lieutenant Thomas "Mr. Spock" Yang was the nerdy kid who wanted to be an *aerial reconnaissance weather officer* when he grew up— civilians would simply call him a meteorologist. Over beers in the officer's club, he'd confessed to Windy that he'd enlisted in the Air Force because he wasn't just reporting on the weather; he was the weather.

"Yang here. You have a question for me, Lieutenant?"

"Yes, Mr. Spock. Thor says the barometric pressure we're measuring here is nine seventy-nine. Ain't that low for this kind of storm? I mean right here in the Eastern Atlantic, this time of year?"

Before Yang could respond, Windy looked at the junior officer and mouthed the word "isn't." She'd taken it upon herself to do everything she could to get her promoted, including washing out the West Virginia from the younger woman's vocabulary. Jazzy smiled at her.

"Actually, it dropped again," Yang said. "It's been dropping steadily since we hit the outer bands of the storm. It's now nine seventy-seven. You're correct, that's low for this time of year and way out here. This is where tropical cyclones are supposed to form, not where you're going to get major hurricanes. We should be seeing nothing more than a tropical disturbance, maybe a tropical depression."

Windy cut in, "What's the wind speed?"

"This bastard is up to 85 knots. That's cat two all the way."

"And the cause? Don't tell me it's sunspots or aliens."

"No, Major. We released a dropsonde into the ocean five minutes ago and it said the water temp averages 27 degrees Celsius, that's cyclone-forming temperature. This is crazy for November."

The aircraft shuddered and the nose dipped as it was slammed by a downdraft.

"Remember the Perfect Storm? Hurricane Isabel?" Mr. Spock said. "They were both cat two storms."

Windy did remember the Perfect Storm. It was 1991 and she was growing up in Boston. She was still a kid and that experience motivated her onto the long road that ended in the pilot's seat on the Weatherbird. She endured years of Air Force training and suffered bullshit jobs flying freight to the Mideast and too many handsy, asshole, sonofabitch senior officers in the O-Club until she finally won this seat. She was proud to be a pilot in the 53rd Weather Reconnaissance Squadron and smiled every time she pulled on her flight suit with her call sign, "Windy," stitched over her pocket.

"Mr. Spock, how often do they even get hurricanes this far east?" she asked.

"Never, Major. No. Check that. There were two small ones, really just tropical storms, earlier this year. Also, in 2015, Hurricane Fred."

"Fred?"

"Roger that, Major."

"Like, Fred? My husband?"

"Yes, Ma'am."

She allowed the nervous laughter from the entire crew on her headset to die down. "What's this one called . . . and don't tell me it's Stacy."

"Sorry Major, no name yet. If you want, I can make a recommendation."

Windy focused on flying through more turbulence. When they hit relative calm, she spoke into her headset. "Mr. Spock? What's the deal with all this hurricane activity now?"

"Well, NOAA, NASA, IPCC, even Defense, all say it's due to climate change. Global warming."

"Seriously?" she asked.

"Seriously."

"And you believe that?"

"Yes, Major. It's as serious as a heart attack," Yang replied.

Another bolt of lightning broke a mere 1,200 feet away dead ahead and interrupted the discussion. The aircraft shook violently, and alarms went off throughout the flight deck. Windy and Jazzy quickly went through another systems check to make sure no controls or instruments were lost. Windy checked the readouts from the four turboprop engines. They purred. She made a mental note to thank the chief master sergeant who oversaw engine maintenance at the base and buy a round of drinks for his crew.

Windy spoke again into her headset, "Thor, how did we do that time?"

"A few auto resets and more breakers flipped, Major," said the sergeant. "About a dozen this time. We're on it. Jackson and I are resetting everything now. Give me a minute." There was no chatter for over a dozen seconds. Then, the master sergeant was in her ear. "We're back. Everything's reset. Uh, Major, just FYI, it's pretty bumpy back here."

"Roger that. I'll slow it down a few knots. We need to make it to the eye of the storm, another ten minutes or so, and then we can turn this bird around. Drinks are on me when we get back to base." She paused briefly. "Tequila shots. Doubles."

"Hoo-ah. Roger that, Major."

"You know, you should never let your horse get in a place where you can't turn around," Jazzy said to Windy.

Windy rolled her eyes. "Is that another West Virginia-ism?"

Jazzy smiled. "Chuck Yeager himself said that to me."

At that moment, the Weatherbird hit another downdraft and dropped two hundred feet. Then, a tremendous gust of wind hit the plane head-on, causing it to buck. Another bolt of lightning flashed across the sky, this time striking the right wing of the Weatherbird.

The aircraft convulsed and the bolt illuminated the cockpit like a glimpse into the sun. An electric charge glowed as it coursed across the skin of the airplane. Almost all of the instruments flickered off, then came back on a moment later, automatically resetting. Alarms throughout the cockpit sounded multiple warnings. A smell, burning oil, reached Windy's nostrils. She could taste it. The pilots immediately began another systems check.

Suddenly, the Weatherbird began yawing to starboard and a sound erupted that made Windy's skin crawl. Warning lights and loud, whooping sirens alerted the pilot they'd lost both starboard engines that were near where the lightning struck.

Windy looked to her right and was sickened to see the propellers barely spinning. The Weatherbird began turning in the direction of the comatose engines, buffeted by the strong winds, downdrafts, and updrafts.

Windy's training went into overdrive, and she pushed on the rudder hard to compensate for the lost engines, pulled the nose up, and simultaneously powered back the two port engines. Her first task was to slow the aircraft to keep it from flipping over.

She struggled to steer the plane, but it was nearly impossible to regain control in the tempestuous storm with her starboard engines out. Buffeted by the high winds, she could not maintain altitude or direction, and the plane was rocked.

As they descended through the hurricane, the altimeter audibly announced the elevation above sea level, in this case the Atlantic Ocean itself. Masculine, terse, and demanding: "Seven thousand feet."

Windy heard the voice of her first flight instructor back when she was sixteen years old: *Stacy, fly the damn plane.* She wiggled momentarily in her seat—Fred said it was her tell when she got excited about something—which she often felt when flying into the mouth of a storm. Her adrenaline pushed her hair on end. *I can do this! Figure it out.*

Her brain and hands were in overdrive as she worked to recover control of the aircraft, but the wind and gravity fought back. As the plane lost altitude, she continued trying to keep the nose up, giving the Weatherbird full rudder to compensate for the loss of her two starboard engines. She moved like the drummer in a rock band playing a complicated percussion arrangement that required her to simultaneously use all of her limbs to play all of her drums and cymbals together. The hurricane provided the dissonant tune. She adjusted the rudders, flaps, stabilizers, ailerons, and anything else on her mental checklist in an effort to straighten out and keep this sick bird flying.

All the while they were buffeted by the cat two hurricanes with no name. She'd never faced anything like this in her twenty years as a pilot.

The disembodied voice interrupted her concentration. "Six thousand feet."

As Windy focused on controlling the aircraft, she knew that her co-pilot's job was restarting the engines. She glanced at Jazzy and could see her frenetic activity at the instrument panel and hear the sickly coughing from the two big Rolls Royce engines on her right. Jazzy's teeth were clenched and bared, sweat poured down the side of her face.

Windy was too busy flying the plane to help. She couldn't assist her co-pilot, but said, "Dammit, Jazz, get those freakin' engines started."

"Working on it, Windy."

"Five thousand feet."

Normally, she could fly the plane without the two engines. She'd trained for that, but that was a white-knuckle ordeal in good weather. As the Weatherbird descended toward the stormy North Atlantic Ocean, in the middle of a crazy cat two hurricane, it would take everything within her, good luck, and the grace of God to get back to an airfield.

In the back of Windy's mind, the same words echoed over and over: *Fly the damn plane, fly the damn plane* . . . No matter what she did, however, she couldn't regain full control of the airplane in this storm without the starboard engines. The smell of burnt oil seeped into her nostrils, her pores.

"Come on, Jazzy. Start 'em up girl." She heard herself say. *Dear God, help her do it.* In this wild storm, that was their only salvation.

"Four thousand feet."

The smell of vomit from the cargo compartment wafted into the flight deck. The Weatherbird pitched through the hurricane toward an unpleasant rendezvous with the raging ocean.

The starboard engines continued sputtering, issuing rheumy coughs like a dying man gasping his last breaths. It was like trying to start a car engine in the winter that just won't turn over. They would catch briefly, then die again. The sound tormented Windy.

"Come on you bastards," Jazzy said.

Suddenly, the Weatherbird hit a microburst. This nightmare scenario caused the plane to drop precipitously, nearly one thousand feet, before Windy regained a semblance of control. The plane continued to descend.

"Three thousand feet."

When they hit three thousand feet, Jazzy hit the automated mayday switch. It instantaneously broadcasted a continuous distress call including coordinates to an Air Force communications satellite located twenty-two miles overhead. The mayday call would be relayed to Air Force command, and search and rescue jets would be scrambled to find them.

At twenty-five hundred feet, they broke through the cloud ceiling and Windy could see the ocean, gray and tempestuous, enraged and wrathful, with swells the height of skyscrapers, and nothing but rough water for hundreds of miles around. Not exactly ideal for a water landing. This would not be Captain Sully and his U.S. Airways Airbus on the Hudson.

The Navy or Coast Guard would dispatch a ship to retrieve them.

If there was anything left to pick up.

CHAPTER 1

JOSH

Have you ever done something that in your guts and head you know is wrong, but you just can't get out of it? You're too locked in, too far down the road. For a long time—and by long, I mean almost eight years—I'd been telling myself I was doing the wrong thing. Like an astronaut ten seconds from blast off who begins to wonder if he's made the right career choice.

I pondered this as I sat in the back of the small auditorium in Houston's Four Seasons Hotel and pretended to pay attention to the speaker, but I was actually flipping through emails on my iPhone. I'd positioned my phone behind the name tag tented in front of me—

Josh Goldberg, Esq.
Bartram, Wynne & Darby

—and piled up the day's worth of handouts to my left. No one was on my right as I was sitting closest to the humongous plate glass window in the last row. I was separated from the raging tempest outside by an inch of tempered glass, but the roar of the wind and pounding of the rain seeped through the glass and walls. At times intense and a moment later slightly less so. Continuous.

Hey hon, how are you feeling

> Not too bad, babe. I made it to Nordstrom's, but I'm so fat and swollen I didn't want to buy anything. I can't wait for this pregnancy to be over. LOL. I mean I can't wait to have our baby. How's the conference?
>
> BORING! I'm thinking about sneaking into our room and cuddling with you.
>
> Well, I've been back for 30 minutes. Come on down if you want to "cuddle"
>
> As soon as I can sneak away—

I never did finish the text. Diane Scanlon sat down in the empty seat next to me and lifted my phone from my hands. She looked at it the way a curious monkey might look at a banana. Diane, in fact, was our department's 2,000-pound gorilla—all 105 pounds of her. She was ten years older than me, with short blonde hair in a kind of a grown-up pixie hairdo, blue eyes, a perfect little nose, and the small boobs and frame of a runner. That was appropriate since she found the time to run in four or five marathons every year. And bill over 2,000 hours a year. And have a three-million-dollar book of business. And be one of our top lawyers. And be chair of our Environmental and Land Development Department. And be on the board of the Philadelphia Ballet. And be vice president of Philly Lawyers Helping the Homeless. You either loved her or despised her. Me? It depended on the day. I wasn't a big fan.

Diane was my boss, and a large part of my job was to be sure I never crossed her, always took excellent care of our clients, and billed a solid 2,000 hours a year unless I had a damn good reason not to. There were very few acceptable reasons to short the time-sheet gods.

She wore a blue tailored suit, with slacks and a white silk blouse—the kind of business outfit a successful woman bought at Neiman Marcus. Also, she wore a tiny gold and diamond pendant around her neck and gold ball earrings.

Diane leaned next to my ear and put her hand on top of my arm which she gripped firmly. "Ah told you no phones, Josh. If y'all can't pay attention to the boring speaker, you have to *pretend* to pay attention. We have people here from the biggest companies in Houston and we paid a shit-ton of money for this event. The least we can do is pretend we're enjoying it."

"Sorry, I was checking on Keisha," I said quietly. "This pregnancy has really taken something out of her. She seems to have morning sickness all day."

Diane looked at the speaker. The PowerPoint slide currently on the screen displayed a large graph. He was offering his predictions of the price of natural gas over the next ten years. In porno movies they would call this "the money shot."

She moved her mouth close to my ear. Intimately close, her hair brushed my face. She wore a subtle scent, fragrant and unforgettable. "You kids—" she rubbed the top of my hand, and her breath tickled my ear, making the hair on the back of my neck stand on end, "Ah, know ah should've talked to y'all sooner about birth control."

She patted my hand a couple of times, then backed away from me and smiled. I suppose she intended the smile to be ironic, maybe knowing, perhaps even friendly. I was sure it was the same smile a shark makes when it greets a baby seal. In this day and age, I wondered whether her comment was even appropriate. How would a junior female associate feel if a big shot male partner suggested to her that she not get pregnant? I knew the answer without dwelling on it.

Diane tapped something on my phone, smiled again, pleasantly this time, and handed it back to me. Then, like a schoolteacher or your mom, she patted me on my shoulder and pointed to the front of the room.

I looked at the screen on my phone. There was no doubt she'd read Keisha's and my texts. Before she handed back my phone she texted:

Hey Keisha, this is Diane. Sorry but I need to keep your boy here for another hour. I can let him go at 4 P.M., but he has to be back by 5 for cocktails. Y'all are welcome to join. Best, Diane

I waited until Diane was patrolling the other side of the auditorium and quickly texted:

Busted

I guess I'll see you at 4

Keisha replied.

I slipped my phone into my suit coat and looked at the front of the room. The moderator for this program was Geoff Roberts. We were in the same department, although Geoff was a real estate lawyer and I was an environmental lawyer. Geoff and I were like a couple of soldiers who found themselves in a muddy trench together. We were both good friends and he was a mentor of sorts to me. He had the dubious honor of being a senior associate with the firm. Being a senior associate meant he had up to three years to become a partner. Or counsel. Or leave. This was the end of his third year as senior associate. Tick-tock.

Generally speaking, partnership was dangled in front of the associates in the way a fish was dangled in front of a cartoon cat running on a treadmill on the old Saturday morning TV shows. Always just out of reach. Geoff was two years and eleven months into those three years at Bartram, Wynne. His time was nearly up.

Over beers and darts after work, we'd speculated on whether he would make partner. He said Diane was hot and cold toward him; he couldn't get a good read on her. One day she seemed to be in love with him. The next, she'd happily stick a knife in his guts. Although most of the partners liked him and his work, one partner, Kelly Larson, despised him. At some point in the last nine years, Geoff failed to follow orders and Larson never forgave him for his high crime. Geoff had been angry and miserable about this for some time, but there was nothing he could do about it. The issue was over the way Geoff handled a real estate matter, which was different from the way Larson wanted it handled. Geoff's way worked and was cheaper for the client, but Larson was pissed off and he never forgave or forgot.

I'd once been told by a senior partner that making partner at our law firm was a "vicious meritocracy." Bullshit. It was more like rushing a fraternity. Even today. One blackball and you were screwed. If one of the big guys didn't like you, you had to hope that partner either retired or had a stroke. That's the way it is. I don't expect anyone to shed a tear for us. Associates in big law firms are overpaid crybabies. Truth.

At thirty-two, I was a seventh-year associate. Far from the lowest of the low anymore, but maybe one to three to years away from a partnership. If I played my cards right, always smiled when Diane talked to me, never said "no" to a partner, continued billing 2,000 hours a year, and never screwed up.

You may be wondering why a bunch of Philadelphia lawyers were giving a seminar in Houston? That was Diane's idea. Every Philly law firm does seminars for clients at some lux hotel in Center City. There's always a fancy lunch and probably an awesome dinner at one of Philly's many fine restaurants. It's a marketing thing. I was there when Diane came up with the Houston idea at a departmental meeting. She said she wanted the firm to sponsor a seminar on Pennsylvania oil and gas law. We all nodded politely. Oil and gas law is a big deal in Pennsylvania and Philadelphia Lawyers all have sharp elbows trying to win the biggest and best clients. Our managing partner happened to be present and was beginning to shake his head "no." Then Diane smiled wickedly and said, "in Houston." Genius.

The speaker was Dr. Somebody, a professor of petroleum economics from Rice University's business school. We got him to speak at this program because he was prominent, well-known to the Houston business community, and cheap. We only paid him an honorarium of $1,500 for his time and nothing for travel or accommodations since he was a local. I suspected he'd given this lecture a dozen times. If I'd been paying attention, his talk might have even been interesting.

Professor Somebody was talking about the price of Pennsylvania's Marcellus shale gas over the next ten years. He predicted the price "most likely" would go up, which was a good thing because for the past decade prices were in the toilet. I watched the audience made up mostly of oil and gas industry people. Many were not paying attention, but for the ones who were, it was like watching a group of alcoholics being told free whiskey was about to be served. I swear some of them were salivating.

Several of our guests were either half paying attention, tapping on their cell phones, or whispering to each other. These students were our esteemed guests, so Diane didn't hassle them. A few wore suits or dresses, but most were dressed casually. All of them came from top companies in the Houston area. Depending upon who's bragging, Houston has either the second or third largest number of corporate HQs in America. Many were clients from in-house law departments, and we provided them with free continuing legal education, CLE, credits for attending our program. They also got a great lunch at the Four Seasons, and all were invited to one of the seven small dinner parties we hosted at Houston's finest restaurants later that evening. In exchange, we got face time with some clients and, as Diane liked to call them, *future clients*. It was a win-win situation.

The only ones who looked super-engaged were the other members of my firm who had all been warned by Diane to look like, and I quote, "every speaker is about to make you cum." We were told to bring our A-game with everyone we met while we were in Houston.

"And therefore, based upon my projections, the price of natural gas in Pennsylvania, per mcf, should go up by a factor of three over the next ten years." He smiled broadly. The next slide read, "Q & A." No one did anything until Diane began clapping. Then, the members of my firm began clapping madly, like freakin' Drake himself had performed on the stage just for us, and a few of the guests clapped too. The professor beamed.

"Any questions?" he asked.

Except for the sound of leaves slapping against the large plate glass window, the room was silent. Finally, wearing her biggest smile, Diane asked, "Professor, what impact will the new west to east pipelines have on the price of oil," pronouncing it *awl* like she'd grown up in West Texas, "and natural gas?"

"A very perceptive question, Ms. Scanlan." The professor smiled warmly at her. It was sunny enough that it made me wonder about the two of them. Diane had a reputation. "That will have a huge impact on the ability to get natural gas to market via pipelines to Philly, New York, New England, LNG terminals and the like. Drilling and pipelines are like a good marriage, interdependent, working together . . ."

***

I plastered on my most interested face but zoned out. My thoughts drifted to the night Keisha and I told my parents we were going to move in together, have a baby, and maybe get married, not necessarily in that order. My brother Ben and his boyfriend were at the restaurant with us, and they were thrilled. The guys shared smiles, handshakes, and hugs with us.

Mom and Dad were sitting next to each other, probably for the first time in years since their divorce, and looked like they'd just been told everyone they loved was on a bus that went over a cliff. They said nothing. Their faces were frozen. It looked like they were trying not to betray their feelings. I mean, they did not say a word until my mom grabbed a waiter and asked if there was more bread.

Finally, I said, "Well, what do you think?"

"What do you mean, what do I think?" said Dad. "I'm sure that girl is nice and a good person." Keisha was twenty-nine years old at the time, sitting right next to me, and my parents had known her for almost a year. "Let's talk this through later."

Keisha's expression seemed neutral, but I could see her eyes had watered. I knew her well enough to know that she was furious. Somehow she held her tongue.

"We'll talk about it now, or we're leaving," I said. I was pissed. Later, Ben told me my face was bright red. "I love Keisha and she loves me. That's all that matters."

"But, she's . . ." I watched my father search for the right word. "African American. Not even Jewish."

"Let's put the Jewish thing away right now," I said. "We were never a member of any temple except for the three months before our bar mitzvahs. We observe nothing except Chanukkah. Don't Jewish me."

"Dear, dear." My mother was desperate to de-escalate the discussion. "We're not prejudiced, it's just, just, what about the children?"

I actually closed my eyes and counted. When I got to ten, I said, "Assuming we even have children, don't worry, we won't bring them by to offend you. You'll never see them."

"No, seriously, no!" My mother was in an emotional tailspin. "We just need a little time to get used to the idea. We want grandchildren. *I* can't wait for grandchildren." She looked at my brother and his boyfriend. "It's just they'll be . . ."

"*Shvartzas*," my dad said mostly under his breath. "I'm sorry to have to say that. It's the truth. That's what our grandchildren will be. That's how the world will view them."

"No!" My mother said. People near our table turned and looked.

In all of the years I can remember, even during the turbulent years leading up to their divorce, I never once saw my mother hit my father or my father hit my mother. Until then. My mother's hand wheeled back and whipped forward. It was an epic sucker punch, landing solidly on my father's face in an unforgettable slap. The crack reverberated around the restaurant, stopping conversations. "Don't you ever utter that word again! Do you hear me? I never want to hear that word. It's awful. We don't talk that way. I'll love those little babies, no matter what."

As a teenager, my family life was chaotic, with my mother and father constantly arguing, and my father frequently staying out late or not coming home. It was the reason I had serious doubts about marriage. Nevertheless, I was unprepared for his statement. Sometimes you have a moment of crystal-clear clarity when your parents disappoint you in a way that colors everything they've ever said or done and everything they'll ever say or do again in the future. This was it.

Putting aside the family issues, I'd known my parents to be reasonably charitable, progressive Democrats. Dad, in particular, had a mouth on him and would argue with friends taking the farthest left, most progressive side. At that moment, I suddenly realized my dad was a hypocrite, a racist asshole. I stood up and Keisha and I left.

I didn't talk with my parents for a month. Ben called the next day and checked in every few days or so. First, he called to tell me how glad he was that I took the heat off him. The whole gay thing. Coming out wasn't easy for him and my parents still didn't understand it. Actually, Ben and I laughed long and hard over that as only close brothers can do. After about a month, Ben called and invited Keisha and me to my mother's condo in Lower Merion. He was able to broker a truce over lox and bagels.

The funny thing was, Keisha's parents gave us a similar reception. From her dad, too. His comments were along the lines of disapproving of a "white boy" marrying his Black daughter. Keisha's mother called me the next day to apologize and said that her husband, my potential father-in-law, felt awful about his outburst. He was taken by surprise and didn't mean what he said. She handed him the phone and he mumbled an apology. I imagined Keisha's mother holding a gun to his head.

Parents. When we decided to have kids, we vowed never to be like ours. The whole business further convinced me that marriage was a terrible thing. It was much better to be together as long as you were in love and no longer than that.

* * *

". . . We have to balance the improved ability to get the gas to market against the efforts by some wrong-headed, so-called liberal politicians to prohibit new construction from using natural gas. My projections took that into consideration. I see overall demand going up, so the new pipelines are baked into my calculations."

But, Professor, if you are going to limit greenhouse gasses, doesn't it make sense to prohibit new construction from using natural gas, too? Otherwise, there's no limit to the increasing demand for natural gas. It's not a liberal or conservative issue. It's a question of human survival. This was the question I thought, but the survival mechanism inside my brain didn't let me ask. I'm so pathetic.

Outside, the rain pelted the windows and lightning rumbled close by. If I said the wind was howling, that would be an understatement. It didn't seem possible, but the roar of the wind was even louder than before, sounding now like a jet engine taking off. The afternoon sky was a weird mix of gray and brown. Dark. Early that morning before I headed off to the conference, the weatherman said this was going to be a tropical storm, not a hurricane, and that it would clear up by the evening as the storm moved toward Mexico. At that point, I wasn't sure.

I waited to see if there were any more questions, then raised my hand. I knew my question might raise a few eyebrows, but I was genuinely curious. "Professor, are you at all concerned that the IPCC, EPA, FEMA, and NASA have been clamoring for climate change regulations and controls for some time? It looks likely that the U.S. will impose some kind of regulation on methane, maybe cap and trade, maybe something else, in the next year or two. Won't those regulations diminish the demand for natural gas and force the price down?"

The professor smiled again. This time it was the smile reserved for the village idiot. *Moi*. I glanced at Diane who was across the room. She put her hand over her eyes and shook her head. I looked around the room. There were lawyers from a dozen oil and gas companies, pipeline companies, and other companies that intensively used the land. Their expressions ranged from shock to downright glee.

"Now you're getting into politics, but we believe climate change regulations will have no more than a negligible impact on price. If I had to guess—" it occurred to me that *now* he was guessing—"if we have a Republican administration in D.C., the price of natural gas will rise even more quickly than I projected. The price will still go up under a *Democrat* administration too, but maybe a bit more slowly." He looked around the room for another question.

I recalled another speaker at a different program. He'd said, "There are no stupid questions . . . just stupid people." Ta da. I should have taken a bow. Thank you, thank you.

Geoff sat forward and looked at his watch. "Well, that was really interesting, but we're out of time, so I have to cut off questions. We're going to take a ten-minute break so you can look at your phones," he made a stage wink to the audience that would've made W.C. Fields proud. "Let's take a bio-break, then grab a cold drink and one of those outrageous cookies they just baked for us . . ."

At that moment, a thick clump of leaves and small branches splattered against the window with a loud bang. Then, a gray ball crashed into the center of the glass. Claws sprang from the ball and scratched the glass for a grip. A gray squirrel. Not the flying kind, but the regular neighborhood type. He was soaked and you could see his heart pounding through his white underbelly. Shit. That dude must have flown about three hundred feet in the air to reach the twenty-eighth floor. Slowly, he slid down the window, his claws leaving scratches in the glass. Finally, he tumbled to the bottom of the window onto a narrow ledge and huddled in a corner of the sill. Shivering.

CHAPTER 2

KEISHA

Keisha Jones propped herself up in the king-size bed in the luxurious hotel room on the twelfth floor of the Four Seasons Hotel and watched the local news. She nibbled on some multi-grain crackers—*hippie crackers*, she thought—and sipped at a ginger ale from the mini-fridge. Surprisingly, the crackers were tasteless and stale, not what you'd expect for twelve dollars a tiny bag at the Four Seasons. The baby, they still didn't know if it was a girl or boy but Keisha always referred to the baby as *she*, was kicking gentle thumps as she did from time to time. Rain pummeled the window. In the distance she could hear lightning.

On the screen, a weatherman stood in the driving rain—of course—reporting on the storm. He seemed to be bracing himself whenever there was a burst of wind. His ball cap sailed off his head a few moments earlier revealing a very white patch of scalp. He was drenched.

A tag at the bottom of the screen read *Stan the Weatherman reporting live from Galveston*. The background was a gray, storm-tossed Galveston Bay with huge whitecaps breaking over a pier. The rain pelted the ground in great sheets.

"At this point, Bill, all we're seeing in the Houston area is an outer band of this unusual November storm. Get this, the National Weather Service has run out of names and is well into Greek letters of the alphabet. So, this one is being called *Tropical Storm Epsilon*. NWS is not yet calling it a hurricane. The storm seemed to lose its punch over the Caribbean and technically it's just a huge tropical storm with sixty-five mile per hour sustained winds."

At that moment, a tree branch twisted in the air ten feet behind him. It was as long as Stan the Weatherman was tall. The branch flew off-screen, but apparently circled back and returned seconds later, sailing past the weatherman's head. The main trunk missed him by inches, but some of the branches scraped the back of his head. He lurched forward. Any closer and he would have been a permanent star on the weather bloopers show—*Tree Impaling Weatherman's Skull.*

Stan ran his hand along the back of his head. "Wow, that was friggin' close." He paused for a long moment, looking at his hand. A stop sign sailed by in a huge gust of wind. "I'm going to move closer to that parking deck you're under, Harry," he said to his cameraman. Stan moved toward the cameraman who likewise stepped back. "Like I was saying, this is still a tropical storm, however predictions are that this will ramp up to a category one hurricane, maybe category two." He ran his hand over the back of his head again and seemed distracted for a moment as he looked at his hand. "The European model says it's going to hit Houston dead-on sometime tonight or tomorrow. The American model says it will largely miss Houston and make landfall at the Yucatan Peninsula in Mexico. Guess which one I'm rooting for? If the European model is right, it will move up the middle of the country all the way to New England. Right now, though, all we're seeing are the outer bands of the storm. In the coming hours, we'll have times of little or no rain and wind, but by tomorrow, if you believe the European model, it will hit us dead-on."

"Wow, that looks intense," said a female member of the anchor team, safely bunkered away in the studio in Houston. "Has the Weather Service given any reason for this late storm?"

A trickle of blood wormed its way down Stan's neck, then began soaking his white golf-shirt collar. "The NWS says intense storms like these are caused by climate change, if you can believe that. I listen to a wide variety of sources and one podcast says it's just good ol' Mother Nature having fun with us. They say climate change, if it even exists, has nothing to do with this." Stan managed a big folksy smile. "Take your pick folks," he held up his mic and his free hand, palm up, exposing a handful of blood. He made the motion like he was weighing something in both. "Your call." Bright weatherman smile.

"Thanks, Stan, you be safe out there," said Bill, the male member of the anchor team.

"I'm a tough old weatherman, Bill. I love this kind of stuff. Throwing it back to Bill and Linda at the station."

The image changed to the studio. A good-looking, overly tanned, middle-aged man with blown silvery hair wearing a dark blue suit and lavender necktie, obviously Bill, sat next to an attractive woman, Linda. She looked like an aging beauty queen, with blonde hair, who wore a bright red dress. Both were exquisitely coiffed. Laptops sat in front of them which appeared to be decorations for the set, not something to be used. Their eyes never moved from the teleprompters attached to the cameras.

"Thanks to Stan the Weatherman," said Linda. "You stay safe out there, friend. Tropical Storm Epsilon is showing us her teeth. According to the NWS, if you believe the European Model, the current arm of the storm will subside in the next hour or so and we'll have calm for a few hours, until we get the next blast, probably late tonight or early tomorrow."

The image flickered back to Stan the Weatherman, who had moved into the parking garage, but was drenched. His shirt collar was red, and blood was running down his neck. Stan's mic was still hot. "Fuck it, Harry, you have to get me to a goddamn hospital . . ." The mic and live stream were cut.

In Stan's place was stock footage of an Air Force Hurricane Hunter WC-130. "In other news, the Air Force is reporting that it has lost contact with one of its fabled Weather Hunter WC-130's," said Bill in his most solemn voice. "Yesterday, the Weather Hunter and its crew of five airmen were taking readings inside the outer portions of Tropical Storm Epsilon in the North Atlantic, when it reported trouble. It's not known whether the plane crashed or managed a landing somewhere. The Air Force and Navy have been scouring a 2,500 square mile patch of the North Atlantic Ocean since the mayday message was received."

"Wow. Those Hurricane Hunters are brave souls. I'm praying on them," Linda said, going off script and getting twangy.

"The bravest, uh, I'm praying on them, too," said Bill, awkwardly following her lead as he bowed his head.

The image changed again to stock footage of a huge concert in a football stadium. Linda's face brightened and her anchor-voice, carefully calculated to have an anchor-person's neutral accent, suddenly regained her El Campo, Texas roots. "In other news, the Houston Livestock Show and Rodeo," *ro-day-oh*, "announced that Tim McGraw and Faith Hill will headline next year's Houston Rodeo . . ."

Keisha turned the volume off and looked again out the window at the sheets of rain splashing against it. She propped her laptop on her huge belly and found TripAdvisor. She searched for flights from Houston to Philadelphia, leaving after 7 P.M. She knew that Josh was stuck in Houston, but she wanted to be back in Philly with her mother, her obstetrician, and her midwife, just in case.

Keisha was not due for another six weeks, but she didn't want to take any chances. She was feeling fine but had no desire to be stuck in Houston in a hurricane in her eighth month of pregnancy. The plan to pop down to Houston toward the end of her pregnancy for a baby-moon and stay in a luxury hotel on the firm's dime, then return a few days later, sounded like a great idea months earlier, but now seemed crazy.

She didn't really want to abandon Josh, but knew he had to stay. He was going to be busy with clients at a dinner party that night and then was speaking at the program the next morning. He was stuck; handcuffed—November was just weeks away from partnership, salary, and end-of-year bonus decisions. If this thing really did turn into a hurricane, they could be marooned in Houston for days.

A day or two apart might be good for us. We need the break. I need the break. I love Josh, he's a good man, but sometimes I feel suffocated. I just need a little me-time. It would be nice to travel together to Philly, but I'm a big girl and can handle that. I'd really like to be back in our little house on Wharton Street in South Philly.

She looked out the window and thought about the endless discussions with Josh about whether to have kids. They both wanted them, but events were arguing against bringing children into the world. There was the whole race thing. Keisha had lost a distant cousin in a cop killing—her cousin was the cop. She and Josh marched at BLM protests, but that seemed like it was pointless; the violence never ended. It was dangerous to be a Black person in this world and she feared bringing a child into it. Still, over the years, she warmed to the idea of having a baby, Josh's baby. He was such a good man, so loving, so open-minded; he'd be a great father. No matter what, he'd always be there.

She was ambivalent about marriage; they both were. His parents, their ugly divorce. She got it. Keisha wanted to be married, but it just didn't seem to be important right now. She and Josh had a solid enough relationship and that was what mattered.

Two months after she stopped taking birth control pills, she'd taken her temperature in the morning and saw she was ovulating. She never forgot the look on Josh's face when he climbed on top of her that night.

"You sure about this?" he said with a huge grin. She didn't say a word, but put her hands on his butt, pulled his hips toward hers, and sealed her lips against his. Two weeks later, the pregnancy test confirmed what she'd known the moment they laid gasping in bed holding hands, side by side, when they were finished.

She returned to her flight options and found one at 7:35 P.M. She had to switch planes in Nashville, but would be in Philly by 1 A.M. There were still a few seats available. Just then, the door opened and Josh entered the room, a smile on his face. He threw his jacket on a chair and kicked off his shoes. He flopped onto the bed and nestled close to her. He kissed the silly tattoo on her bare ankle, the one with her nickname that she and her whole sorority had gotten at 1 A.M. after a night of serious partying, then he snuggled up to her until he was under her arm.

Keisha loved his smell. He didn't overuse aftershave or cologne, but she could still smell a lingering scent from this morning, plus his usual odor, warm and inviting. He smiled at her and looked so hopeful.

"We only have forty-five minutes, hon, anything you'd really like to do right now? I mean immediately? That *cuddling* thing we texted about, maybe?" He kissed her cheek and gently ran his hand along the side of her belly.

His intentions were obvious. Her obstetrician said there was nothing wrong with it and normally, she was up for it. Instead, she said, "Actually, babe, we have to talk."

CHAPTER 3

JOSH

The rains had paused briefly, however, the street in front of the Four Seasons was still wet. The hotel's maintenance workers were wasting no time sweeping up branches and leaves from the entrance plaza. Houston's city lights illuminated the low clouds which rolled quickly to the north in the early evening sky. At least the winds were now light. Thunder rumbled in the distance. It reminded me of the storm scene at the beginning of *The Wizard of Oz*.

Keisha and I stood under the large awning of the hotel. I'd already tipped the bellman, so we stood next to the limo, ignoring the swirl of activity around us and the leaves whipping by. I hugged her as tightly as her basketball belly would allow.

"I feel like a jerk not going with you," I said.

"You're not a jerk, you're an associate at a big law firm," she said smiling.

"Isn't that the same thing?"

She kissed me warmly, enough to turn heads on Lamar Street. Obviously neither of us cared. Besides, we didn't live in Houston. Let them talk.

"I have to admit, I'm a little scared about this trip," Keisha said. "I Googled around, and it looks like I'm going to be just ahead of the storm. If that European model is correct, it could hit Houston in a couple of hours. One of the websites I found actually talks about travel conditions *en route*. They predicted a bumpy ride the whole way home. The first thing I'm going to do when I get to my seat is pull out the air sickness bag."

We paused while a red Houston Fire Department High Water Rescue truck screamed down Lamar Street. It went two blocks then turned the corner.

"Are you sure you don't want to wait it out here with me? It's not like Houston is some hick town. They have pretty good hospitals here. I'd rather you were lounging by the indoor pool or snuggling with me in our bed than bumping around at 30,000 feet."

She kissed me again. "I've already taken off more days than the principal is happy about. I really need to be back in school by Monday. If that hurricane hits, it's entirely possible you'll be stuck here all weekend and not get home till Monday or Tuesday. Also, you know me, I'll want my own doctor and midwife if the baby comes early. Don't worry about me. I'm sure I'll be okay."

Just then, lightning lit up the sky. It wasn't too close, but it illuminated the low-hanging clouds. I counted off ten seconds before I heard the roll of thunder. The lightning was two miles away.

I pulled her closer. "I want you to text me every step of the way. Just before takeoff, after you land in Nashville, and when you get to Philly."

"What are you, my mom?"

"No, just your guilt-ridden fiancé. It'll make me feel better knowing that you're a step closer to home."

"I'm sure I'll be fine," she said. "You'll be home Friday night. We'll be okay."

The stretch black Cadillac limo idled quietly near us. Abdul Mohammed, the owner of At Your Service Limos, stood by the door, holding it open for Keisha. He wore a blue blazer over casual clothes and was busy working his phone. I'd met Abdul on my first trip to Houston. I was waiting for my luggage, and he approached me at the luggage carousel and asked if I needed a ride into town. He said that the person he was waiting for never showed up and he was driving back to Houston anyway. He promised a great rate, fifty bucks, which was about the same as a taxi. It was a comfortable ride in a very clean car, and I tipped him twenty bucks. He gave me his card and asked me to call him whenever I was coming to town. I did.

I love guys like Abdul. He got to this country from Jordan ten years ago and is proud of his heritage. We talk about Jordan and Israel often when he's taking me around. They are civil conversations. Here's a man who came to this country with very little in his pockets and drove someone else's limo fourteen hours a day. Now he owns a thriving business with a dozen drivers. How American is that? He loves America.

I helped Keisha get into the car and leaned over to give her a kiss on the cheek. Abdul gently closed the door, and I paid in advance, giving him a $50 tip. He took the tip so discreetly; he wouldn't even know I over-tipped until he got home. "You take good care of my woman, okay?"

"Ms. Keisha is in good hands, Mr. Josh, I'll have her at the terminal in forty minutes, maybe less, depending on traffic. I'll help her as far as I can into the terminal. You can count on me."

I knew I could. I shook his hand. On one of our many rides, he told me he and his wife had been trying to have a baby for years. Unsuccessfully. We continued this discussion every several months. He was a friend, of sorts, and I trusted him implicitly. I noticed he discreetly glanced at Keisha's belly, and I felt badly for him.

Abdul waited for a break in the traffic and pulled the long, black car onto Lamar Street. I waved to Keisha.

When I turned around, Geoff Roberts was standing behind me. "Is Keisha bailing, bro?" he said, watching the limo as it disappeared in the traffic. He was wearing the same suit he'd worn all day at the conference. So was I, although I didn't put my necktie back on after I visited Keisha in our room. Geoff is a seriously good-looking dude. He has that whole Heisman Trophy-star-running-back thing going on. Think Regé-Jean Page from Bridgerton, only more pumped. Also, he's easily six-foot-two. I've seen women, and men, hit on him while we sat at a bar. Me? Not so much. If Adam Driver and Jonah Hill had a baby, I'd look like that.

"Well, she's eight months pregnant and wants to be home, I can't blame her. I'm hoping we'll be able to leave tomorrow, but who knows?"

"There are worse things than getting stuck at the Four Seasons Hotel for a few days." Geoff and his wife, Imani, have five children. Five. Who does that anymore? They love kids. He told me they actually were considering adopting. I couldn't blame him if he needed a break for a few days, and not surprisingly, he made sure his mother-in-law would stay at his home to help Imani with the kids.

"Is Diane still mad at me?" I asked.

"You mean because you ignored general order number one and ditched the cocktail hour? Or because you asked that lame question about climate change having an impact on the price of natural gas?"

"Exactly."

"I don't know if she's mad; she doesn't share with me," Geoff said. "But it did look like she was counting heads at the cocktail party. We lost quite a few guests who probably wanted to avoid the storm rather than eat jumbo shrimp and drink Glenlivet with us."

"Well, at least she won't be having dinner with our group. We can relax a bit."

Geoff grinned at me. "Maybe you forgot general order number two? Bring your A-game. I'm not sure we're allowed to relax."

"Doesn't mean I can't have a cocktail and enjoy myself. Are you ready to head to Luke & Francesco's?" I asked. "We should be on time."

"I don't know if you checked your emails," he said, "but Madeline sent us an email a few minutes ago saying two of our guests have canceled. I guess the opportunity of having a two-inch thick steak was outweighed by the possibility of getting stuck in a hurricane."

We found a taxi and fifteen minutes later were ushered into a private room in Houston's best-known steakhouse. There was a large window overlooking a lush garden that was drenched with rain. I chatted with the head waiter who quickly removed two place settings, then moved our tables together so the remaining six of us would be able to talk. We ordered two bottles of Silver Oak Cellars cabernet sauvignon, from 2016, and watched as the sommelier opened both so they could breathe while we awaited our remaining guests. We chatted and sipped on some of the wine when my phone rang.

Keisha. It was 7:30.

CHAPTER 4

KEISHA

Keisha arranged the seat belt around her belly and settled in for the ride to the airport. Her legs weren't particularly long, but she appreciated being able to stretch out. Traffic in Houston was slow, but Abdul zigzagged onto side streets to avoid the congestion. He managed to sandwich himself between two eighteen-wheelers as he pulled onto an eight-lane highway and finally was able to speed up to fifty miles an hour in the Houston traffic.

When he'd settled the car into a lane, he glanced into the rear view. "Ms. Keisha, would you like a bottle of water? Help yourself; it's in the compartment in the center console."

"Thanks, I'm okay. If I drink any water, you're going to have to stop every five minutes to find me a place to pee."

She saw his grin in the rearview mirror. They drove silently for the next few minutes.

Keisha texted Josh.

> So far, so good. On highway. On time. How's the dinner

> A lot of cancellations. Ppl afraid of getting stuck. It may end up being just Geoff and me and 2 or 3 guests. LMK when you are on the plane. OK?

Keisha stopped looking at her phone and watched Houston's mediocre scenery. The route to the airport took them past chain restaurants, Walmarts, Dollar Stores, bars, rental stores, furniture stores, miniature office buildings, small houses, a large church, and nothing particularly scenic or noteworthy.

The rain began again, first as a drizzle and a moment later as a heavy downpour. The wipers on the big car had trouble keeping up with it. Keisha was glad that a professional was at the helm, someone who knew his way on these highways and who could deal with the crazy Houston drivers. Then, they slowed in traffic to twenty miles per hour and, after five minutes of crawling in traffic, sped up again to sixty. A large overhead sign said *Bush Intercontinental Airport* with an arrow. Abdul pointed the car in that direction as the highway divided and they continued toward the airport.

Since early that afternoon, the lightning had never really gone away. Keisha recalled Stan the Weatherman saying it was unusual to get lightning this time of year, something to do with the atmospheric conditions. Fortunately, the lightning seemed to be behind them.

Again, the traffic slowed and, this time, came to a stop. Abdul was watching the rearview mirror as the traffic had to stop quickly. Directly behind, a semi screeched loudly, its breaks and tires squealing on the slickened highway. The grill of the big truck filled the rear window. It stopped just inches behind them.

"Crazy." Abdul shook his head. "Crazy-assed driver."

Abdul turned the rearview mirror so he could see Keisha. "I apologize for my language, Ms. Keisha. I know a shortcut. It takes us off the highway for a few miles, but we will get back on fairly close to the airport. The people on this highway are insane. If I take the shortcut, I can still get you to the airport with a lot less traffic, way ahead of boarding time. If I don't, I can't guarantee I'll get you there on time. What would you like me to do?"

"What would you do?" she asked.

"I'd take the shortcut."

"Let's do it."

Abdul swerved onto the shoulder and then drove about one-half mile to an exit ramp, which he took. He turned the limo onto a commercial road, in an area of warehouses and, surprisingly, small ranch houses. *Houston. Who would want to live next to a warehouse?* There was much less traffic and the limo sped along at forty-five mph in the rain.

"We should be okay," said Abdul, smiling into the rear-view mirror. "I've taken this road many times and it's never that busy."

Keisha sat back and the seatbelt snugged around her belly. It would not loosen. As cars and trucks zipped by just feet away in the opposite lane, she took it off, let it retract, and enjoyed the moment of freedom. Then, she extended the belt and clicked the latch into the buckle, tucking the webbing under her belly.

She noticed the road went from four lanes down to two. Now it was more congested and there were many more cars than before. Traffic coming toward them included many semis, no doubt heading to the warehouses that clogged both sides of the road.

As Keisha pulled out her cell phone to text Josh, an oncoming light blinded her, and she looked up. A tractor-trailer, going too fast on the slick road, was headed straight for them.

The semi's air brakes shrieked, and the trucker leaned on his horn, blaring a frenzied warning.

Abdul's knuckles were white on the steering wheel, his eyes wide open, his teeth clenched and bared.

He cut the wheel first right, then left, then right. The big car fishtailed and skidded sideways across the shoulder.

Keisha yelled, "Oh God!"

She grabbed the overhead strap with one hand and covered her face with the other.

She waited for the impact.

The limo's tires squealed.

The car skidded onto the shoulder toward the embankment.

Keisha held her breath awaiting the impact. There was none. The semi continued without stopping or hitting anything. The limo, however, hit some debris as it slid on the shoulder.

Keisha first heard, then felt, the blowout.

Abdul continued pumping the brakes and working the wheel to keep the limo going straight. It was a masterful job of driving and if it weren't for the blowout, they would have been able to continue to the airport. They slowed and he pulled off the road, two wheels in the grass near a guardrail and two on the shoulder.

The limo idled quietly as they sat saying nothing for several seconds. Finally, Abdul turned around and looked at Keisha. "That son of a pig. Are you okay, Ms. Keisha? The baby?"

Keisha breathed heavily as she evaluated her status. She seemed okay, but the limo had lurched back and forth several times. The seatbelt was snug below the baby, and she hoped there was no damage. "I think I'm fine. I just want to get home."

The traffic picked up and motored past the limo as though nothing happened. Abdul waited a moment, then got out of the car and walked around checking for damage. He disappeared as he bent down to look at the tires. Finally, he returned and pulled the door shut. Water dripped off him.

"We have a blowout. My right front tire is shredded. I don't know what we drove over, but the tire is in pieces. It was a new one, too."

"Can you change it?"

Abdul laughed. "Even if I could, it would take an hour. These tires are heavy-duty and aren't meant to be changed with a jack and a lug wrench. Let me see what I can do."

He pulled out his cell phone, pushed a few numbers, then began talking rapidly in Arabic. Finally, in English, he said "thank you."

He turned in his seat and said, "I spoke to my cousin, Ibrahim. He's on the highway, not far away. He was going to the airport to pick up a customer but was taking the highway route. He'll get off and meet us. He should be here in about ten minutes. We'll switch you to the other limo and get you to the airport. You should be there on time. Are you sure you're feeling okay, Ms. Keisha?"

Keisha nodded. "I think so."

Abdul got out of the car, opened the trunk, and took out a flare, which he lit and laid on the shoulder about twenty feet behind the limo.

Keisha watched him and thought about texting or calling Josh. Then, she decided all she would do was worry him. She felt okay and, as planned, would text him when she was on the plane. She kept thinking about the lights from the truck shining in her eyes, aimed straight for the car. The whole incident probably didn't last for more than five seconds, but she had a hard time not thinking about it in slow-mo.

A full fifteen minutes later, another black limo pulled in behind them. Abdul got out in the rain and sat in the front seat of the other car. After several minutes, he and the other man transferred Keisha's luggage to the new car. Then, Abdul opened the car door for Keisha and held it with one hand and an umbrella in the other. She staggered a step, and he grabbed her by the elbow.

"Are you certain you're okay, Ms. Keisha? If you want, I can take you back to Mr. Josh or to the hospital to be checked out."

Keisha glanced at her phone. She still had time to get to the airport and make her flight, barely. She just wanted to be home.

"No, no. That's okay, Abdul. I'll be fine. Just get me to the airport."

Abdul spoke to Ibrahim and then held the door for Keisha in the second limo. Ibrahim stayed with the first limo and Abdul got into the driver's seat. They made it to the airport barely thirty minutes ahead of Keisha's boarding time.

The departure terminal was a nightmare with people escaping Houston just ahead of the storm. Cars were lined up everywhere, some triple parked, and the police struggled to keep traffic moving. Abdul looked at Keisha. "I need you to play along with something. This will be the fastest way to get you to your flight. I need to find my friend, Mr. Jefferson, who works here. I'll be a minute."

Keisha had no idea what he was talking about but waited while he got out of the limo and disappeared into the crowd, entering the terminal. Thirty seconds later, an airport traffic cop tapped on the window and Keisha rolled it down.

"Where's the driver?" The cop had a pissed-off look that must have been permanently glued to his face. "You need to move this limo or I'm going to have it towed."

"Sorry, officer, I can't help you," Keisha gave him her winningest smile. "I'm just the passenger."

As they talked, Abdul came up behind the officer. With him was a porter, an old Black man, pushing a wheelchair. "My apologies, officer. My passenger is an invalid."

The cop looked at Keisha, made a face, shook his head, then stood in the traffic and directed cars around the limo.

"Ms. Keisha, this is Mr. Jefferson," he nodded to the old man with the wheelchair. Mr. Jefferson wore a gray work shirt with a patch over one pocket that read, *Airport Services—Curbside Attendant*. Over the other pocket was a patch that read, *Ted*. Although she didn't feel she needed any help, Abdul helped Keisha into the wheelchair. Clearly this was not a first time for Mr. Jefferson, as he deftly pulled Keisha's rolling luggage behind him while he pushed her in the wheelchair with his other hand. Abdul walked as far as the terminal entrance then said, "Are you sure you're okay?"

Keisha smiled at him. "You're very sweet, Abdul. I'm fine. Thank you for everything."

Abdul leaned over and whispered to her, "I already gave him ten dollars, no need to tip him again, but if you do, five would be plenty." Then he touched his hand to his forehead in a salute and watched as Keisha and Mr. Jefferson headed into the busy terminal.

"Don't you worry, Miss Keisha. I've got you," Mr. Jefferson said in a strong southern accent. "Do you happen to have PreCheck?"

"Sorry, no."

Keisha looked over her shoulder and smiled at him. She couldn't tell if he was fifty or seventy. He was thin as a rail with short white hair. Some men are like that. He navigated the terminal as though he were in his backyard. She didn't know if it was the wheelchair or Mr. Jefferson, but it was like they had a golden ticket and Keisha was quickly ushered through ticketing and baggage check. They approached the security line with hundreds of impatient, anxious travelers which snaked around a rope line, then down the hall. Mr. Jefferson went to an unmarked door and swiped his employee badge in the control device. The door clicked. He pushed the wheelchair down a long hallway lit by old fluorescent lights. They passed doors marked just with numbers and letters, A-430, A-1028, before they made several sharp turns. *Where the hell are you taking me?* She looked back at Mr. Jefferson, and he smiled.

Finally, they came to a door. He swiped it and the door opened next to her gate. "How did you do that? What's going on?" Keisha said.

Mr. Jefferson just smiled. He talked briefly and quietly with the gate attendant. She told Keisha one seat was available in first class and, without asking, the gate attendant reassigned her to it. When it came time to board, she was the first one on. Keisha pulled a twenty-dollar bill from her pocket and turned around to thank Mr. Jefferson, but he was gone. He'd disappeared into the whirl of frenzied people rushing to catch their flights out of Houston.

The airplane was delayed and sat in a conga-line of planes on the tarmac for forty-five minutes. The rain poured. Keisha felt a tightening across her belly as she pulled out her phone and called Josh. It was 7:30.

"First thing, babe. I'm okay. I'm sitting on the airplane."

Tears started to streak down her face as she struggled not to sound like she was crying. She told him about the blowout but not the semi. She ended the call in under a minute. saying the flight attendant told her to power off her phone.

As she put her phone on her lap, the tears began flowing in earnest. She buried her face into her hands and sobbed. Without asking, a flight attendant brought her a small pack of tissues, a blanket in a plastic bag, and a cup of hot tea. Keisha smiled thanks at her but couldn't bring herself to utter any words.

Outside, the rain pelted the 737 and lightning flashed in the distance. Finally, they began rolling down the runway and the jet climbed steeply through the clouds. The raindrops seemed to be blown from the window. Keisha could see nothing other than mist, dark clouds, and a blinking red light on the wing.

The jet felt like it was going over rumble strips as it ascended through the stormy sky. Keisha sat back in the seat and wondered about the tightening in her belly.

CHAPTER 5

JOSH

The rain pounded against the restaurant and all of eastern and central Texas as we sat in the private room. The small garden outside our window was flooded and looked tropical. With each crash of thunder, it became clearer that our clients had abandoned our party. Forty-five minutes after we expected dinner to begin, as rain continued to pelt the restaurant, and after a few text messages containing apologies, we asked the waiter to remove the remaining settings for our guests. I texted Keisha but received no response. I expected she was in the air. I assumed I'd hear from her in Nashville within the hour.

As we waited for the clients who would never show, we'd been sipping on wine from one of the bottles of the Silver Oak cab. Once we knew that all of our clients bailed, we felt we could risk something more potent, so Geoff and I ordered cocktails—Bombay martinis, very dry, shaken, not stirred. I was always careful with martinis. Even though I loved them, if they were large-sized, the first one made me buzzy. The second was my truth-serum. The third, if I got that far, was my knockout punch. I'd known Geoff long enough to know that alcohol didn't seem to have an effect on him. The drinks came a minute later and were Texas-sized and so cold that a nearly microscopic sheet of ice formed on top. Three gigantic olives winked at me from the glass. I allowed the piney juniper smell of the gin to invade my lungs and slowly enjoyed the bite of the alcohol and the burn in my throat. How could a drink burn and yet be so smooth? I didn't have martinis often, but when I did, a dry Bombay martini was my go-to.

Midway through our martinis, we ordered nice dinners: eighteen-ounce ribeye steaks, mine medium rare, Geoff's rare. The smell of the still-sizzling steaks was glorious. We ate and worked on the first bottle of the Silver Oak cab. As expensive as the dinner was, the wine cost twice as much as our food. The firm was paying for this and neither of us gave it a second thought. I wondered how that came to be.

It's an amazing thing. At twenty-five, if you have a conscience, you begin practicing law in a firm knowing there are things you will do and other things you will not do. You create a line in the sand you will not cross. Yet when you're in as deeply as I was, part of your brain just shuts off. The annoying nag goes away. You get to a point where there is no internal debate: *should I, shouldn't I?*

When advising my clients, I always followed the letter of the law. Every bit of advice I provided was legal. Every one of my clients said they wanted to be guided along a lawful path and claimed they did everything according to the laws and regulations; complicated laws which I interpreted for them at five hundred dollars an hour. Yet I knew that something about what some of them were doing was wrong—coal mining, fracking, development in wetlands, constructing huge warehouses on farmland, emitting pollutants from giant smokestacks, all of it. And I was doing the legal work, work that at times troubled me, some that I regretted doing. Worst of all, I *wanted* to succeed, to win, so I worked hard to make sure my clients got their way.

On top of that, like everyone else at my firm, like every lawyer in private practice in a firm such as mine, I wanted more of it. More work. More clients. More success. I didn't feel I deserved the perks but didn't hesitate to enjoy the bounty of my labor. Why? I knew I was complicit in whatever devastation they wrought. Had I simply smothered everything I once so strongly believed in? Where exactly was my line in the sand? By the time I was thirty, I no longer knew the answer to that question. What the *fuck* happened to me?

As we ate dinner, the rain pelting the roof of Luke & Francesco's sounded like uninterrupted cannon fire. I assumed—hoped—that

Keisha's plane was high above the clouds and that in a short while she'd be in Philly. I wasn't worried or anxious; I just hoped everything would go according to plan for both of us. Over dinner, Geoff and I had a weighty discussion regarding the crappy management of the Philadelphia Eagles. That morphed into a discussion of Geoff's unhappiness at the firm.

"Bro, I've been waiting to get the good news about becoming a partner for four years now." Geoff sniffed at his wine then took a deep sip. "I know it's not going to happen."

"Don't be so sure," I said, inhaling the rich bouquet of the wine. "You're a great real estate lawyer."

"That's Josh, always the optimist. Have I first-chaired fifty and even hundred-million-dollar development projects? Yes. Under budget, too. Do the clients love me? Yes. Do Krakowski and Larson hate my guts? Also, yes. That's two partners who are not going to vote for me right there . . . and the vote usually has to be unanimous or the magic doesn't happen."

"Krakowski's probably a racist and hates everyone," I said. "The rest of the partners know that, and I've heard they ignore his vote."

"Uh-huh. And Larson?"

"He's a serious dude. Heavy hitter. Maybe Diane can talk to him so at least he abstains," I said.

"Diane, yes Diane." Geoff took a long time looking into his glass, then sipped more wine before he refilled his glass. A generous pour followed by a big gulp. "She and I, well, let's just say we have a long, complicated relationship. Multi-faceted."

"Complicated?"

Geoff waved a hand back and forth. End of topic.

"Have you noticed that her southern accent seems to be getting stronger the longer we're in Houston?" I asked.

"Sure, but isn't she from down south somewhere?"

"Sort of. McLean, Virginia. Hardly the deep south. More DC and northeast than Mississippi." I said. "I found out she attended Sidwell Friends in DC, then Phillips Academy in Massachusetts. That was before she attended Amherst and Yale Law. None of those are places where you intensify your southern accent. I don't recall her having *any* southern accent during my years with the firm."

"Now that you mention it, I've noticed that she breaks out the *y'alls* when we're talking with clients from Texas."

"That's what I'm saying. The accent disappears and reappears depending upon the person she's talking with. It seems kind of phony to me."

Geoff laughed. "Bro, you know an awful lot about her."

I shrugged. "If you know the enemy and know yourself, you need not fear the result of a hundred battles."

"Yogi Berra?"

I laughed and shook my head. "Sun Tzu . . . I admit, she does kind of fascinate me."

"Like a moth is fascinated by a candle the moment before it flies too close?"

"Perhaps." I took a deep sip of the wine. It *was* good. "So, what about a counsel position with the firm?" I asked. "You're too valuable and they won't want you to leave. I'm pretty sure you'll make counsel. That's a raise and a promotion, right?"

"Josh, Josh, Josh. I don't want to suffer the ignominy of being *promoted* to counsel. Even if no one else knows I was counsel because I didn't make partner, *I'd* know. I've wanted to be a partner in a law firm ever since I decided to go to law school. When I was a freshman at Penn, I didn't decide to become a fucking *counsel* in a law firm. I wanted to be a *partner*."

Somehow, he'd finished the glass, his third, and emptied the dregs from the bottle into his glass.

"So, what's next?" I asked. "You told me a few weeks ago you were thinking about making a switch."

Even though we were alone in the room, he looked at the closed door. "Yes, basically it's a done deal. I've been talking with our client, Bowman Real Estate Investment Trust. I've been doing their real estate work for five years and they love me and want me as their new GC. I'm just about there with my decision."

"You can't do that, bro," I said, shaking my head and smiling. "If you leave, then who am I going to complain to about Diane?"

He smiled at me.

"Bowman REIT?" I said, "In Bala Cynwyd? The General Counsel job's got to be a good gig. Probably pays pretty well."

"It does."

"When do you have to decide?"

"Monday," Geoff said. "Then I'll tell Diane and the firm. Assuming I do this, I'll make everyone happy." He smiled weakly.

"You too. Right?'

He shrugged.

He got up and looked out the door of our private room. I heard him ask for the second bottle of wine. As he sat, he said, "Enough about me. How about you?"

The sommelier lightly tapped on the door. She was a lighter brown-skinned woman, maybe thirty years old, who, like the other staff, wore a blue cowboy-style shirt and a clean black apron, folded at her waist, over black slacks. She brought in a cart with four round glasses. She'd opened the bottle earlier but wasn't done with preparing our wine. The lady knew her stuff and she precisely poured a tiny amount of wine into a glass which she tasted, then she nodded at Geoff. She gave us fresh glasses and did this thing I'd never seen before where she put a few drops of wine in each glass, "to prepare the glass," she said, before swirling it around and dumping the drops into another glass. "I'll pour a small amount now, so the rest of the bottle gets some more air. Is that acceptable?" Geoff nodded. Then, she poured wine into two glasses and began to leave the room.

"One sec," I said. "How's it look outside?"

"Not good, sir." She nodded to the large window which overlooked the small garden. "The parking lot is full of water. We're getting heavy rain and wind. There's flooding all around."

"I guess business is down?" I asked.

"We have maybe ten percent of our usual crowd."

"You'll be able to get home okay?"

She half-smiled. "*Si*, I live in an apartment nearby." She nodded and quietly left the room, taking all of the debris with her. We thanked her as she left, and I made a mental note to leave the waiters a larger than usual tip at the end of our meal.

"Nice presentation," Geoff said. We clicked glasses.

"Cheers."

"My situation is different," I said as I enjoyed the first sip of the new bottle. "You know, I have my opinions about environmental issues, strong opinions, but I keep them to myself. I've always considered myself an environmentalist, yet here I am, working as an environmental lawyer for a big law firm that represents chemical, oil, and waste disposal companies. I've convinced myself that I'm still doing the environmental thing. I mean the C-Suite guys in the boardroom pay us a shit-ton of money for our advice and I try to steer them in the right direction. I like to believe they pay more attention to me than the people protesting outside wearing the paper mâché Guy Fawkes masks. At the end of the day though, my guts tell me I'm working on the wrong side."

"How can you live with yourself doing that?" Geoff asked. "I mean, I do real estate law and for the most-part that's morally neutral. Don't you help companies get around the law?" He laughed.

I squinted my eyes. "Them's fightin' words, pardner. No, I don't do that. I don't have to tell you that regulations are really complicated. Most companies just want to have someone, me, us, figure that out for them. I've never knowingly helped a company violate the law."

"So, all you're doing is helping companies to comply with the law so they can legally rape and pillage the environment?" He smiled.

I shrugged. "What's the line from *The Big Chill*? 'Then there's the money.' I hate to admit that. My views were strong at one time, college, law school, but when the firm offered me the job, I figured I'd better take it and keep my values to myself. The starting salary was $160,000. *One sixty*. Way more than my father ever earned, and I didn't know squat. My total student loans when I graduated from law school were over $300,000. One month after graduation, I had to begin paying $2760 a month to pay that off. Do you know how that limits your choices?"

"No one told you to go to Haverford and Georgetown Law."

"Yeah, and when I was seventeen years old, no one told me *not* to. Everyone said I should go to the best schools I could get into. My parents paid for some of college, but law school was entirely on me."

"Don't whine. It's beneath you—"

"Says the kid who grew up in Chestnut Hill and went to private school starting in kindergarten."

"So, what are you going to do about this?"

"I know a guy in Harrisburg working for the state doing environmental law at DEP. He started at thirty-five-K, but he's doing well and doing good. Now, here I am, seven years later, in friggin' Houston trying as hard as I can to lure in an oil company as a new client. It's so screwed up."

Geoff made a face. "You're no different than most other lawyers. You have a family to think about, school loans to pay, a mortgage, and all of that. You're not chained to a desk here. You have what, three years to finish paying off your student loans? Work out your finances, bro, and you can move on whenever you want. Go work with your buddy in Harrisburg for the state if that makes you happy."

I nodded and texted Keisha again. Normally she replies in seconds, but not this time. I set the phone on the tablecloth, waiting for it to ching, and drank some more wine. It occurred to me that one sip alone of this elixir probably cost ten bucks. Worst of all, I enjoyed it. I liked my office with its view of City Hall, the clothes from the fancy men's shop on Chestnut Street, the nice vacations, and the house Keisha and I bought. I liked that I was paying off my tuition loans without suffering too much. And yet, I was not happy.

"I feel an overall malaise. Most lawyers my age would kill for my job and here I am, whining to you about it."

"No one's forcing you to do anything, Josh. If you're not happy, move on . . ."

"Says the guy at the firm who's probably moving on in three days," I said.

He made a face. "Yes, ninety-nine percent chance of that. But it's not making me entirely happy to think about it."

"Seriously, why are you at all hesitant?"

He looked into his glass as he swirled the deep purple liquid. "Partner. The partner thing. I'm hung up on it."

"If I guaranteed you right now that you'd become a partner tomorrow, would you be happy? Would you stay here? As a partner with Diane, Krakowski, and Larson, the whole crew?"

"Yes, then I'd quit the day after tomorrow. I'd have won. I'd have won the whole damn game. Being a partner in a big law firm is about winning the game, dude. What happens after that is irrelevant." He paused and we looked at our wine.

"The whole partner thing is a farce," I said. "It's bullshit. Who cares, really? A handful of guys at the Union League walking around in Italian suits with squash racquets shoved up their asses? I mean, seriously bro, what difference does it make?"

"Do you know who the greatest baseball player of all time was?" He asked.

"I don't know . . . Babe Ruth?"

"Right. You could argue it was Willie Mays, but let's say it was Ruth. He retired at forty in 1935. Did you know he died thirteen years later in 1948?"

I shook my head.

"Do you know what he did for those thirteen years?"

I shrugged.

"Exactly. He couldn't get another job in baseball, drank and ate himself sick, played a lot of golf, and died of cancer. Do most people know or care? No. What happened to him after he retired is irrelevant."

We both drank.

"And you?" He poured us more wine.

"I think I know what I *want* to do," I said, "but I remember something my father once said. *Golden handcuffs*. Or maybe it was a gilded cage? Same deal. I know how I feel, but over the years I've decided I want to make it here, too. Becoming a partner never meant anything to me until I started thinking of it as the finish line. All of that college and law school. Year after year of 2,000 plus billable hours. Putting up with all the crap the clients and partners dish out to the associates. Partnership has become the goal post. Somehow that became important to me. I keep my values in the closet on the shelf next to my plans to hike the entire Appalachian Trail and backpack cross-country for two months."

We finished eating and ordered brandy to top off the dinner. When the bill finally came, Geoff took it and, with a laugh, put the charge on his firm AMEX card. We were so drunk; it took both of us to figure out how to calculate a thirty percent tip.

Finally, I ordered an Uber and once outside it became immediately clear the storm had ignored the models and picked Houston, not the Yucatan Peninsula, to come ashore. The driver slowly navigated streets full of water. Some side streets were flooded. The highway wasn't bad since it was relatively high and well-drained, but we were in the midst of a serious storm. We made it back to the hotel around 10:30.

I'd talked with Keisha briefly from the restaurant at 7:30 when she called. I texted her again from the Uber but received no response. The wine and brandy continued working in my system, and I barely remembered undressing and climbing into bed. I didn't exactly black out, but I didn't remember getting into bed either.

* * *

It was after midnight and Josh was sound asleep when Keisha's text came through. He and Geoff had drunk martinis, two bottles of cabernet sauvignon, and a glass of brandy each, and he probably wouldn't have heard a klaxon fire alarm if one sounded in his room. Deep in his cups, he ignored the cricket noises chirping from his phone. He rolled over and covered his head with a fluffy Four Seasons pillow.

> **Hi Babe, no problem here. My flight was diverted to Cincinnati. Ugh. The airline is booking me on a flight early in the morning to Philly. No hotel rooms. I'll camp out in the airport. Don't worry, I'm fine. Love you. Keish**

CHAPTER 6

JOSH

Damn me! Of course I didn't hear my phone chirp when Keisha's text arrived in the middle of the night. I may as well have been dead. For sure, I was unconscious. With the clarity that only a good, pounding hangover can bring, I lay in bed and asked myself why I drank so much the night before. I had no answers. I texted her at 7:30 from bed.

> **Sorry I missed your text last night. The restaurant was really loud. Cincinnati? R U OK? Call me. I'm moderating the first program in an hour and won't be able to look at my phone until 9:30. I always screw up the central time zone thing, so I think that's 10:30 to you. Right? Or are you in my time zone? Love, Josh**

When I got to the bathroom, I ate two ibuprofens and drank a full glass of water to tamp down my hangover. As I dressed, I watched the rain pelting the window in sheets. The weatherman on TV said the storm was coming ashore between Galveston and Corpus Christi and would not hit Houston dead on. Nevertheless, the city would experience severe hurricane-force winds. Just before I left my hotel room, I called Keisha again. The phone went directly to her voicemail, and I left her another message.

The conference room was nearly empty. The day before, we'd had about forty guests at our program. Nearly fifty people including lawyers and speakers. That morning I counted three guests and six of our lawyers. Geoff was a no-show. I knew better than to call his room or bang on his door. He was doing exactly what I wished I could have been doing. I grabbed a mug of coffee and started sipping.

We'd flown three speakers from Pennsylvania to Houston and put them up at the hotel. They were chatting with each other or eating breakfast. The hotel had put out a breakfast buffet for fifty people and it was clear that a lot of bagels, scrambled eggs, and bacon were likely to go to waste. I hoped there was a shelter somewhere that would get the food.

Madeleine Billingham, our event coordinator and a friend, came over to me and put her forehead close to mine. Nearly touching. She whispered, "Almost every one of our guests has bailed. No one wants to venture out into the storm. They all wanted to work from home. Who can blame them? Diane explicitly said we would not do a virtual or hybrid program, since she wanted all of them to be here with us. A couple of people did make it in, but we don't have much of an audience."

"What does Diane want to do now?" I noticed again that Madeleine's resting face was a smile. I'd seen partners completely melt down over some perceived disaster at an event and Madeline always managed to maintain her composure, smile, and grace. Whatever the firm paid her to be our event coordinator, it wasn't enough.

"Her exact words were, *fuck it, the show must go on*." Madeline smiled and her cheeks reddened, like a schoolgirl who was compelled by the principal to tell her exactly what another kid had said in class. She never talked that way. How could you do anything but like her?

I found Diane talking with a client. She was wearing a different outfit from the one she had on the day before. I, on the other hand, was wearing the same suit with a different shirt and tie. Somehow, I managed to hang it up the night before and not leave it in a ball on the floor. As I approached her, she briefly touched our client's arm and smiled in a way that suggested much more than what you might get from a mere acquaintance. Classic Diane bull. She broke off her conversation and walked me to the corner of the room. In an instant, her smile transformed into a scowl.

"This is a shit-fest," she whispered loudly. Age lines formed in the corners of her eyes as she talked. "We've spent so much money and made so many plans. Came all the way to Houston to meet with the *awl* and gas folks, now this. Fucking hurricane. We have to go on." She paused and it was as if I saw the wheels spinning in her head. "You're moderating the first program, maybe we'll do it a bit differently. Do more of a conversation than a presentation. Can you pull that off? Hopefully, a few more hardy souls will dribble in. *Crap*." She held my eyes with hers. I was afraid to look away.

Diane's face was screwed up in a rage. I wondered *at whom*? It wasn't like any person had done this to her, to us. It was the roll of the dice. And, oh yes, while we were suffering in the Four Seasons Hotel, most people were stuck somewhere in the storm, getting totally screwed over. Flooded out. Homes destroyed. Lives endangered. We were suffering in the freakin' Four Seasons. This was so typical of Diane. She assumed everything was about her.

"Got it." I nodded and headed for the opposite corner of the function room, which had seemed small the day before but cavernous at that moment. We still had a few minutes to go before the program. I pulled out my phone and saw I'd received no response from Keisha. I quickly texted her again.

Hey babe, what's going on? I'll be speaking in 5 mins

My first speaker was a professor from the University of Pittsburgh, Dave Bastogne. He was an outspoken climate change scientist, nationally known, who appeared on CNN as one of their resident experts. If you saw his face, with his signature scraggly beard, unkempt balding hair, and tired eyes, you'd know him. Bastogne was munching on some fruit salad from a china plate. He'd placed his coffee mug on the wide buffet and smiled when I approached.

"Professor, I hope you had a pleasant evening last night." I shook his hand.

"In fact, I did. I had dinner with a colleague from the University of Houston. You may not believe this, but not everyone in Texas is a climate change denier." He looked around the room. "I'm going to assume that the small number of people here has to do with the hurricane and not my presentation."

I smiled at him. "Even the other side," I nearly said *enemy*, "wants to hear from people with your perspective. The smart ones do anyway. They want to learn about what you're thinking so they can be better informed."

"Do you really believe that?" He displayed a sad smile.

"Well, three of them do anyway." We both laughed. "Diane has suggested that we do this differently. More of a roundtable than a presentation. Do you mind if we change it up?"

"Makes sense. I may still want to use a PowerPoint slide or two, but we can do that."

The hotel staff had already brought a few chairs to the front of the room, off the riser, facing the audience.

Just before we began, I checked my phone again. No messages from Keisha. Seriously worried now, I went against everything I'd learned as a public speaker and left my phone turned on.

Madeleine hurried around the room like a friendly sheepdog and gently ushered our guests to their seats. She encouraged them to sit toward the front. Diane's lips had curved into a smile, but her eyes narrowed malevolently, as she made head nods at our lawyers who got the message and joined the other guests.

I moved to the front of the room and stood and waited until everyone quieted. "Apologies for the storm," I said. "We're very fortunate to have Professor Dave Bastogne from the University of Pittsburgh as our next speaker. Due to cancellations resulting from the storm, we've called an audible and instead of his prepared presentation, we're going to do this as a roundtable. More Q&A than lecture. Okay?" I didn't wait for a response. "One more thing, my very pregnant wife," I didn't say fiancé, "is traveling and got diverted to Cincinnati. I haven't heard from her this morning, so I've left my phone on in case she calls. So, apologies in advance."

I introduced the professor and spent a few moments talking about his very serious credentials. Degrees in physics and climatology. One of the youngest full professors at the University of Pittsburgh. A member of the United Nations IPCC. He'd written dozens of peer-reviewed articles and two respected books on climatology. His research on the effects of carbon from fossil fuels on the climate was cited in hundreds of other papers. The professor was the real deal, not some pompous, self-righteous ignoramus on TV with a degree in political science from Dartmouth.

"Thanks, Josh, you read that introduction exactly as I wrote it." Muted laughter for the ancient joke. "You can blame me for the storm. I wanted to make a point about climate change and stood on the rooftop of the hotel dancing around and praying for rain." A few people laughed out loud. "Actually, it's fortuitous that I'm here today in Houston." He pointed to the window. Outside, the rain was coming down in sheets and debris was flying down Lamar Street. "On August 9, 2021, the U.N.'s Intergovernmental Panel on Climate Change, the world's most renowned and respected research organization on climate change, issued its sixth report on the physical science aspects of climate change and predicted storms just like this one . . ."

While he spoke, I saw Geoff come in through a rear door. He grabbed a mug of coffee and found a seat all the way in the back of the room. He was dressed okay, but from across the room, I could see his face looked like hell. He leaned back in the chair and drank deeply from his coffee mug. He rocked his chair back until he was tilted against the back wall.

"The report stated it was *unequivocal* that human influence has warmed the atmosphere, ocean, and land. Let's stop for a moment and think about the term *unequivocal*. Understand that scientists almost never use the word. Albert Einstein wrote a *theory* of relativity. Charles Darwin wrote a *theory* of natural selection. Even though they are theories, most scientists accept Einstein's and Darwin's. The IPCC's scientists used the term *unequivocal*. This means the IPCC's statement that climate change is man-induced is more credible than Einstein or Darwin's theories." He smiled at the small audience.

"Wait a minute, Professor. I'm J.B. Leach, Deputy General Counsel for North Texas Oil and Gas." Leach was a tall man with an imposing gut who wore a white western-style shirt. His high cowboy boots disappeared under his khakis. "This is the United Nations talking? A lot of us have difficulty believing anything coming out of the U.N. It seems like this is a bunch of scientific wannabes tryin' to make a name for themselves. Put down the USA. No one gives them any mind. Especially here. I've talked with one of our *geologists* and he says this whole climate change thing is a bunch of bullcrap."

The professor smiled placidly at Leach. "Keep in mind, Mr. Leach, that hundreds of scientists from around the world participate in the IPCC, which is under the auspices of the U.N.'s World Meteorological Organization. This isn't a bunch of left-wing, granola-eating, Birkenstock-wearing crazies. They collectively represent thousands of years of academic research. Hundreds of PhDs from all of the major universities in the world. This is as mainstream as it gets."

"Well, you're entitled to your opinion," Leach said. He looked at the middle-aged woman in a bright yellow dress who sat next to him and gently nudged her with his elbow. They shared a quick laugh.

"And you're entitled to your opinion too, Mr. Leach. My opinions are based on thousands of hours of research I've personally conducted, and I've read hundreds of journal articles on climate change. Your comment reminds me of something John F. Kennedy once said. *Too often we enjoy the comfort of opinion without the discomfort of thought.*"

I tried not to show any facial expression. I did spot Diane standing with her back to the wall. She was rubbing her forehead with her hand. I'm sure she didn't appreciate our speaker insulting one of our guests, regardless of who threw the first punch.

The professor continued. "Human-induced climate change is already affecting many weather and climate extremes in every region across the globe. Evidence of observed changes in extremes such as heatwaves, heavy precipitation, droughts, and tropical cyclones, and in particular, their attribution to human influence, has strengthened over the past five years."

The woman sitting next to Leach had some heft to her. Despite the stormy weather, she was wearing a bright yellow dress with a modest hem below her knees and stylish leather boots. "Hold on there. You're talking about weather. I'm sure I don't have to tell you that there's a difference between weather and climate. Weather is variable. I Googled *bad storms* and there have been plenty of them over the past century. If you want to find a so-called trend, it all depends on what years you pick. If you pick a few bad years, it looks terrible. If you pick a few good years, it looks great. I think some of these so-called climate scientists are just cherry-picking their weather events to make it look like the climate is changing for the worse." She smiled at him as though she had just scored a point. I noticed she bumped Leach with her shoulder.

"Let me explain, Doctor . . ." he paused.

"It's Wendy McDonald, like the fast-food chains. I'm with American Interstate Pipeline Corporation."

"And you are a meteorologist, I presume?"

She smiled. "No, another lawyer." Some laughter filled the oversized room.

The professor smiled pleasantly at her. "In a limited way, you're right. Weather is a specific event—like a rainstorm or hot day—that happens over a short period of time. Weather can be tracked within hours or days. Climate, on the other hand, is the average weather conditions in a place over a long period of time. Generally, we climate scientists think of it as trends taking place over thirty years or more. Understand that we're now able to relate trends of weather events to climate and climate to weather events. When you look at the storm raging outside," he pointed to the window and all heads turned, "a highly unusual, very late, strong tropical cyclone or hurricane, the only scientific cause for that is climate change."

McDonald frowned at him.

"You may not like it," the professor continued, "you probably don't hear that on Hannity or Tucker. It may not conform with your pre-set political mindset, but that's a fact. You're a lawyer, so I presume you can read. Spend some time reading the IPCC's summary reports instead of wasting your time watching the blabbermouths on Fox News."

I was sure the professor was getting ready to insult our remaining guest when my phone rang. I pulled it from my pocket and saw it was an 859 area code and a number I did not recognize. I held up the phone and said, "Apologies, I think this may be my wife calling, hopefully from Philly."

I hurried from my seat and to a doorway. "Keisha, is that you? Are you okay?"

"Hi babe. Yes and no. I'm still in Cincinnati and I'm still waiting for a flight to Philly. This place is a friggin' madhouse. I'm supposed to leave here in an hour, but they've been canceling flights left and right. A whole bunch of planes were diverted here, so there's no way everyone's getting home today. It's raining up here too and the wind started to blow a few hours ago."

"How are you feeling?"

"Meh. I've been better. My belly has been aching ever since the accident, but I don't think it's anything serious."

"Aching? Are you sure it's not contractions?"

She paused, then slowly said, "I don't think so. I've never had contractions, so I don't really know. Abdul really had to yank the car back and forth when that tractor-trailer nearly hit us. I think I'm just feeling where the seatbelt cut across my belly."

I shook my head. "What? You didn't tell me about that last night. You said he had a tire blowout."

"That too. Really, babe, it's nothing."

"Are you kidding me? A tractor-trailer? You should have told me you were in an accident. Can you find a doctor? I think you should be checked out. I'm not kidding. This is your health and our baby's, too."

"Chill out, babe. I will. When I get back to Philly. Look, I'm using a payphone. My phone ran out of juice sometime last night and I didn't realize it until I woke up this morning, sitting in a chair in the airport. My charger is in my luggage, God knows where. I was finally able to borrow someone's charger, but the outlets are all taken. Then, I realized I ought to go old school and found a payphone. Other people are in line to use the phone. My cell is probably charged up enough now and I should be able to receive and send texts."

"Look, I'm not happy about this. Do they have an urgent care at the airport? Can you see if they do and just have someone take a look at you?"

"You're such a worrier! I'll try to find out. It's kind of a mess here now."

I heard shouting from the professor and J.B. Leach. "Crap. I think my speaker is having a smack-down with one of our guests. Okay, stay in touch. I want to know if you find a doc and when you're on that flight to Philly. Love you."

I hurried back to the program. The professor was standing.

"I have a PhD and thirty years of research behind my opinions," the professor was shouting. "What do you have? A couple of hours of listening to Alex Jones?"

"I'm just saying that all you're stating is your opinion," Leach yelled. His face was red. "It's not fact."

Diane was rushing to the front of the room. I beat her. "Well... okay, everyone," I said. "Let's get back on track."

Diane cut me off. "Actually folks, it's 9:15 and time for y'all to take a break. I want to thank Professor Bastogne for his interesting and maybe controversial presentation. Our next speaker is from Western PA Drilling Company who will be talking about the difficulty of drillin' in Pennsylvania's complicated geologic environment. Spoiler alert, even our geology loves drillin'. We don't have many earthquakes either, at least not as many as they have in Oklahoma."

The audience laughed.

Diane turned and looked at me. Her expression resembled the one an executioner might give the honored guest at a guillotining a moment before a black hood is placed over their head.

CHAPTER 7

JOSH

I grabbed a fresh mug of coffee and found a seat next to Geoff in the back row. Close up, he looked like he'd aged a few years. He'd cleaned up and was wearing a different suit from yesterday's, but his eyelids were drooping and it was evident he needed more sleep. He wore a crisp white shirt and a knock-your-socks-off bright Ermenegildo Zegna necktie. It was a good thing too—the tie drew your gaze to his neck, not his bloodshot eyes.

As I sat down, Geoff greeted me with, "Urgh."

"Good morning to you too, sunshine." I lightly punched him on the shoulder and smiled brightly.

We sat like two juvenile delinquents in the back of the classroom. Hands behind our heads, legs splayed out, slumping in our seats. Every now and again Diane would turn and glare at us and both of us smiled and waved back.

J.B. Leach strode out of the room immediately after Professor Bastogne's presentation, no doubt insulted by his comments. Now we were down to two clients in the audience. Outside, rain continued to pelt the windows and leaves, branches, and other debris flew through the air. I noticed the squirrel was gone. Either he'd managed to climb down the wall or he'd been blown away.

One of our partners, Brad Allen, was doing his best to have a conversation with the vice president of Western PA Drilling Company. The

VP was using a laser pointer, shining a bright red dot onto a screen showing images from his PowerPoint. As Brad and the speaker chatted back and forth, I wondered if anyone in the audience really cared. I certainly did not.

"I'm getting too old for this shit," Geoff said quietly, looking forward and pretending to pay attention.

"What? Drinking?"

"No, I enjoyed every drop of that wine last night." He looked at me and smiled. "I mean this bullshit with the firm. I hate marketing and I hate having to grovel for clients and partners. I'm sick and tired of begging for business and pretending I like people I hate. Don't get me wrong, I enjoy the legal work, I just despise everything else about firm life."

"Except for the expense account," I said.

Geoff nodded.

"And the money," I leaned close to him when I said that.

Our firm had a policy. Our managing partner wanted all attorneys, not just the partners, to feel a sense of ownership of the firm. This meant the associates received the same financial data as the partners received. I knew how much our highest producing partners made, how much Geoff made, and all bonus amounts. Likewise, Geoff knew what I made. Basically, we had complete transparency within the firm on this topic. There was also a hard and fast rule that we never discussed this information outside the firm.

After fifteen minutes of pretending to watch the program, Geoff tapped me on the shoulder and said, "Can you come with me?"

We stood in the hallway, just down from the conference room door. Geoff looked around making sure no one was near, then said, "I've decided to do it. Take the position with Bowman REIT, as their new general counsel."

I nodded. "I can't say I'm surprised. What pushed you over the edge?"

"Last night. Talking this through with you. There's no reason to stall. I'm going to tell everyone on Monday."

"Is Imani okay with this?"

"More than okay. She's been rooting for it. She says I need a change. It will be good for me and good for our family."

"Well, I'll miss you. It's like the humans are getting beamed up from the planet. I'll be the last one left . . . stuck with them." I gestured with my chin toward the door to the conference room. I meant it. Almost everyone else had drunk the Kool-Aid. I felt like a cup was waiting for me.

At that moment, the door opened and Diane looked out. We froze. It was like we were caught by the principal smoking in the boys' room. "I'd appreciate it if you didn't sneak off. There's almost no one here and we need the bodies." She held the door while we retook our seats. I looked at Geoff and touched my finger to my nose.

I had just settled into my chair when there was a terrific bolt of lightning. The wind picked up and the sound was that proverbial freight train noise. A moment later, a metal trash can smashed into the huge plate glass window, causing it to crack and form a giant and intricate spider web in the broken glass. Somehow, the tempered window didn't shatter.

"Holy shit," said Brad, jumping to his feet.

We all stood and backed away from the window. Everyone looked at each other not quite knowing what to do.

A few moments later, the door opened and one of the hotel employees came rushing in. She went to the window and pulled the heavy curtain shut. "We're going to have to move you," she called out. "The storm is picking up and we can't have you in a room with windows. We have interior rooms and will accommodate you as best as we can under the circumstances."

I noticed our two remaining guests bolting for the door.

"I never should've come today," said Wendy McDonald, the lawyer in the yellow dress who bickered with the professor. I'm getting the hell out of Dodge. Sorry, Diane."

"Me too," said our last guest on his way out the door. "My office is next-door and I'm going to try to make it there and ride out the storm."

The door closed behind them, and Diane said loudly, "Shit. goddamn storm. Shit. Shit."

I watched Diane and Madeleine as they talked with the woman from the hotel. The program was set to end in a couple of hours with lunch. It was pretty obvious that it was over now.

I texted Keisha and told her I would try to get out of town. My flight was at 4 P.M., but I had a feeling all flights were going to be canceled. After I texted her, I worked my iPhone and was not surprised to see that not only was my plane canceled but every other flight out of Bush was also canceled. I didn't even bother checking Houston's other commercial airport, the much smaller Hobby Airport. It made no sense to venture out. Then, I wondered whether the hotel would extend my reservation. I found a house phone and called the front desk. They were very accommodating, and I extended my reservation through the weekend.

While the storm raged outside, I worried about Keisha. What was going on? Why didn't she respond to my texts?

CHAPTER 8

JOSH

I hadn't heard from Keisha for hours. I texted her as soon as the conference broke up and received no response. I texted again after I extended my reservation at the Four Seasons Hotel. After a while my texts simply said:

Keisha?

I sent her five texts just like that. When I called her number, it went directly to voicemail. My hope was that she'd gotten on a flight and turned off her phone. The flight from Cincinnati to Philly was about two hours long and I should have heard from her within about two hours.

I knew she would take any airline she could find to get to Philly. I dialed the number for United and was advised by a robot-like voice that all of their operators were busy. The voice said they really, really, *really* valued my business and I should have heard from her by the time she landed. After fifteen minutes, I hung up. I tried the other airlines and got the same thing. While I was on hold, I went online and saw that most flights out of Cincinnati had been canceled. There was no way to determine where in the world Keisha was at that moment.

There's nothing worse than being stuck far from the woman you love and not being able to do anything to help her. I was so worried and helpless; my stomach clenched painfully.

I pulled out my laptop and worked the airlines' websites. Literally every flight out of Bush and Hobby that day had been canceled. Although all of the airlines showed flights departing beginning at 5 A.M. the next day, Saturday, I figured they were probably fully booked or the airline hadn't yet gotten around to canceling them yet. It all depended on the storm. The TV news showed scenes of Bush Airport full of nervous, tired passengers sitting on their luggage. Going nowhere. Complaining. Everyone complained. Some whined. The reporter speculated the earliest things might return to normal was Sunday or Monday. *Shit.*

I was sick of just sitting around doing nothing. A thought occurred to me, and I spoke to my phone. "Hey Siri, how long does it take to drive from Houston to Cincinnati?"

Siri was very accommodating and, a second or two later, she responded, "Traffic from Houston to Cincinnati is light, so I'm estimating the travel time as 15 hours and 12 minutes by I-69 North." I looked out the window of my hotel room and the rain was still pummeling Houston. Small trees along the streets swayed back and forth like those inflatable twenty-foot-tall tube men. If the traffic truly was light, that was only because few people were insane enough to be on the highway right then.

I lifted my phone again and dictated into Google, "route from Houston to Cincinnati." Google differed from Siri and showed a route taking 15 hours and 44 minutes. I worked my phone and found another route that took thirty minutes less time. The difference was the longer route was on Interstate highways and the shorter route was on a combination of Interstates, US routes, and even some Texas back roads. The shorter route was more direct, I supposed, but I was much less confident in the maintenance of all of those US and state routes in a storm. I really wanted to see a paper map so I could visualize it all at once. No matter what, assuming bad weather and a stop or two for coffee and to pee, it would take at least sixteen hours.

The distance was 1047.7 miles. If I could rent a car and leave at 8 A.M. on Saturday, that meant I would get to Cincinnati by about midnight.

If I could find a car to rent.

If the road was clear.

If there was no traffic.

If I didn't stop to eat or piss.

If I had the strength to drive nonstop to Cincinnati in a hurricane.

If there was no hurricane.

That was a long drive to do in one day and I was pretty sure no one from Philly would want to go with me. According to Siri, it would take another eight hours and thirty-nine minutes to drive from Cincinnati to Philly. I began to brace myself for a long, solo drive.

I knew Geoff had a supply of speed and addys. He said he used these only when he needed to stay up late to work on some deal. Supposedly they kept you up and focused. The strongest drug I'd ever taken was ibuprofen, so I figured taking speed would be a really bad idea since I had no idea how it might affect me. Instead, I decided I'd load up on coffee and maybe some of those five-hour energy drinks.

The more I thought about it, the more I hoped Keisha was on her way to Philly. It occurred to me that by the time I got to Cincinnati, Keisha could be back home. The scenarios were driving me crazy. Before I started calling car rental agencies, I decided to check out the possibility I'd been trying desperately not to think about.

I looked up hospitals near Cincinnati International Airport. It turns out the airport is in northern Kentucky. Who knew? The first two listings were for urgent care facilities in Erlanger, Kentucky. The next was for St. Elizabeth's Hospital in Florence, Kentucky. The map indicated it was a couple of miles from the airport. With one click, I could dial the hospital.

I paused. I was sure I was being overly dramatic. This was something my parents would do. *Oh crap*, I thought, my *parents* wouldn't do this, my *mother* would. I was becoming my mother. My finger hovered over the button on the screen as I debated what to do. I knew there were two very real probabilities. Keisha's phone could have run out of juice again and she was unable to recharge it. The other was she was on a flight and couldn't receive calls. I seriously doubted she was in the hospital.

At the same time, another voice was telling me she'd passed out in the ladies' room, cracked her head on a sink on the way down, and had been transported to St. Elizabeth's Hospital. She carried a small backpack for the plane with her ID, credit cards, keys, and a little cash, but if the EMTs didn't pick it up, she'd have no identification. If she was unconscious, they could see she was pregnant, but they'd know nothing else about her. Right now, I imagined some Jane Doe, Keisha, was lying on a gurney, unconscious, in the emergency room at St. Elizabeth's Hospital in Kentucky.

While this was going on, her asshole of a boyfriend was lounging on a king-size bed at the freakin' Four Seasons Hotel with his laptop propped up on his legs and the television news playing mutely across the room. I thought perhaps I should order a pitcher of martinis from room service to complete the picture of the selfish, callous boyfriend. With the storm raging outside and no transportation, I felt helpless. This was the least I could do.

Perhaps I really had become my parents. Not the racist part, but the overly concerned part. What the hell was wrong with me? I knew what I needed to do, even if I perhaps *was* becoming my mother. My finger hovered over the icon of a telephone receiver and the word *call*. Finally, I tapped my phone, which then provided me a second chance to change my mind, asking me if, in fact, I *really* wanted to call the number. I clicked the call button.

The phone rang six times. Finally, a woman's voice came on. Her words were memorized and appropriate, but her delivery was taut, hurried, even angry that I interrupted her. "Thank you for calling St. Elizabeth's Healthcare, how may I help you?" It came out sounding like one long word—*ThankyouforcallingSt.Elizabeth'sHealthcare, howmayIhelpyou?*

I had to think for a second. "Hi, my name is Josh Goldberg. Can you tell me if you have a patient named Keisha Jones or maybe she's registered as Keisha Goldberg? I'm her boyfriend and I haven't heard from her in hours. I'm worried she may be in the hospital."

"Hold on." I could hear clicking in the background as the operator typed on a keyboard. The static from the phone competed with the sound of the wind whipping around the building.

"No one with that name has been admitted. It's a madhouse here. We've already had victims of the storm brought in from down south. People are piling up in the emergency department. Everything is delayed, so please check back in an hour—"

It sounded like she was about to disconnect me.

"Wait, wait a second. Maybe she's listed as Keisha Jones-Goldberg? Goldberg-Jones? I don't know how she would have been recorded on admission."

More typing. "No one with any of those names has been admitted here. I have six calls blinking for me on my screen, so if you could call back later—"

"Please wait. How about the records in your emergency room? Maybe she's down there?"

A sigh escaped the lips of the operator. More clicking. "Like I said, they're really backed up. I suppose she could be sitting in a chair waiting to be triaged and she might not yet be in my system. No one here has any of those names. I really have to take the next call—"

I imagined Keisha passed out on the floor of the ladies' room in the airport. Unconscious. Unable to talk. No ID. "Wait a minute, please, one more thing. Maybe she was unconscious. Keisha is 5'4", light brown skin, African American, with black, curly hair braided to her shoulders. Very beautiful and sweet. And pregnant. Eight months."

The operator paused. I pictured a middle-aged woman, probably a mother herself, overworked and underpaid, who sat at a keyboard for eight hours a day.

I heard myself say, "I love her, and I'm scared to death for her."

More clicking. "Hold on. I've got one more thing to check. Her voice seemed to soften. Okay?" Long pause, maybe twenty seconds. "Hang on, I'm looking at an alert that says we had an anonymous African American woman brought in from the airport about two hours ago. Unconscious. Pregnant. We still don't have any ID for her."

"Oh my God. That's got to be her."

"Take a breath, sir. We get more than a dozen patients a day from the airport. Black, brown, white, male, female, pregnant, you name it. Does she have any other identifying marks or characteristics?"

I closed my eyes and thought. "Yes. She has this little tattoo above her right ankle. It was a sorority thing." I thought about her tattoo. She'd told me the sorority had been partying one night and thought it would be clever to get their nicknames tattooed on their legs for some kind of sorority picture. She'd regretted it as long as I've known her, but I always thought it was cute. I never call her by that name. "Her tattoo says, *Boo-Boo*. B-O-O-B-O-O. It's small, just two or three inches long."

There was more clicking as the operator worked her keyboard.

"Checking... Mr. Goldberg... Okay. She's here. I'm going to transfer you to the head nurse in the emergency department."

CHAPTER 9

KEISHA

Keisha dozed fitfully in the hospital. About an hour after she regained consciousness, she placed a brief call to Josh, just long enough to establish proof of life. Josh had asked if he should drive from Houston to Cincinnati and she had enough wits about her to tell him that would be crazy and under no circumstances should he do that in the storm. Then, she went back to sleep. As she drifted off, she was thinking about Josh. The minute she began to doze, a nurse would awaken her to check her pulse, take her blood pressure, or perform some other mundane task. A hospital was no place to get rest.

In the early afternoon, a doctor and nurse woke her up and examined her. She was half awake and still groggy from passing out at the airport but could see the stitching on the doctor's white coat, *Edith Match, M.D. Internal Medicine*. Match lifted Keisha's gown and pressed her hands into Keisha's belly, feeling the baby.

"The good news is the septicemia is abating. Still, I'm not going to be comfortable until you've had a good five days of bedrest, maybe more."

"I'm not sure if it says this on my chart, but I'm from Philadelphia and I have no family in the Cincinnati area. I have no idea where I can stay if I need days of bedrest here."

Dr. Match smiled. "Don't worry, we won't put you out into the storm. We can work it out."

She spent a few minutes filling out the electronic chart, then said, "I'm going to send in an ob-gyn. I want you to be evaluated by those folks."

"I'm not going anywhere."

Keisha fell back asleep for a few minutes, waking when an attendant placed a tray of food on the stand next to her bed. The smell of the food—a piece of chicken and mixed vegetables—turned her stomach. Keisha wasn't hungry and ignored the food; she closed her eyes and managed to drift in and out of sleep. As she dozed, she recalled that morning when one of the doctors wanted to catheterize her so she didn't have to get out of bed to pee, but Keisha had begged, and they agreed she could get out of bed briefly to use the bathroom. Nevertheless, she had tubes stuck into her arm, a monitor on her belly, and a trip to the bathroom involved pulling an IV bag full of antibiotics on an IV stand and a monitor cart with her.

Her phone played her mother's ringtone, Tupak's *Dear Mama*. She'd called her mother after she'd been awake for about half an hour to let her know she was in the hospital. She was able to get off quickly that time when she lied and said a doctor was coming into her room to examine her. She knew she had to talk with her now. Pleasantries lasted ten seconds, then her mother started in.

"Keisha, I'm just so mad. I feel helpless. There you are stuck in Cincinnati in the middle of this storm and all alone. I can't believe you went to Houston with just six weeks to go in your pregnancy."

"No one expected a hurricane in November, Mom. We were staying at a fancy hotel and Houston has great hospitals. When the hurricane hit, I just felt it would be best to go home."

"Well, I'm angry that Josh didn't go with you."

"Mom, I explained that to you. He had a program to do in the morning, today, and it was me. I insisted that he stay. I was the one who wanted to get back to Philly. He wanted me to wait until the program was over and we could travel together."

"You should've listened to your husband."

"Okay, Mom, he's still my fiancé and I'll think about that next time. It's not very helpful now. Look, I'm in St. Elizabeth's Hospital near the airport in Kentucky. I Googled it and it's a good one. Don't worry about me, I'll be okay."

"Kentucky? Oh great. You're in a hospital in Kentucky. Do they even have medical doctors in Kentucky?"

"Mom!"

"Maybe I'll get your father to drive us out there. It can't be all that far."

"That would be insane, Mom. I've got the news on, and the storm is headed your way. It's going to become a nor'easter when it hits the coast. Please don't give me something else to worry about."

"Well, you're going to learn soon enough about your kids, honey, I've been worrying about you for thirty years. That never goes away. I love you and I can't wait to hold your baby. You tell that Kentucky doctor to take good care of everything."

Keisha imagined her mother making air quotes when she said the word *doctor*.

When the call was finally over, she laid back down and felt her belly. For the past few months, she got nervous when she hadn't felt the baby move or kick for a while. Now, it had been hours since she felt the baby. Maybe her little girl was sleeping. She'd already received two sonograms in the hospital, one just a few hours earlier, and the docs claimed that everything was all right. She was hooked up to a fetal monitor and the constant beeping reassured her.

Due to her condition, however, they were afraid that she might go into labor and the baby would be born six weeks early. Hence, the bedrest. Dr. Match said if Keisha could hold out for another three weeks or so, it would be better for the baby. As a result, she was facing at least a month of bedrest. At some point, the hospital would have to throw her out. She knew they could find a hotel or Airbnb nearby but had real anxiety about being away from a place that could quickly deal with her if she went into labor.

Keisha felt the presence of someone in her room and opened her eyes. A doctor stood at the foot of her bed and lightly tapped the wall. Keisha studied what little of him she could see behind his surgical mask and black surgical cap. He was a Black man, about six feet tall, wearing blue scrubs and a long white doctor coat. His name and specialty were stitched on his coat: *Anthony Sudor, M.D. Obstetrics and Gynecology*. Only his eyes were visible. It was hard to tell, but he appeared to be smiling.

"Hello, Keisha. I'm Dr. Sudor. Dr. Match sent me to see you . . . remember me?" He pulled down his face mask and smiled broadly.

Keisha threw her hands over her mouth and gasped. "Anthony! What, what the heck are *you* doing here?"

He put a warm hand on her shoulder and squeezed. "I'm an attending. I'm sure you heard I did my residency at Ohio State in Columbus and liked it enough to stay in Ohio. I've been working in Cincinnati for a few years now."

"Oh my God, you are so out of context I didn't recognize you behind the mask. You became a gynecologist?"

Anthony had a deep laugh. He tugged at his coat and pretended to read the stitching. "Yes, that's what it says. I guess I finished the program after all. You know, I always liked lady parts." He laughed again.

"And ladies," she said, frowning at him.

He looked at his iPad. "Ouch. Well, Dr. Match wanted me to examine you to see how you're doing and assess how long we should make you stay in bed." He looked up from the iPad and winked at her. "As I recall, you were able to stay in bed an entire weekend if the hotel was nice enough."

"Anthony!"

"Just kidding. I'm acting very unprofessionally. I'm just really happy to see you." He sat on the edge of her bed. "Believe it or not, I was thinking about you recently and wondering how you were doing. Trust me, the last place I expected to see you was in a bed in my hospital. Do you ever think about me?"

In fact, she had. Keisha's relationship with Josh was always just simmering. Never a full boil. It wasn't that she didn't love him. She did. She expected this was what some would call mature love. Whatever that meant. Her relationship with Anthony while he was in medical school in Philly had been white hot. She hadn't forgotten that. Her hormones were raging, and she was madly in love with him. It helped that Anthony had been a particularly talented and skilled lover. He wasn't someone she could ever forget. Every now and then she caught herself daydreaming about him. Not that she didn't love Josh and his capabilities in bed, but Anthony . . . Anthony had been an unusually special man in her life for a time . . .

. . . Until she found out he was sleeping with another medical student.

"Not really. I mean, sometimes I go past Thomas Jefferson Medical School and remember getting drinks at Doc Watson's bar, but that's about it."

Anthony's shoulders slumped.

"Well, Ms. Jones, considering we had a prior relationship, the right thing to do would be to rustle up another gynecologist. I'm the only one on duty right now. We're supposed to have at least two attendings during the day, but my colleague couldn't make it in due to the storm. As soon as she comes in, I can have her examine you."

"I go by Jones-*Goldberg*," she said immediately, lying.

"Got it."

Keisha thought for a moment. "No, that's okay. We can be grownups about this. You're a doctor and I'm a patient."

"You may be okay with that, I know I am, but the ethics board would have my hide if I did that. I have a physician's assistant who I trust. I'll get her in here for the internal exam."

He winked at Keisha. "Let me just check on the baby."

"Well alright then." He pulled her blanket and sheet up to her neck and put his hands on her belly over her gown. He felt around carefully. "The baby is pointed in the right direction, that's good. Everything seems to be where it ought to be" He felt her more. Much more than any other doctor who had ever examined her before. A light touch. Warm hands. Something very familiar about the way he touched her. "I'd say you're thirty-three weeks pregnant."

"Anthony, you *are* good. That's exactly right."

He laughed loudly. "Actually, that's what it said on your intake chart." He continued feeling her belly. His hands had a loving familiarity.

"Okay, Ms. Jones-*Goldberg*, we need an internal examination. Hang on."

He went to the door and opened it. "Loretta, can you help me for a few seconds?" He pushed the door shut.

Keisha had her knees up and Anthony brought a chair near the foot of the bed. A woman in scrubs came into the room and looked at Anthony. "Anthony, Dr. Sudor, did you need me?"

"Loretta, this will be a minute. This is Ms. Jones-Goldberg. Can you do a quick internal exam?"

"Sure." She looked at Keisha and smiled. "Hi, I'm Loretta, Dr. Sudor's P.A. This will just take a minute. Okay?"

Keisha smiled and nodded.

Loretta snapped on examination gloves and touched Keisha's knees, which she parted at her touch. Anthony stood near Keisha's head and put his hand on her shoulder and smiled during the examination. A flood of memories invaded Keisha's mind. She gasped the moment Loretta began her examination and both the doctor and PA glanced at her before she controlled her breathing.

As the PA examined her, Keisha tried not to think about the flashbacks of her and Anthony, like a PowerPoint of pictures set on overdrive. *Well, this will be interesting.*

When the examination was over, Anthony said he had several other patients to visit, but that he would be back. He placed his hand on Keisha's shoulder and stroked it gently.

"Loretta said you're fine for a lady who is eight months pregnant. Now, I've got patients in a hospital to visit, so I'll see you in a few," he said.

"Minutes, hours, or days?

He smiled then left.

Keisha lay still and thought about Anthony. One memory after another. Good memories. Fond memories. Sensual memories. They all crashed into the stone wall of the moment she caught him in bed—their bed—with that other medical student. Still, she had so many memories. They all came flooding back.

After thirty minutes of indecision and reverie, Keisha decided she needed to text Josh. She tapped out a text, then revised it twice before she sent it.

I'm feeling pretty good, all things considered. Do you want to hear something hilarious? You'll never guess who my ob-gyn

is here. Dr. Anthony Sudor. You probably remember hearing about him. Isn't that funny? I can't wait to see you, but don't do anything stupid. If you need to stay over somewhere until the storm is over, do it. I'm in good hands. Love you babe, Keish

CHAPTER 10

JOSH

Hurricane Epsilon continued to rage. With nowhere else to be and nothing else I could do, I sat at the bar of the Four Seasons Hotel with Geoff, my phone in front of me while I kept an eye on the television, which was broadcasting the weather full-time. The hotel staff had placed large plywood boards over most of the plate glass windows, leaving a six-inch gap at the top. I was grateful for the gap as it gave me a small, real-time view of the storm.

I'd talked earlier with Keisha's doctor in the emergency room and filled in whatever history I could. They felt she would need to be hospitalized for several days. They were concerned both for her and the baby. So was I. I was marooned in Houston and completely helpless. I took a sip of iced tea. That was the strongest thing I planned to drink until I figured this out.

"So, Epsilon came ashore early this morning as a category two hurricane." Stan the Weatherman was broadcasting from the safety and comfort of the studio. Occasionally, he would turn his back on the camera to point to the weather map, revealing a large white bandage on the back of his head covering the ten stitches he had received the day before in Galveston. At some point, he had described in exaggerated detail his injury and profusely thanked the doctors and the emergency department at John Sealy Hospital in Galveston. The patch made it look like he was wearing a white yarmulke. Even though he was not impaled by the tree branch, he still made the weather bloopers show, focusing on the pool of blood dripping from his hand after the branch scratched his head.

"A cold front originating in Canada is pushing down on the hurricane, slowing its northern advance and causing it to turn more eastward than predicted. The storm from Canada is a rare, late season *derecho* which is combining with the hurricane. At the same time, Epsilon continues to pick up warm water from the Gulf which is feeding the storm. So, we have the worst of all worlds. It's a gigantic, rare, late-season hurricane, moving slowly, gathering intensity and moisture from the Gulf."

Bill, one of the anchors, had an eyelid that drooped. I hadn't noticed it the day before, but he'd been on air for thirty-six hours straight and as each hour went by, it drooped more. He and his co-anchor Linda were stuck at the station and had been broadcasting live for most of the previous day and a half. I'd left the news on throughout the day in my room and Bill and Linda seemed to be on screen whenever I turned my attention to it. "Any idea when this is going to move out of here?" Bill asked. He sounded like he needed a nap.

"Originally, Bill, we'd hoped it would move through Houston and Texas quickly," Stan said as he shook his head back and forth. "Now, with this cold front pushing down from Canada," he motioned with his hands hovering over the map, "the hurricane has slowed, and it continues dumping rainwater on us. The Weather Service is saying we can get six to twelve inches of rain, but I think that's just a wild guess. We've got sustained winds of sixty miles an hour with wind gusts to eighty miles an hour."

Linda's eyelids were sagging and wrinkled, and no amount of stage makeup could cover the gravel in her voice. She had aged a few years since the day before. Her shoulder-length blonde hair was frazzled. "And you're still saying that good ol' Mother Nature is causing this?"

Stan the Weatherman paused and looked to the right, not toward a camera, but as though he were looking at someone. "I'll be honest with you, Linda. I'm coming around to the climate change way of thinking. We've had too many awful storms in the past few years and our temperatures have been way too extreme for this just to be Mother Nature. That November storm we had in 2020, the one that took out the power grid and left so many of us cold and miserable for weeks? The awful rain event in August 2022? Neither were hurricanes. Just awful, severe storms. Nothing like it ever before; it's exactly like what the climate scientists have been predicting. I studied the Intergovernmental Panel on Climate Change reports and other serious journals. Sure, some fringe scientists are saying this is normal. Just Mother Nature. That's BS, there's nothing normal about it."

Stan put his hand to the right side of his head and a moment later pulled the earpiece from his ear. It dangled from a clear coiled cord. "Call me a convert. I suppose it doesn't matter what the cause of the storm is; it's big and horrible and there will be a lot of pain and suffering during and following. I hate to think how it's going to impact the folks here. Our neighbors. I'm just calling it as I see it."

The weatherman turned back to the map. "So far, the European model has outperformed the American model. This storm is here, not cutting across Mexico." He looked directly into the camera. "Can you believe that? The European model is outperforming the American, right here in Texas." He shook his head in disbelief. "Anyway, as you can see, the hurricane is going straight up the heart of the great state of Texas and will turn east. It's going to be a slow mover with very damaging wind and rain. Expect tornadoes. They've already seen them up in the Dallas area and in Oklahoma." He paused and shook his head. "Back to you."

Linda was staring blankly, straight at the camera, "Let's go to those clips of Corpus Christi where the storm came ashore early this morning." The scene changed to a nighttime shot, illuminated by a bright light, of heavy rain and waves rolling into houses built entirely too close to the shoreline.

It was early afternoon and there were maybe a dozen people in the bar. I guessed all of them were stuck due to the storm. I sipped my iced tea and Geoff nursed a beer. He had an empty shot glass that had held Jack Daniels but had finished that a while earlier. To his credit, he turned down repeated offers from the bartender for a fill up. He wore jeans and a loose cotton sweater with running shoes.

"So, exactly what did this doctor tell you?" Geoff asked as we both took our eyes off the weather report.

"Keisha has this thing called septicemia. I've heard of it but don't entirely understand it. Basically, it's an infection throughout her whole system. It may have been triggered by some internal damage she received when Abdul had to make all of those evasive moves to avoid the truck. That caused some kind of infection. The doc put her on massive antibiotics and bed rest. They're watching the baby with a fetal monitor. It's not good. If she gets worse, they may want to perform a cesarean even though the baby would be six weeks early. I talked to her briefly a couple of hours ago, but she was dopey. She didn't sound too bad, just tired. She's going to be in the hospital for the next three or four days at a minimum."

Geoff patted my arm. "I'm sure she'll be okay, bro." He thought for a moment. "Are you still thinking about driving to Cincinnati?"

"I don't really want to do that. It will be an awful drive through all of this crap." I waved in the direction of the boarded-up windows. "I really want to be with her but driving a thousand miles through a hurricane seems insane."

"Yep, brother. It is."

"There are exactly zero flights for the next day or two. I can't stand the fact that I'm here and she's a thousand miles away. I feel like an ass . . . and stuck."

He nodded. "Did you have any luck renting a car?"

"Zero. Zip. Nada. There was nothing online and I couldn't even get through to any of the 800 numbers for any of the rental companies. I did manage to connect to Thrifty at the airport, and the lady told me that when it became apparent the airlines were canceling all of their flights, people rushed the counters and websites, and the cars were all rented out in a few minutes. Everyone wants to get home, even in the storm . . . especially in the storm."

"Seriously, though. Would you risk it? Driving, I mean?" He nodded with his chin toward the boarded-up windows. "God knows what's going on out there."

"I want to say, hell yeah, I'm going to drive for a whole day through the worst freakin' storm of the century to get to my girlfriend who's in the hospital about to have my baby. That's the fearless, risk-taking part of me who doesn't think about the consequences of my actions. Another part of me is saying that would be incredibly foolish. No one in their right mind would drive one thousand miles in a hellish storm when you could fly to Cincinnati a day or two later, safely."

"So?" Geoff let his question hang over the bar like the smell of stale beer.

We stopped talking and listened to debris pelting the plywood. I could see the rain splattering across the small portion of the window visible at the top. Lightning flashed and I only got as far as two-Mississippi when I heard the roll of thunder. Close.

My phone chirped. Crickets. A new text from Keisha:

> **I'm feeling pretty good, all things considered. Do you want to hear something hilarious? You'll never guess who my ob-gyn is here. Dr. Anthony Sudor. You probably remember hearing about him. Isn't that funny? I can't wait to see you, but don't do anything stupid. If you need to stay over somewhere until the storm is over, do it. I'm in good hands. Love you babe, Keish**

I studied it. Geoff was looking at me.

"Is she okay? Is everything alright?"

I showed him the text.

"Dr. Anthony Sudor?" Geoff looked puzzled. "Do I know him?"

"Do you remember I told you there was some asshole Keisha once dated? A med student. They lived together until she walked in on him screwing another med student in their bed."

"Okay..."

"She broke it off immediately after that. It was maybe five-ten years ago, but I don't think she ever really got over him. I needed her passport to get our plane tickets for that trip to Mexico we took last year. I was rummaging around in the back of her dresser drawer and came across a pile of pictures of her and the guy. The med student. She still had the freakin' pictures after all those years. That was less than a year ago."

"Okay..."

"That was him. This guy." I held up the phone. "Anthony Sudor. Her gynecologist in Cincinnati."

"Whoa." Geoff held up his beer as though he was toasting the storm. Outside, more lightning crashed and the lights flickered for a moment. "What are you thinking?"

"I'm driving to Cincinnati in a fucking hurricane."

CHAPTER 11

JOSH

"Seriously? Because of this? Him?" Geoff pointed at the phone.

I pressed my lips together. "I wanted to do it, but just didn't have the balls for it. Now I read that Sudor, the last guy Keisha truly loved before me, has got his hands in . . . in . . . her parts and I'm a thousand miles away. Shit, no one in their right mind wants to drive through a freakin' hurricane. But I don't want to leave her alone with him for any longer than necessary. Keisha's been wavering and I don't want him to take advantage of that."

"Seriously? You trust Keisha, right? I mean, she's eight months pregnant with your baby, bro. It's not like she's going to jump into bed with him. I doubt she'd do that even if she wasn't pregnant."

"I *do* trust her. I also know that she's kind of unsure about us right now. Everyone thinks *I'm* the reason we're not married. *My* screwed-up childhood, *my* parents. That's partly true. The other part is Keisha. She hasn't wanted to commit. I thought when she became pregnant that would be it. She'd want to get married. I was wrong. The further along she's gotten, the more indecisive she's become. I mean, I don't trust this guy."

Geoff nodded at me. "Bro, tell me. Who is it you don't trust?"

I slowly nodded back.

Geoff waved his hand once in the direction of the bartender. "Two Jack Daniels. Shots. Two beers."

A moment later, the drinks were in front of us. I pushed aside my iced tea. Geoff held up his shot glass and said, "It'll work out, bro."

We clicked glasses and he tossed his drink back and followed with his beer. I sipped mine slowly, allowing the whiskey to burn my throat.

"Maybe you could buy a car?" Geoff said. "I'm surprised they're even renting cars in this weather. It's one thing if a car already is on the road, but it's another to rent out a car under these conditions."

I shook my head "I'm guessing all of the dealerships are boarded up. Not to mention I don't have a spare thirty thousand dollars to buy a used car. I sure as hell wouldn't want to buy a new car and drive through this."

I rested my eyes on the giant TV screen across the room. It had an image of a roof being pried up by the wind from a house in a place called Sugar Land, south of Houston. Just then, a middle-aged man walked between the TV and me pulling his luggage. He was wearing a trench coat, unbuttoned, with a blue suit underneath and a ball cap with the Houston Texans logo pulled down tight on his head. He was dry.

"Where do you suppose he's going?" Geoff asked.

The man headed for the door of the bar. I jumped off the bar stool and caught up to him near the door to the lobby. "Excuse me, you're not heading out into this, are you?"

He had short hair and a red, jowly face. "Damn straight I am." He said with a twangy Texas accent. "That idiot Millennial manager of ours wanted to do a mandatory weekend retreat with yoga, group hugs, and all that crap. New age bullshit. I didn't have a choice but figured it couldn't be all that bad if it was at the Four Seasons. Got here last night and the meeting was canceled this morning. F those bastards. I'm heading home."

"You're going to drive? In this weather?"

"Hell no. I got a limo to pick me up. I live in Katy, about fifty miles west of here. The guy's charging me double, but it's worth it. I got flooded out back home in that goddamned storm two years ago and we saw a shit load of high water in that storm in August '22. I want to make sure my new generator and sump pump are working." He looked through the door toward a limo driver standing in the lobby, a black man wearing black slacks and a black raincoat. He wore a ball cap that said, *Excellent Limo Service,* and held up a clipboard with the name *Taylor* scrawled on it. "There's my guy." He waved to the man who began approaching to take his luggage.

"Good luck," I said. "*Namaste.*"

He gave me a dirty look, then continued into the lobby.

The driver took his luggage and rolled it to the car, which sat under the hotel portico as rainwater dripped from it onto the pavement. It wasn't a stretch limo, just a regular-sized Cadillac Seville. The logo for *Excellent Limo Service* was stenciled on the door. As the man headed for the car, the wind took his Houston Texans cap and sent it into the air, revealing a wide bald patch with long strands of brown hair fluttering in the breeze. He made a grab for it; his moves were comical as he chased his hat. Then, he must've realized how pointless it was trying to go after it and watched it sail down the street. They drove out into the driving rain.

"What's going on?" said Geoff when I returned.

I smiled broadly. I could see myself in the mirror behind the bar. I looked insane. "What about a limo? What if I take a limo to Cincinnati?"

Geoff nodded thoughtfully. "You know that Tesla you told me you hope to buy some day when you pay off your tuition loans, the model S? They cost about one-hundred grand. A limo ride to Cincinnati might cost you half that much."

I thought for a moment. "What if I drove? Maybe I could rent a limo from Abdul? I could pay him a couple thousand dollars which is a lot more than I'd pay Hertz or Avis. Also, unless there are other desperate people who want a ride home in this weather, he's not making anything over the next couple of days anyway."

"Do you really think your friend will want to rent you a limo? Also, are you sure about this? It's about a twenty-four-hour drive."

"Nah," I said. "Siri says it's only sixteen hours. Plus, it's all Interstate driving. Houston to New Orleans, then north to Nashville, and finally northeast to Cincinnati. Easy-peasy as Keisha likes to say."

Geoff shook his head. "You're crazy. Is that driving time with or without a category three hurricane the whole way? That's a long way to drive by yourself. At some point, you'll need some rest. I don't care how much coffee you drink; it's not going to be an easy drive."

I sat looking at the continuous weather report on the TV screen. A map showed the storm covering the entire southeastern part of the United States. Something clicked in my brain.

"Didn't you once tell me you had family in Nashville?" I asked.

Geoff squinted at me. "Yes," he said slowly. "My sister, but we're not close."

"Wouldn't you like to see her again? Reconnect? See your little nieces and nephews? You do have nieces and nephews, right? Have them get to know and love their Uncle Geoff-y. You know, Christmas is around the corner."

"You're forgetting I have a wife and five kids in Philly that I really want to see. I'm sure they don't want me taking a freakin' road trip in a hurricane. Worst case scenario is I'll get out of Houston on Monday, maybe Tuesday, and get a direct flight back home. I'll be back in Philly no later than Tuesday night."

"Or, and hear me out," I said. "You drive with me to Nashville. Spend a day with your sister and cute little nieces and nephews, then fly back to Philly on Monday. That's a day earlier than flying out of Houston. I believe we call that a win-win."

Geoff slowly shook his head no. "You're a no-good, shit-eating, low-life bastard, asshole scum, bro. I can't believe I'm saying this, but if you can convince your buddy Abdul to rent you a limo, I'll go with you. I'm not paying for gas. Plus, when we get back to Philly, you and Keisha are taking Imani and me out to dinner at Barclay Prime. And you're going to buy a bottle of Screaming Eagle Cabernet Sauvignon with dinner."

I smiled broadly. "Deal. You're a friend. Thank you." I held out my hand and waited a long couple of seconds until he shook it.

**

Abdul answered the phone on the second ring. "Mr. Josh. All of the flights have been canceled. Are you calling to reschedule?"

I quickly outlined my proposition. He said nothing for several long seconds. "You want me to drive you to Philadelphia? Pennsylvania?"

"Not exactly. No driver. I'll drive and you'll rent me just the car. Of course, I'll pay all of the tolls and gas. When the storm is over, we'll figure out a way to get the car back to you. I may hire a driver to bring it back, but one way or another I'll get it back to Houston."

There was another lengthy pause.

"Actually," said Abdul. "I have a cousin in Brooklyn. I was planning on selling him one of my limos. It's an old Town Car, not a stretch limo. I was trying to figure out how to get it to him. He's not buying a new car; it's the oldest one in my fleet."

"Keisha told me your cousin Ibrahim lives here."

"I have many cousins. This one is Asad."

"Well, what do you think?"

"I think this is crazy, Mr. Josh."

"I'd like to leave first thing tomorrow morning. No later than 8 A.M."

"In the storm? Are you crazy?"

I explained in detail the medical situation with Keisha, leaving out the old boyfriend part. He was silent for a long time. "Does that have anything to do with the truck, the near accident?"

"I don't think so." Actually, I thought it did. If Abdul hadn't taken those crazy evasive maneuvers, however, I suspected the accident might have been deadly. Somehow, Keisha's uterus was injured and that was causing the septicemia. I hoped she and the baby would be all right, and I knew they would be if I was with her. *I* would be better if I was with her.

"Let me be sure I understand this. You want to take my limo into the crazy storm and drive to Philadelphia?"

"Actually, Cincinnati, where she's in the hospital. Then Philadelphia."

He paused again. "That's what, about 1,500 miles?" He asked.

"Give or take," I said.

Yet another pause. "You've been a friend to me, and you've sent me lots of business. Plus, I feel terrible for Keisha. Also, my cousin wants the car." Long pause. I could hear thunder rumbling on his end of the line. "I'll do it." He paused and I waited. "How about $1,500?"

"No, $3,000," I said.

Abdul laughed. "Mr. Josh, you've not spent any time in the *souk*, I see. That's not how this works. I give you a price, then you give me a lower price. We argue for a few minutes, and you tell me how worthless my car is, you wouldn't transport pigs or your mother-in-law in it, you don't really need it, blah, blah, then we agree in the middle."

I laughed. "I know. But you're doing me a huge favor. It's worth it. Just make sure the car has decent tires and oil."

After making the arrangements, we signed off. I looked at Geoff who was drinking another beer, his third or fourth. A Lone Star from a bottle. Before 4 P.M. "Looks like we're going to make a buddy movie, compadre. We're rolling out tomorrow at 8 A.M."

Geoff didn't look at me or say anything. Instead, he caught the bartender's eye and made a hand gesture. Two fingers up, like a peace sign, then he pointed at the bar. A moment later, the bartender laid down two shot glasses in front of him and filled them with Jack Daniels. Geoff handed one to me. We clicked glasses then knocked them back.

Geoff looked at me and exhaled whiskey fumes. "Yee-ha. Nashville, here we come."

As if on cue, lightning flashed and a scant two seconds later we were assaulted by a momentous crash of thunder. I shook my head and thought, *Hurricane Epsilon, here we come.*

CHAPTER 12

JOSH

Geoff and I decided on an early dinner in the hotel restaurant. Keisha and I had talked earlier, and she told me the doctors wanted her to have IV antibiotics and complete bed rest for five days, so I knew where she was going to be. She didn't mention Sudor. That was bad. I knew her well enough—if nothing was going on, she would have said *something* about him.

I desperately wanted to be with her and the baby. I really wanted to be there just in case she went into labor. And to put myself between her and her old boyfriend.

There was another thing. I wanted to get her back to Philly and finally marry her. We'd postponed marriage way too long and it was time. With the baby coming, I decided now was the time to marry. Finally.

I told Geoff I wanted to get to bed early, so I'd be as refreshed as possible for the long ride. It was early for dinner and there weren't that many patrons in the restaurant. Also, I guessed quite a few had headed home by then. The restaurant itself was lavish, modern style, the kind of place where lawyers and oil company executives went to splurge. Not surprisingly, no one was dressed up. I was surprised, and not surprised, that they were running a full menu in the storm. This was the Four Seasons, after all. Geoff suggested we get a bottle of wine, but I told him it might be better just to have a glass of wine with dinner. We were going to have a long day on Saturday. I didn't need to start it hungover.

I wanted a clear picture of the route and obtained maps of Texas and the Southeast from the concierge. The trip was a fairly straight shot on I-10 to New Orleans. We'd bypass NOLA, then take I-59 north to Nashville. It was just four hours from Nashville to Cincinnati. Google Maps confirmed the plan.

Although New Orleans had recently suffered greatly from several hurricanes, we figured by traveling east to New Orleans, we wouldn't be hit by any of Hurricane Epsilon until we were near Birmingham. That was only about a three-hour drive from Nashville, so we'd be relatively close to Geoff's sister's place if we had to hunker down for a while. The total drive time would be about twelve hours to Nashville. Assuming we only stopped for gas and pit-stops and for takeout along the way, we'd be there around 8 P.M.

The drive from Nashville to Cincinnati would probably be right through the hurricane. Depending on how I felt, and weather reports, I figured I'd either start out immediately after dropping Geoff or I'd crash at his sister's place and get an early start on Sunday morning. The plan felt right. Geoff seemed like he'd be a good travel companion and the trip was doable. It was 7 P.M. on Friday. If everything went according to plan, I'd see Keisha the next night, Saturday, by around midnight.

As we were finishing dinner and I folded up the maps, I looked up and Diane was standing between us. She was wearing jeans and a clingy green scoop-neck sweater showing off some of her limited cleavage. She wore a thin smile. Diane could turn heads.

"I've heard a rumor that you boys are driving to Philly tomorrow. Is there any truth to that?" She smiled at us. Her shark smile. All traces of her southern accent were gone. "You know, I need to be in Philly on Monday morning for a meeting with Niles Lindstrom, the billionaire and new owner of Liberty Chemical Company. It's a big deal."

I looked at Geoff and he barely contained his eye roll.

"Actually, we're driving to Nashville tomorrow. We'll get there by around 8 P.M. if all goes according to plan. I'm going to drop Geoff at his sister's house and then continue to Cincinnati. Keisha's in the hospital there and I need to be with her."

Diane shook her head. "Cincinnati's no good. I need to be in Philly on Monday morning."

"In that case, you're better off trying for a flight on Sunday from here," I said. "The storm will have passed through by then and you can hop a flight directly to Philly. Also, considering that there's a major hurricane going on in Houston and you're stuck here, maybe Lindstrom can postpone the meeting a few days? Maybe do it virtually, if nothing else works."

Diane shook her head and made a face. "Lindstrom is coming in from goddamn Norway on his private jet. He's looking to buy another chemical plant on the Delaware River. A hundred-year-old facility with *beaucoup* environmental problems. I've talked with him several times about doing his environmental work and this guy is a no-bullshit zone. The work will keep us busy for years as we sort out the legal issues with the DEP and EPA. He wants to meet me at 8 A.M. on Monday and then is flying to LA in the afternoon. There are three other firms in Philly that are auditioning for this work. I've got to be there at 8 A.M. on Monday for the beauty pageant. My best chance for being able to do the meeting in person is hopping a ride with you boys." She smiled and put her hand on my neck. She laid it there lightly, casually, like it was the most natural thing to do. I felt sweat form down my back.

"Really, Diane, I don't think this is going to work," I said, trying not to sound disagreeable. "I'm going to Cincinnati, not Philly. Cinci to Philly is almost a nine hour drive itself, assuming good weather."

Diane pursed her lips and looked away. She looked back a moment later. "I know. Maybe you can drive me to Philly and then you drive back to Cincinnati. That way, I'll make my meeting and you can hang out with Keisha."

Diane was in her early forties and, to my knowledge, had never been married. I'd seen her at firm functions with good-looking men escorting her. When she took a vacation, it was always to some fabulous island or ski slope, and she loved to show pictures of her and the man who accompanied her. She had no trouble getting dates, but I had no doubt why she'd never married. She only cared about herself and no one else. There's a reason some people never marry. In Diane's case, she was too freakin' narcissistic.

"Well, Diane, if I did that it would take at least another sixteen hours to drop you off and circle back to Cincinnati. Honestly, I'm not going to leave Keisha alone in the hospital for an additional sixteen hours." I held eye contact with her.

She stared at me. It was a cold stare, and I tried my best not to break it off. The light touch on my neck turned into fingernails and pressure until I shrugged her hand off.

Finally, Geoff said, "Why don't you come with us? We're going through several big cities and I'm sure there will be flights to Philly. We can drop you at whatever airport has a direct flight. Birmingham, Nashville, Cincinnati. I'm sure one of them will have a flight to Philly."

I looked at him and widened my eyes. *What the hell, Geoff?*

Diane's lips, which were naturally thin, were pursed together like she wanted to say something, but it looked like she was restraining herself. She squinted, then said, "Good. What route?"

I briefly shut my eyes and shook my head. Oh, crap. This was going to be awful. "I-10 to New Orleans, then Interstates direct to Nashville. It's the easiest."

Diane rolled her eyes. "No way. I've looked it up. You picked a route that goes a long distance out of the way." She smirked and shook her head. "There's another route due north from Houston, on Interstate 69, that goes through Texarkana then hopscotches to Nashville. It's about an hour shorter and more direct. We should take that route."

I pulled out the map. "Look here, Diane," I said, pointing at the map. "Just a few miles north of Houston, I-69 turns into a US Route 59, then the route becomes some kind of state route, a two-lane road in places, not even a highway. If we take your route, we'll be on crappy little roads most of the way to Texarkana. I suppose theoretically it's a little shorter, but who knows what kind of maintenance they have on those roads? Also, your route just about follows the track of the hurricane. If we go through New Orleans, we'll miss most of it."

Diane frowned and shook her head. "I checked Siri. My route is about an hour shorter. I'm sure the roads will be kept clear. Also, my route goes through Nashville, too, where we can drop Geoff. Maybe somewhere along the way one of those Podunk airports will have a flight to Philly. That's as far as I'm willing to compromise. I-69 to Texarkana."

It hadn't occurred to me that we were negotiating a route or that I even had to compromise. It was *my* idea to drive to Cincinnati. *I* arranged for the car. *My* girlfriend was the one in the hospital. *My* baby was about to be born. If Diane wanted to get to Philly in time for a meeting with some Norwegian billionaire, she should figure it out herself and not intrude on my personal life. I was really steamed. *Screw you,* my brain screamed.

The medulla in my brain kicked in. My survival instinct reminded me that Diane was the person most responsible for my future as a lawyer at the firm. As department chair, she had a huge say in my end-of-year bonus, next year's salary, and partnership track. All of that would be decided in the next four weeks. Diane remembered the freakin' necktie I wore to my job interview eight years earlier; she'd remember in December if I ditched her in Houston. I'd have to find another hill to die on. *Fuck me.*

"Well, okay," I said brightly, trying my best to smile. "I-69 to US Route 59. I always wanted to see Texarkana."

Diane smiled and rubbed my shoulder. I couldn't figure out the meaning of the unnecessary touches. It was more than a pat, anything but affectionate, and way too long.

She started to go. "By the way, did I hear we're leaving at 8 A.M.?" She shook her head as she spoke. "That seems a little late, doesn't it?"

"That's the earliest we can get the car," I said. "We don't have many choices." She made a face. "We're wheels up at 8 A.M."

She continued shaking her head, then turned on her heels and stalked off.

"Crap," I said under my breath. When Diane was out of earshot, I said, "You're welcome, Diane. It's my pleasure to drive you all the freakin' way to Cincinnati, you asshole."

I raised my hand and a waiter appeared, "Buffalo Trace, doubles, water on the side. Two of them."

"Bourbon or rye?" the waiter asked.

"Bourbon."

"Now you're talking," Geoff said. He rubbed his hands together. The drinks were delivered to our table less than a minute later. Geoff raised his drink and swallowed about half of it.

I was tempted to shoot the whole thing back at once. Instead, I tried to sip my drink. This was going to be bad. I knew it.

CHAPTER 13

JOSH

Houston, Texas, 779 miles to Nashville.

I stood under the portico of the Four Seasons and listened as Abdul walked me around the Town Car, giving me instructions. It was a 2010 limo with 350,000 miles on it, a regular-sized Town Car, not a stretch. Still, it was large for a car these days, a lot bigger than an average-sized auto, but you could still fit it into a parking space. It was in reasonably decent shape despite its age—a few dings, but not much else showing on the body. Despite the wet weather, it looked as though Abdul had detailed it; the car gleamed under the lights of the portico.

The wind had abated somewhat but was still blowing hard. The air had a decidedly sea-smell, no doubt because all of the moisture coming from the Gulf of Mexico a mere fifty miles away.

According to the weather report, the winds were gusting up to eighty mph, but the sustained winds had calmed to between forty and fifty mph. That was still strong enough to blow you into the next county. You could be impaled by a passing branch, street sign, or lamp post. The rains continued unabated, and I was glad the portico was wide and deep. Plenty of rain was blowing on us, and I wished I had more than a windbreaker. Worse yet, we'd be fully immersed in the storm soon enough and for most of our trip.

"Mr. Josh, there's a switch on the dashboard to open the trunk, or you can just push this button." He showed me the button on the key fob and the trunk popped open to his touch. He picked up my suitcase—I had one rolling piece—and put it into the trunk which was obviously designed to hold many pieces of luggage.

"I really appreciate this, Abdul. You can only imagine how worried I am about my wife."

"I get it. Our wives and families, they mean everything to us." He looked at the black Cadillac idling quietly a few feet behind us. An attractive woman, early thirties, with brown eyes and long straight brown hair, sat behind the wheel. Abdul waved to her, and she waved back. "My wife. I told her I'd get my cousin to drive the second car today, but she insisted."

We smiled at each other.

I heard the sound of a rolling suitcase and looked toward the building. Geoff pulled his luggage out of the hotel. In addition to his suitcase, he had a heavy-duty garment bag and juggled a large cardboard cup of coffee. Abdul took the suitcase and put it into the trunk. He laid the garment bag on top.

"Remind me again why it is that we're leaving a perfectly good five-star hotel with a nice restaurant and bar and driving out into the nasty hurricane?" Geoff asked.

"Because you're a great friend and comrade," I said. "The best." I lightly punched him on the shoulder.

Abdul began to close the trunk when I stopped him. "We have one more passenger." I looked at my watch. It was 8:15. I recalled Diane saying she wanted to make an early start. We stood chatting for another five minutes when, finally, I saw a bellman helping Diane as she walked through the sliding door. The bellman had three pieces of luggage on a hotel trolley which he maneuvered toward us. One was large enough that you could have slept in it and the other two were smaller, normal sized. Diane was talking rapidly on her iPhone. She was using her "Don't fuck with me" tone of voice, so I assumed she was on a business call, although with her, she could have been talking to her mother. At 8:15 A.M. On a Saturday. When she noticed us, she held up her pointer finger and continued talking.

"It's a good thing we have a limo," I said when she finally clicked off. "I'm not sure we would've fit all of this luggage into a compact rental car."

Diane shrugged and said, "Whatever. I assume it's okay if I sit in the back. I've got some work to do." She held up her briefcase, a sleek, shiny leather thing that resembled an oversized purse.

"Are you planning to help us with the driving?" I asked. I suspected she'd be happy to let Geoff and me do all the driving so she could bill the entire sixteen-hour trip. At her billable rate, she'd bill over $10,000 while we drove.

"Yeah, sure."

Abdul held the door for her, and she climbed in the back with her iPhone and briefcase. Before the door closed, I saw her pull out a pile of papers and set them on the seat next to her. It looked like she had a week's worth to get through.

I leaned next to Geoff and said quietly, "I have a feeling she's going to spend the entire trip back there."

"And you're saying this because you're unhappy? Explain."

I shook my head and smiled.

Abdul gently closed the trunk and that was when I first noticed his license plate. *Kalypso 2.*

"Kalypso? Is that Arabic? How'd you come up with that?"

"It's Greek. Calypso was a goddess who could grant immortality. I spend a lot of time in my cars with a lot of crazy drivers out there, in all kinds of weather. I felt I could use a little assistance from a mythical goddess. When I came to this country, I couldn't afford cable. After driving all day, I would turn on the television. I liked Jacques Cousteau's program. It was very soothing. An interesting show about the sea. He named his ship Calypso. If it was good enough for Cousteau, it was good enough for me."

"Wait, that was with a 'C', right?" I asked.

"Yes, but the DMV said that was already taken, so I spelled it with a 'K'. This was actually my second car. My newest one is Kalypso 9."

He gave me a second set of keys for his cousin in Brooklyn, which I jammed into my jeans pocket. Then we shook hands, and he held the door for me until I was in the car. He closed it as only an experienced chauffeur could. Despite the wind, he shut the door the same way a mother would close the door to a sleeping child's room. Softly and quietly. Barely a click.

The interior was spotless. I knew it would be. Abdul's cars were always clean. It had long ago lost its new car smell, but had no odor of cigarettes, mold, or anything nasty. Nothing out of the ordinary except for the Armor All. It looked like Abdul had recently cleaned the dashboard and leather with the stuff. Again, I appreciated Abdul's automobile-OCD. I wasn't sure if that was for us or his cousin in Brooklyn. It didn't matter. I decided when I got to Philly, I'd have the car detailed for his cousin. If for no reason other than to honor Abdul.

As we settled in, I texted Keisha for the second time that morning. I'd called her at a reasonable time the night before and awakened her, so I decided texting would be best.

I'm on my way. If all goes according to plan, I hope to see you around midnight. I can't wait to be with you. Give your belly a pat for me! Call me when you're up to it. Love, Josh

Geoff was sitting in the shotgun seat. I turned on the radio and was glad to see he had Sirius XM. I found a station with Foo Fighters and turned up the volume. A Dave Grohl guitar solo, loud and bluesy.

"You're kidding, right?" Diane said, poking her head forward. This was the first time she looked up in five minutes. "You're planning on driving all the way to Nashville listening to that noise?"

"Well, only as far as I drive. When Geoff takes over, he can put on whatever station he wants," I said.

"I'm into old-school hip-hop," he said. "Run D.M.C., Tupak, Public Enemy, all the greats. We're lucky, there's a satellite station that plays just the old-school hip-hop songs. If we didn't have that, we'd have to listen to country music and gospel on the local radio stations. We should be able to listen to the good stuff on satellite all the way to Nashville with no commercials. Hopefully, Abdul won't discontinue his subscription until we're home." He grinned broadly.

"I don't want to listen to any of that crap," Diane said. She set down some papers and a gold pen on the seat and crossed her arms. "How am I supposed to work? Why don't we compromise and listen to that pop-rock blend station?"

I shook my head. "Sorry, the driver picks the station. If you want to listen to ABBA, be my guest, but you have to drive. That's the rule. Driver's choice."

"You're kidding me, right? Who made this rule?"

I looked at Geoff. "Time immemorial itself," he said. "It goes along with calling first for shotgun and who gets to pick the fast-food joints. It just is."

Geoff and I grinned at each other.

Diane shook her head. "I don't fucking believe this," she said under her breath, quietly, but loudly enough that we could hear it. "Does this car have one of those glass dividers between the front seat and back? I want to roll it up."

"Sorry, no. The best I can do for you is adjust the speakers, so the music just comes out in front."

"Un-fucking-believable. I'm driving all the way to Philadelphia with two sixteen-year-old boys."

"All the way to Nashville with the two of us," I said. "Then to Cincinnati with me."

"Yeah, right." She shook her head and looked disgusted. Then, she reached into her briefcase and pulled out a pair of earbuds. She held them up for us to see. "You guys are morons. Here's my plan B." She plugged them into her ears. I watched as she tapped on her iPhone.

"Diane, Diane," I said looking forward and in a normal speaking voice. She didn't respond.

I looked at Geoff and said, "I think she has her music on and must have noise-canceling earbuds. She can't hear us."

"Don't be so sure," he whispered.

I pushed the button on the trip odometer until it registered zero. Then, on the Waze app, I tapped in Geoff's sister's address in Nashville and noticed it predicted we'd be there in thirteen hours. Awesome. We were already way behind schedule. I plugged my phone into the charger, then settled myself. I pulled out onto Lamar Street and immediately felt the wind buffet the car. The wipers could barely keep up with the rain.

"This is going to be awesome," Geoff said looking forward, I assumed so Diane couldn't read his lips. "The Lincoln Lawyers."

Awesome, indeed. "All-righty then," I said. "Giddy up."

CHAPTER 14

JOSH

Cleveland, Texas, 45 miles from Houston; 734 miles to Nashville.

The wind was relentless. Merciless. Brutal. Savage. Although the storm was coming up from the south, the wind would unexpectedly blow at us from every direction. I was glad we were in a large, heavy car with six cylinders, and not some compact piece of tin likely to be blown off the highway.

There seemed to be few eighteen-wheelers on the road. Thank God. They were like giant sails. The occasional semi we saw was having a hard time going in a straight line. I watched one in front of me swerve from lane to lane. I was sure he wasn't doing that on purpose. Most were traveling about forty-five mph, although there were always a few insane truckers doing seventy or eighty. Crazy bastards. Whenever I caught up to one, I stepped on the gas and passed it as fast as I could. Something I learned from my father fifteen years earlier when he taught me to drive was "If you're going to pass, then pass." He was right. I was afraid the wind would shift, and some no-good SOB would swerve right into us. Passing, or being passed, by any tractor-trailer was an adventure.

Houston drivers, or maybe this applies to all Texans, are insane. It's like they've all taken amphetamines and drunk several cups of espresso before getting behind the wheel. They went fast and changed lanes without hesitation. Keisha had accused me of being a "crazy Philly driver," but I could never drive like a Texan. Maybe I was a little jealous of their speed and dexterity.

Some of their highways are sixteen lanes wide. Sixteen. In Philly, the major highway in and out of the city is the so-called "Expressway." It is actually four lanes wide—as in two in each direction. They can be jammed at any time of the day or night. The highways in Houston, with all of their lanes, really aren't a whole lot faster.

Despite that, everyone in Texas seems to think they're driving on some twenty-lane superhighway with an unlimited speed limit. Like it's a God-given right. More than once, I got honked or high-beamed to move out of someone's way because I wasn't doing seventy-five. I expected that in the midst of a hurricane, the Texas drivers would behave differently. They didn't. For the most part I stuck to the right lanes, except when I had to get around a semi.

I was shocked that the state police or Rangers or whatever they call them in Texas hadn't altogether banned these trucks from the road during the storm. I know they hate the government in Texas, but as best as I could tell, the only governmental rules and regulations the authorities seemed to be relying on was the insanity rule. The sane drivers had parked their cars and rigs until the storm was over. Only the insane ones were on the road. Along with the insane limo drivers.

I-69 wasn't too bad. The highway was raised way above grade and well-drained. In Houston, we could see down into the neighborhood streets with water flooding the ranch homes and businesses. Those streets were miserable, and I felt awful for the people there. I knew that in August 2022, the interstates flooded, too. I hoped that wouldn't be the case today. I was able to keep the car at between thirty-five and fifty mph on the highway. Normally, it would take roughly forty-five minutes or so to get from downtown Houston to Cleveland, Texas, where the interstate ended and US 59 took over. Although the traffic was light, it took us over an hour in the storm.

As we traveled north, the Houston suburbs gave way to farms and ranches and finally woodlands and what I'm sure was pretty countryside. You could hardly tell. The constant rain made it difficult to see very far off the highway. Also, I was afraid to allow myself the distraction of glancing at the scenery as I needed to devote my full attention to driving.

I was glad to see the interface from Interstate 69 to US 59 was seamless. The US route looked exactly like an Interstate highway, albeit with occasional pull offs in weird places. A gas station here, a roadside church there, someone's driveway. The difference between an Interstate and a US route, I suppose.

I was focused on the driving and glanced around quickly as we approached Cleveland. I'm guessing some ex-pat from Ohio landed here a hundred years ago and needed something to remind him of his far-off rust-belt hometown in the wilds of Texas. There was nothing remotely similar about the Ohio city on Lake Erie and Houston's distant suburb. I decided I would Google it up some day.

"Cleveland is up ahead," I said loudly. "Anyone need to stop?"

I saw Diane pull an ear bud out. "No. I think we ought to go as far as we can without stopping. You're not covering much ground."

I smiled into the mirror. "And you're not driving in the hurricane, Diane. That's the plan. I was just asking to be polite."

She smirked and dug the ear bud back into her ear.

"Diane, Diane," I said quietly. She didn't respond. I glanced at Geoff. "Maybe I'll just stop here to piss her off."

He smiled.

As we blew past Cleveland, the woods closed in around the highway, which narrowed to two lanes in each direction. I could feel the sweat forming in my armpits as I picked my way along at fifty mph. Trees were blown over to the edge of the road and the remnants of trunks littered the side of the road. A few miles north of Cleveland, I watched in horror as the wind toppled a large tree just ahead of us. It crashed onto the shoulder and, without looking, I jerked the big car into the left lane. I drove over some branches doing forty. Crap, I was fortunate no one was trying to pass me. The highway department seemed to be playing a losing game of whack-a-mole with the tree limbs.

We drove through the wooded areas, and I repeatedly glanced from the road to the nearby woods to see if any more trees—weakened by the pounding rain, their roots exposed and protective soil cover washed away, challenged by the relentless wind, and just tired of hanging on for dear life—would decide to give up the ghost. I expected another tree to fall in front of us as we drove by. I would've loved to check my blood pressure then. Generally, it's fairly normal, but I was sure it was through the roof. I tried to breathe serenely. Like yoga. *Namaste.*

The satellite radio station we'd been listening to had moved on from Foo Fighters. It had played a number from Soundgarden and now was playing one of my favorite songs by Red Hot Chili Peppers—*Californication*. I turned up the volume. Actually, I'd turned up the volume several times since we left the hotel. Although the Town Car had really good sound insulation, the noise from the storm and trucks was loud, drowning out the music. I needed the music to distract me and help calm my nerves.

"Isn't that loud enough?" Diane said from the backseat. I glanced in the rearview and saw her removing her ear buds. "I can hear that crap over my music and noise-canceling earbuds. Can you turn it down?"

"Actually, no," I said. "This is the most screwed up driving I've ever done. I need the music to keep me as chill as possible. I need to be able to hear it."

"Well, *I* need to work. That noise is distracting me."

"Anytime you want to take over driving in the nice hurricane, be my guest. You can listen to whatever station you want if you're driving. You could listen to Lawrence freakin' Welk for all I care." I stopped ranting for a moment. "What music do you listen to, anyway?"

Diane thought for a moment. "Survivor, Paul McCartney, Toto, Milli Vanilli, Elton, all the pop music greats. I know you think my music is lame, but I like to rock out too." She made a dance move with her hands, first to the right, then to the left.

I threw Geoff a look. He responded with an eye roll.

"I suppose some of those are okay," Geoff said. "Some of them have pretty good songs. Not as good as Dr. Dre or Snoop, but you can dance to those."

"See. I'm sure there's a station we'd all be happy with." I could see Diane manufacture a broad smile in the rear view.

"Yes," I said. "It's called driver's pick. Any time you want to take over, you can pick the station."

Diane frowned, shook her head, and plugged her earbuds back in. She picked up her pile of papers and studied them. I focused on driving.

I'd been able to speed up to sixty mph in the right lane as I came upon a semi. He was going slower, maybe forty. Even at forty, the wind was causing him to weave from one side of the lane to the other, occasionally crossing the dashed line. He splashed a tidal wave of rainwater behind him. Great. All I needed was to be sideswiped by 80,000 pounds of truck.

I took a quick glance in the rearview and stepped on the gas. Seventy, eighty, eighty-five miles per hour.

"What the fuck are you doing, Goldberg?" Diane yelled from the back seat as she held onto the overhead strap. "Are you trying to kill us?"

I ignored her. Despite the headwind, the powerful motor propelled us past the truck. I hoped I wouldn't hydroplane from all the water. As we came even with the cab, Geoff said loudly, "Shit, that bastard is looking at his phone. Unbelievable."

I clenched the steering wheel more tightly and kept speeding up until I put at least a quarter mile between us.

I continued driving and began wondering if the wheels were unbalanced or the car was out of alignment since we kept pulling, first to one side then the other. At one point, the winds must have died down a bit because the car drove just fine. It occurred to me that the pulling was from the force of the intense wind.

The terrain changed and the woods again gave way to farms and ranches. At least, I decided they might be ranches since we were in Texas. This was good and bad. There were fewer trees to worry about. For now, it was much less likely that some half-dead tree would fall across the highway and kill us. At the same time, as we came upon a field or pasture, the winds rocked the car. I thought about Keisha and kept driving.

Ahead, I could see taillights from mostly trucks and a few cars in the right lane. There was a police car with blinking red and blue lights on the shoulder. A row of orange traffic cones corralled traffic to the right lane. Standing on the shoulder was a man in a yellow raincoat, with a yellow cowboy-style rain hat waving a bright light. I slowed to a stop behind a semi. The man's raincoat had the words "Deputy Sheriff" printed in big black letters. He had a sheriff's badge stenciled on his raincoat. Above that was his name, A. Elias.

I rolled down the window an inch or so and was greeted by intense wind and rain which blew onto my face.

"What's going on, Sheriff . . . Elias?"

The guy was big and beefy, his face slick with rainwater and rain dripped off his hat. Weirdly, he wore clear ski goggles. This was the last guy I expected to see on some ski slope. As I considered this, the wind blew more sharply, and they made sense. He was protecting his eyes from flying objects.

"That's *Deputy* Elias, thank you. We're stopping the big rigs and cars here," the officer spoke with a thick Texas accent. "Y'all are about a mile from the Trinity River and an open bridge crossing the river. We've had accidents there in the past. Two years ago in that big goddamn storm, we had a truck get blown clear off the bridge into the river. Took out an SUV when he went over. We're stopping everyone here and asking them to wait until the wind dies down before we let some go through. The trucks have got to wait. A lot of the cars are waiting for a break in the wind."

"So, I don't have to wait if I don't want to? I have a long way to go today."

"Everyone wants to be somewhere else. Get home. Work. Man, I'm telling you it's dangerous. The winds on that bridge are like a whirlwind. The bridge is completely open, and the winds are a lot more intense than what you've been driving through. I think it's crazy to cross that bridge now. Those winds'll blow you back to Houston. If I were you, I'd wait. But this is Texas, and you have a God-given right to play the fool. We'll let you through, but it's on you." He looked down the highway. "If you're in trouble, the best I can say is we'll fish you out of the river when the storm's over, but that's it."

I looked at Geoff. "What do you think? I mean we could sit here for hours if we wait."

Geoff bounced his head from side to side like he was weighing his choices. Finally, he said, "Giddy up."

"Well then, hang on. I don't know whether it'll be better to go real fast or real slow across the bridge. I'm not sure there's a right way."

I looked at the deputy, who waited in the rain, and said, "Deputy, I appreciate your concern, but we're going to try it. Thanks."

I waved to the deputy and noticed he keyed a mic that was fixed to his shoulder and talked into it. He moved a traffic cone so I could pull out. I angled into the left lane and drove past dozens of trucks and a few cars, waiting for the signal from the police that it was safe to go through. After about a minute of driving slowly, the bridge loomed ahead. It was one of those flat highway bridges. Unimpressive. It was not the kind with towers and suspension cables, just a flat top. On an ordinary day, you'd cross it in a few seconds and not know you'd been on a bridge.

Another raincoat-clad sheriff held up his hand and stopped me. He was also wearing clear ski goggles.

"You the one who talked to Deputy Elias at the back of the line?"

"Yes, sir. Is it better if I take this fast or slow?"

The cop shook his head. "It's better for y'all to wait a spell. If you're bound and determined to take it, though, I'd go slow. Real slow. This ain't no rodeo. Be prepared for hard wind that'll look to blow you right off the bridge clear to Galveston. Even in this big car. Just be prepared for it." He looked toward the bridge and waited for the wind to calm a bit. Then he said, "Okay, pardner. You're up." Like in a rodeo. I was the one sitting on an angry bull with his balls bound up.

I thanked him and rolled up the window. I drove about twenty miles per hour. When we reached the opening for the bridge, the winds, which were already roaring, picked up and the car rocked violently. The bridge wasn't long, maybe a quarter mile, flat, cement, four lanes with a divider, and a rail on each side at about waist height. A red sign with big white letters at the entrance to the bridge read:

TRINITY RIVER
WARNING: DANGEROUS WINDS

The sign was whipping back and forth like it wanted to unscrew from the ground and fly off. I was sorely tempted to step on the gas and rocket across the damn bridge.

I started venturing across tentatively, slowing to maybe ten mph. When I was a few dozen feet across, the wind picked up even more and the car began to rock. I mean serious rocking. I glanced at Geoff. He was holding the above-head grip with one hand and had his other on the dashboard. I glanced in the rear view. Diane had put down her work and had her hands on my seat to brace herself.

I tapped the gas and sped up to thirty. The rocking eased a bit. When we were about half way across, a big gust coming downstream hit us from the side. The car began to go up on two wheels. The front and back wheels on my side felt like they weren't gripping the deck. The wind was like a giant fist, pushing us off the bridge onto the narrow shoulder. As my wheels were pushed, the noise from the concrete corduroy strip on the shoulder warned me we were approaching the edge of the bridge. The car felt like it was going to roll onto its roof and over into the river.

"The hell with it," Geoff shouted over the wind. "Get off the damn bridge."

I stomped my foot on the gas and the car shot ahead. It was all I could do to keep the wheels on the bridge. I turned the steering wheel hard to the left, as though I was making a left-hand turn, to keep from getting blown off the bridge. The tires squealed on the wet pavement above the noise of the wind. When I got to the other side, just a few seconds later, I quickly had to correct the wheel and the car swerved wildly as we rocketed onto the highway doing at least seventy. A seagull shot past the windshield. Not flying. It was like it had been launched from a canon.

"Holy shit," Geoff said.

I must've looked insane. As I pumped the brake, Geoff said, "You should see your face, bro, you look mad. I mean crazy-mad."

There was a pull off on the other side of the bridge surrounded by scrubby trees. It looked like someone's driveway. I braked hard and pulled way over, almost in the grass away from the travel lane, and put the car into park. The Town Car purred quietly. A gust of wind buffeted us from time to time. We rocked back and forth with the trees.

On the southbound lanes, a line of trucks waited for the opportunity to run the gauntlet of wind. The deputy monitoring the traffic looked at our car and shook his head. His expression told me all I needed to know about what he thought of us.

"Just give me a second," I said, looking at Geoff. "Man, I could use a drink."

Geoff immediately pulled a small metal flask from his jacket. He smiled at me and wiggled the bottle back and forth. "Seriously? You want some Makers?"

I shook my head. "Nah. It's just a figure of speech. I need all of my wits for the rest of the drive. I'm just unbelievably tense."

Unexpectedly, a pair of hands reached out and found my neck. Slender hands, warm and experienced. Diane dug her fingers into my neck firmly. She expertly worked my trapezius muscles. I immediately tensed up as she pressed my neck, but her touch was hard, yet tender. Relentless, like her. This was not a cursory neck rub, but a serious therapeutic massage. It took me a couple of seconds to begin relaxing. Before I dropped my chin to my chest, I stared straight ahead and gave Geoff a sidelong glance and could see he'd raised his eyebrows as he looked at the road. I didn't say a word as Diane rubbed my neck and the back of my head for at least thirty seconds. It was weird, I mean, this was my boss. Freakin' Diane. And excellent. Really, just what I needed at that moment. Except that it was . . . Diane. Finally, I said, "Thanks, Diane, that felt wonderful. I really needed that."

"I took two courses on massage on my last trip to St. Barts." She continued stroking my neck, her hands reaching to the top of my chest. She touched me lightly, making the hair on the back of my neck rise. "Sports massage and erotic massage." Neither Geoff nor I responded. "I aced both courses."

"Awesome," I finally said. She gently touched the back of my head, running her fingers through my hair and stroking it for several seconds. She finished with a pat on my shoulders.

Suddenly, she grabbed the hair on the back of my head with her fingers and pulled it back toward the headrest. Hard. "Now, will you change the fucking channel?" She asked with a smirk in her voice. Then, she smoothed my hair gently and tickled my earlobe with a finger.

"Sure." I found The Blend and the first song it played was *In the Air Tonight*, by Phil Collins. Always a quid pro quo with Diane.

We sat at the pull-off for another minute as I collected myself. I looked at the trip odometer. We'd driven sixty-two miles from the hotel. It took us over two hours.

Crap.

CHAPTER 15

JOSH

Dybbuk, Texas, 105 miles from Houston; 674 miles to Nashville.

We continued north on US 59 through an area that was a mixture of woodlands and farms. The winds continued gusting ferociously, buffeting the car. There were times it was all I could do to keep the car in the lane. After a while, it felt like the wind may have been dying down a bit. I had a feeling that was temporary. It would start up again a minute later. The one good thing about the police holding up traffic near the bridge was that truck traffic had diminished considerably—many of the trucks were stuck on the south side of the river.

"So, Geoff, do you want to hear my entire riff on why climate change is causing the storm?" I asked.

"Do I have a choice?" Geoff shook his head. "I guess we're stuck in a car for another twelve hours, so why not?"

"I mean, you don't need to be a climate scientist to buy into the fact that this gigantic storm in mid-November is entirely wrong." I took a hand from the wheel and waved it around. "I mean it's got the unusually heavy winds, incredible rain, tornadoes, even snow up north. The whole thing is like a freakin' disaster movie."

"I hear you. Look, I'm a real estate lawyer. I watch ESPN, not the climate change channel like you do. If a client wants to buy a house next to the seashore, I'm not going to lecture him about climate change and tell him that his property could be washed away. That's not on me."

"Are you sure about that?" I asked. "You're an ethical guy. I know you'd counsel a client if the house was infested with termites or had some other dangerous condition. That's the law. Do you think you might have an obligation to tell your client that the beachfront property he's considering buying might end up being an island? Worse yet, it may end up being Atlantis."

"That's not the law. I don't have any special knowledge regarding climate change. They can read those United Nations reports as well as I can. If a house is built on quicksand and I know about it, I must disclose it. If the question is whether the ocean might rise two feet and swallow someone's house, I don't see that as being on me or their agent."

Suddenly, the wind picked up in a staggering gust and I had to turn the wheel hard to stay on the road. I'd become complacent over the past half hour but still had to concentrate. When the gust died down, I took a deep breath.

"Jesus, Josh, can you please keep the car on the road?" Diane from the back seat. "Boys, if you don't mind me jumping in, there's another thing. I know that Josh doesn't feel this way, but I look at climate change as something more like an interesting theory, not a scientific fact. Maybe just science fiction."

"Science fiction?" I said. "Seriously? I know you have to agree with our clients when they're around, I suppose, but this isn't just us talking. Can you really dismiss the IPCC report and the other hundreds and thousands of studies that have been done?"

"You talk like there's only one position. There's another side. There are many notable scientists who believe that what you're calling climate change is nothing more than natural oscillations in the wobble of the earth, normal cycles in temperature and precipitation, that kind of thing. I've read some reports, too. Fox News. They say the so-called climate scientists are cherry-picking their data. I don't have the studies at my fingertips, like you, but they're out there."

"Diane, respectfully, that's bullshit. I agree there've been a number of reports that have been written by some fringe-y people. Not all of them are scientists . . ."

"You mean like the former vice president . . ."

"I put him in the category of cheerleader. Not everyone can be the quarterback. You know, Gore did get the Nobel Peace Prize for his work. You can't dismiss the work that's been done by the United Nations, the NWS, NOAA, NSA, NASA, the Department of Defense, all of those agencies. Not to mention the literal thousands of scientists who have taken a stand. They all conclude the same thing. They may disagree on how fast the impact will be from climate change or how large, but the IPCC says we only have until the end of this decade to make serious changes, then it's too late."

"You have your scientists, I have mine." Diane made a laughing noise, like a snort. "I've talked with plenty of scientists at the energy companies we represent, and they have an entirely different perspective."

"I'm sure you could talk with the scientists at the tobacco companies, and they'll tell you cigarettes don't cause lung cancer. Really, I don't think they're the most objective arbiters."

We drove for another minute being buffeted by wind and pummeled by rain. I'd gotten the hang of driving in this awful weather and although it was stressful, I learned to anticipate a gust of wind and to avoid spending time too close to any other vehicles, especially trucks. It helped that we were driving in a massive car. I pondered briefly how much carbon we were spewing, but there was nothing I could do about it.

Now, we were way north of the Trinity River and had driven through the towns of Chester and Corrigan. A highway sign said that the city of Dybbuk was a few miles ahead and Lufkin about twenty miles further. I glanced at the odometer and realized we'd only traveled about 110 miles. It was already past noon. At this rate we wouldn't get to Nashville until after midnight, and only if we made up time somewhere else. The big gas tank in the Town Car was still over half full, but it occurred to me it wouldn't be a bad idea to keep it topped off. The last thing we needed was to run out of gas in a hurricane.

"I'm thinking we might stop in Dybbuk or Lufkin for gas and lunch. I could use the break. We could switch drivers, too. Any objections?"

"Sounds good to me," Geoff said immediately.

"You do know at this rate we're not going to get to Nashville till tomorrow sometime," Diane said. "If we stop, we'll be even later. I still need to be in Philly for my meeting on Monday."

"I hear you, Diane, but I need a break. We're going to have to switch drivers. We may as well fill up the tank and take a break at a luncheonette for twenty minutes or so."

I picked Dybbuk, the Lumber Capital of East Texas, because US 59 went straight through the town. According to the map, the highway went around Lufkin. I figured stopping in Dybbuk would be faster. I pulled into Paulie's gas station and when none of my passengers moved, I got out and looked for the credit card reader on the pump. A handwritten sign said it wasn't working and to pay inside.

I jogged to the store through the rain and wind and stamped my feet as I closed the door. The old linoleum was broken and worn. Dust and grime covered everything. The place smelled like an old bar with the lingering odor of cigarettes and stale beer. Most of the shelves were empty. The whole place was shabby, like it was ready to be demolished.

Sitting on a bar stool behind the cash register, a teenage girl was on her phone. She was maybe sixteen years old, and her blond roots showed under dyed green hair. She wore one of those tank tops that clung to her body, showing off her limited contours and mini boobs, which seemed odd to me considering the temperature was in the fifties. Despite her attempt to achieve some kind of look, I didn't think it was working. I waited for over a minute until she finally acknowledged me and ended her call.

"Yeah?" the girl said, looking me over.

"I'd like to fill up at pump number four," I said, handing her my Visa card. She slid it into the reader.

"Y'all come back after you fill up and I'll give it back to you."

I went back outside. Even though the tank wasn't half empty, it still took almost ten gallons. I was glad we were in Texas where gasoline was relatively cheap. As I stood in the cold drizzle, I noticed the station had an attached garage. The bay door was open, and a car was on a lift inside. An orange and purple tow truck with the logo, "Paulie's Garage" written in script, sat in the rain to the side of the garage. Everything about the place looked sad and decrepit.

When I got back into the store to collect my credit card, the girl was gone. She may have been in the ladies' room, but I had no way of knowing. "Hey! Is anybody here? Hello!"

After a good thirty seconds, a man came out from a door that connected to the garage. He wore grease-stained blue coveralls with the name "Paulie" stitched on. His face was grizzled, but the most noticeable thing about him was his eyepatch. Black and held on with an elastic cord. He looked like a pirate. Not one you would hope to see at Disney World. "Yeah?"

"I gave the girl my credit card and filled up my tank. I need my card back."

"Yeah? Which girl?"

"I don't know, blonde and green curly hair, shoulder-length, young, thin, tank top, maybe sixteen or seventeen."

He smiled a weird smile at me and said, "You like 'em young, mister?"

"What? No. I just said she was young. What the hell do you mean?"

"Don't mean nothin'." He shrugged and smiled and went to the cash register. "Name?"

He picked up what looked like a stack of credit cards and started shuffling through them. It was a big stack, like a deck of cards. That was not very reassuring.

"Joshua. Joshua Goldberg."

He looked at me and said, "Goldberg. Uh-huh. You from New York?"

"No, Philly, Philadelphia. Does it matter?"

"Don't matter to me."

He went through the cards, and I was certain he was going to tell me it wasn't there before he pulled the one off the top and handed it to me. "Here you go, Mr. Goldberg."

"Thanks. I looked around at the empty shelves and general filth of the place. "You got a restroom here?"

He laughed. "Yeah, but it's out of service. Most people, guys anyway, girls too, just go out back. Feel free."

I shook my head and went back to the car.

"Do they have a restroom?" Diane asked.

"Not exactly. Only if you want to squat in the weeds out back. This place is weird. Let's get the hell out of here and find somewhere to eat. It creeps me out."

We drove further into town. Many of the storefronts were empty. Finally, we found a luncheonette on a corner, Priscilla's Diner. I pulled into a parking spot, and we all hurried through the weather into the restaurant. I was glad it was open. There were a few people inside.

A waitress came over almost right away. None of us took seats. "You want drinks, hon?"

I said, "Coffee, black."

Geoff said, "Make that two."

Diane looked around the small place with its booths and art from Sears and said, "Any chance you can make me a macchiato, maybe a latté?"

The waitress closed her eyes and shook her head. "Dang it, fresh out. I've got regular coffee and decaf coffee, hon. Maxwell House. That's it."

Diane nodded and said, "Give me a Diet Coke."

We all made our way to the restrooms. I was out first and sat in the booth facing the street. I was glad to see my coffee was waiting for me and had a sip. It had been a while since I had a plain Maxwell House coffee and I'd forgotten that it actually tasted quite good.

Geoff came out and sat across from me. He took four bags of sugar and dumped them into his cup.

"You want a little coffee with that sugar?" I asked.

"It's my metabolism. My body eats the stuff up."

As we glanced at the sticky menus and waited for Diane, two girls, not quite women, came in with ski parka hoodies pulled tight over their heads. They shrugged off their wet parkas and sat at the counter. I guessed they were no more than seventeen or eighteen years old. Jeans, skimpy tops, ski parkas. I thought it was too cold for tube tops and too warm for ski parkas. I recognized the one girl, skinny with her green hair, as the cashier at Paulie's Garage. They obviously knew the waitress as she came over and they shared a laugh.

After a moment, the two girls started looking at Geoff and me. Smiling at us. The one girl put her mouth next to the green-haired girl and they laughed. Then they both got up and the dark-haired one, slender, attractive, with unartful tattoos on her arms, approached me, while green hair approached Geoff.

"Hey there, boys" dark hair said with a Texas accent. "Y'all passing through?"

"In fact, we are."

"Well, what're ya'alls names?" she said to me. "Why don't you introduce yourselves like proper gentlemen?"

I glanced at Geoff. "Joshua, Josh."

"Well, I'm Nancy, Joshua Josh," said the dark-haired one. I couldn't tell if she was mocking me or really thought my name was Joshua Josh. As she talked, she placed her hand on my arm. "Hey Joshua Josh. You work out?" she patted my bicep. "Nice."

"Oh yeah, I work out. They call me *the Rock* back home." I grinned. Geoff rolled his eyes and shook his head.

The green-haired one put her hand on Geoff's shoulder, "How about you darlin'? You got a name?"

"Snoop. Like the rap star." He smiled broadly at me. "I had that name before the other Snoop did."

I looked at Geoff and made a face.

"Snoop?" asked the green-haired one. "I've never been with someone named Snoop before. I mean, I've been with Black dudes, but never anyone named Snoop. I'm Alice."

Snoop/Geoff held out his hand and shook Alice's.

"You guys like to party?" Nancy asked, pushing her way onto the bench next to me and placing her hand on my knee. She rubbed it gently, moving her hand to the inside of my leg. "I know a place we can go to party. The fun begins in ten minutes."

"Well . . . We're just traveling through," I said. "This is just a quick stop."

"Quick is good," said Nancy. "Alice and me can arrange a party that's as quick or as long as y'all like. We can do a foursome, threesome, one-on-one, you boys can watch us do it too, we don't care." She leaned in close; she smelled like strawberries on steroids. "A hundred bucks in advance, total, Joshua Josh, for whatever you boys like. Up to an hour of fun."

I looked up and Diane was standing behind them. "Oh, shoot, busted. Snoop, look who's here. I guess the party's over."

Nancy didn't miss a beat. She looked Diane up and down. A long and shameless look. "For an extra twenty-five dollars we can add your mama."

We pushed our way out of the booth, and I threw down a ten-dollar bill. We bolted for the car and Geoff got behind the wheel.

"Exactly what was that all about, the thing about the extra twenty-five dollars to add your mom?" Diane asked. Geoff and I were laughing too hard to respond. "And what's the deal with *Snoop*?"

Every time one of us started to talk we burst into deep belly laughs. Uncontrollable.

We drove through a town that reminded me a little of the one in *The Last Picture Show*, except without all of the hope and charm. We found a Sonic Drive-In on the other side of town and ordered bags of food and drinks, then headed back onto US 59. The rain and wind had eased some more, and I hoped we'd be able to make up for lost time.

As we reached the outskirts of town, I turned and looked through the rear window to see if we were being followed. Satisfied that we had the road to ourselves, I helped myself to a greasy French fry.

CHAPTER 16
KEISHA

Keisha lay in her hospital bed, ignoring the TV which she'd muted, and mentally blocking out the noise from the storm raging outside. Finding reassurance from the sound coming from the fetal monitor, she focused on herself. Her body was swollen from her face to her toes. Three months earlier she had to pry her rings from her fingers. She knew Josh would have to cut them off if she'd waited another few days. At that time, he said he would buy her an engagement ring, but she said it was "too soon." He said if they waited much longer it would be "too late." They both laughed.

Mostly, she focused her thoughts on her belly and the baby developing ever so slowly inside her. Keisha urged her daughter, she was convinced it was a girl, to grow. Keisha's mother had told her she was only six and a half pounds when she was born. That seemed like a reasonable weight and as long as her baby weighed that much, Keisha was sure she'd be okay. Not that he spent much time looking at it, but once Josh had shown her some Jewish text, maybe from the Talmud, which said every blade of grass on earth had an angel hovering over it that whispered to it: "*grow*." Right now, she hoped there was an angel hovering over her baby, whispering, "*grow*."

As she lay in the hospital bed, she spent a few moments thinking about Josh and a lot of time thinking about Anthony. She'd just finished her education degree at St. Joseph's University in Philly's Wynnefield section and was a rookie teacher at Gompers Elementary School. She'd met Anthony at a party, and he'd bragged that he was in medical school at Thomas Jefferson University. At first, she thought he was full of himself—and he was—but he was handsome and sweet, and she managed to overlook his arrogance. One date led to another and a month later she moved into his apartment in Philly's hip Manayunk section.

Keisha's family was middle-class, but Anthony came from a wealthy family in Cheltenham, a suburb north of Philly. Both of his parents were doctors and he'd gone to private school his entire life. She wasn't ready to settle down but enjoyed living with him. Sometimes his attitude got in the way of their relationship, and she was never sure he respected her career choice. But when she was offered a prestigious job as an elementary school teacher at Friends Select School in center city, he urged her to take it. She did and never regretted it.

They were together for almost two years. Long enough for all her relatives to meet him and all of her friends to urge her to marry him. She thought she might be ready to get married but wasn't sure he was. Besides, he hadn't asked, and she was traditional enough that she didn't ask him.

Life with Anthony was an adventure. When he wasn't crazy-busy studying, they managed weekend escapes. He had money and always paid, even though she told him she would pay her way. The three-day weekend in Paris was the best time. Anthony gave her less than a day's notice and they went over Columbus Day weekend, when they both had an extra day off from school.

As a lover, he was better than any man she'd been with, not that she had excessive experience in that department. He could bring her to wonderous heights. His breath, his touch alone could make her tremble. She'd never tell Josh, and she sure as hell wasn't about to remind Anthony, but no one, including Josh, had ever made her feel the way Anthony made her feel. But all of that was in the past—she thought that more than once.

The end came the day she came home early from school. She'd caught some virus from one of the children, began coughing, and the headmaster ordered her to go home. When she arrived home at around 11 A.M., she heard a noise in the bedroom. It was exactly what it sounded like—Anthony and some woman from his class whom Keisha had met several times at med school gatherings. Their clothes were strewn on the floor. The woman was naked and riding Anthony. Keisha never forgot Anthony's expression when he opened his eyes and saw her standing in the door, tears flooding down her face. That was it. She fled to her parents' house and moved her belongings out the following Saturday.

Eight years ago. In many ways, it felt like yesterday. The pain was like an old toothache that subsided but never went away.

She wondered at the attention she was now receiving from her former lover. He had visited her three times the day before and already once today. He knew she was pregnant with Josh's baby, and she'd told him all about Josh, but that didn't divert him from popping in. Nearly every time he would feel her belly, sometimes above and sometimes under her gown. In a weird way, she felt flattered. Here she was, looking her worst and this attractive doctor was giving her lavish attention. She assumed they both knew it ended here.

She had zero interest in Anthony or any man other than Josh, she told herself. Beyond the fact she was about to have Josh's baby and she wanted and needed him. She continued to have her doubts about their relationship, but at least for now, he was the only one for her. She didn't need another, a different, man in her life. Period.

Keisha loved Josh, she did. Nevertheless, there were times over the past year when she wondered if she really was ready for a long-term relationship with him or anyone else. She hated herself for even thinking that. It took months of anguish for her to admit that. At times, she was angry at herself for even having those thoughts. "What's wrong with me?" she thought from time to time. She had little cause for guilt, but these thoughts could make her miserable and sad.

Outside, the winds and rain picked up. In addition to rain, for the past hour, big, fat snowflakes fell from the sky, covering the grass and cars. Keisha had a view of the parking lot and could see road signs twisting back and forth, gyrating. The leaves had long since disappeared from the trees, but the small ones bent in the wind and the large ones swayed back and forth, some precariously. Occasionally, a piece of trash would fly across the driveway until it got hung up on a car or tree.

Every car that pulled into the parking lot had its wipers going full blast. The driver would find a space to park and the passengers took their time getting out. No doubt they had to steel themselves against the onslaught of the wind, rain, and sleet. Most people didn't bother with an umbrella but made a mad dash for the hospital entrance. Every now and again some fool would open an umbrella only for the wind to turn it inside-out or have it yanked into the sky like a kite.

About every thirty minutes, a weather report would interrupt whatever show was on the TV. The announcement music was always a dramatic beating of drums or some other pulsating sound. Duh-da-da-dum, duh-da-da-dum. The station she was half-watching always had a "BREAKING NEWS" logo in bright red, splashed across the screen when the weather came on. Keisha got it. She expected all of the other watchers did too. The hurricane had been going on for about a day in Northern Kentucky and Ohio, so anytime the weather came on it wasn't exactly "breaking news."

The last time she watched the weather report, the meteorologist, a plump, middle-aged white man who went by the name Dr. Joe, showed the latest radar and radar projection. She hadn't seen Dr. Joe trying to do a weather report outside, like Stan the Weatherman in Houston, so he was at least a tad smarter than his Texas colleague.

Dr. Joe said that the Cincinnati area was still receiving the outer bands of Hurricane Epsilon and the worst was yet to come. The storm was massive, reaching from Texas to Ohio. The radar showed an angry orange and red center which meant wind speeds were at least eighty mph. Dr. Joe reported that gusts were up to one hundred mph. He warned of thunderstorms and tornadoes. The north-western-most reach of the hurricane, just west of the Cincinnati area, was bringing heavy snow, a blinding blizzard dropping two inches an hour. He called it a "bomb cyclone," adding this was the worst he'd ever seen.

Keisha worried about Josh, who was in the middle of the storm, and wanted him to be with her but wished he'd stayed in Houston. She thought she understood Josh and his need to be with her. Prayers didn't come easily to Keisha, but she prayed for Josh and that the baby wasn't going to be born prematurely.

She worried about her parents. They promised her they wouldn't try to drive to Cincinnati, but she thought they might try to do that anyway. When the TV showed the storm track, it hooked to the east. It would come right across Pennsylvania like it was following the Pennsylvania Turnpike to Philly. That was exactly the way her parents would have to come to Cincinnati. She thought back on her conversation with her mother the night before.

"Keisha, your Daddy and I will get in the car and come to you. We'll just be on the Turnpike most of the way. We want to be there with you."

"Mom, the weather is awful, promise me you and Daddy won't try to drive here."

"Well—"

"Promise me, please, promise me you won't try to come here until the storm is all over."

"Sure, honey, but your Daddy really wants to and he's a great driver—"

"Mother, please. I don't need any more stress and if I have to worry about you being in the storm for twelve hours . . . I just don't know. Please."

"All right honey. I promise."

Keisha half-expected they might drive anyway. She was already worried enough about the baby and Josh and didn't need the additional aggravation of her parents trying to navigate their way in a hurricane. At the same time, a part of her hoped she would look up and see her mom and dad standing at the door, big smiles on their faces.

Every now and again she had to move. She got sore laying in one position for too long. The day before, her nurse, an older Black woman, had given her instructions:

"Honey, it would be best for you to do a little in-bed exercise to help prevent a blood clot. We don't want that."

Keisha nodded.

"Now, honey, flex your legs and feet." She pulled the sheet off and moved her legs into the stretch position she wanted Keisha to take.

"Good. Now, I want you to pretend you're at the gym and do some curls with your arms," Keisha complied.

"Okay, honey. This is the best one. Put your arms to the sides, plant your feet flat, and arch your back," She waited for Keisha to do that, then she put her hands behind Keisha's lower back and pushed it up another inch. "Can you do that?"

"Now, honey, I have these lovely socks for you to wear."

"Those are awful."

"Yes, but they'll help prevent a clot. You don't want that, do you?"

The nurse tugged the leggings up over Keisha's calves and attached them to an automated air pump. Every few minutes, they filled with air. As the air was released it sounded like a balloon deflating. It was very annoying.

In Keisha's mind, however, every movement she made potentially opened the door to her uterus. She dreaded having to go pee and at times she wished she'd taken the catheter. It had been days since she pooped, and Keisha wondered if she could go six weeks without emptying her bowels. The last thing she wanted to do was push.

She looked at her phone and saw it was 2:15 P.M. "Where was Josh?" she wondered, and debated whether she should text him. The last time she had, he was driving, and Geoff texted her back. She liked Geoff, his wife, and his family, and his text gave her a good laugh. At the same time, she didn't want to seem like she was nagging. It didn't matter. She was texting him anyway:

> **Hey babe, how's the road trip? Are you, Geoff, and Diane playing nicely together? I hope the conditions are OK. I can't wait to see you. Love ya, Keish**

Two minutes later, she received a reply.

> **Hey hon, it's slow going. It took us almost 4 hours to go 120 miles. We just drove past a town called Lufkin. At this rate I won't see you until sometime on Sunday. We stopped in a crappy little town called Dybbuk for gas and food. I have a hilarious story to tell you when we get together. Geoff's driving now. It's still raining, but the winds have let up a lot. If it stays like this, we**

may be able to get to Nashville by midnight. Please tell that little pumpkin inside you to stay put. I love you so very much. Josh

As she put down her phone, Anthony was standing at the door carrying two cardboard coffee cups. He wore his scrubs and a big smile.

"Hey, Keish. The coffee bar downstairs is surprisingly good. Let's see if I remembered right. Double latte, extra foam, three Sweet 'n Lows. Right?"

She smiled, sat up, and accepted the coffee. Josh had heard some stories about Anthony, the kind you might tell your new boyfriend about an old boyfriend. Not any sultry details. Certainly not the steamy parts. Not the parts she woke up dreaming about from time to time. It occurred to her she still hadn't told Josh that over the years she continued to think about Anthony.

Her gynecologist.

CHAPTER 17

JOSH

Garrison, Texas, 162 miles from Houston; 618 miles to Nashville.

The rain and wind slackened considerably. Although there was still a constant breeze, it felt like the average wind speed had dropped to maybe twenty mph. It was still gusting from time to time, but nothing like what we'd been through. The road was covered with leaves, branches, the remains of cardboard boxes, a few trash cans, live bait signs, and other crap. In places, you could see where water flooded the highway. Most of that had stopped.

There was almost no rain. Occasionally, we drove through mist or a few drops as though we were being blessed by a priest with holy water flung from an aspergillum. I rolled down my window a couple of inches and breathed in the air. It was about sixty degrees and humid. After the wind and rain we'd been through, it wasn't all that bad. The hurricane seemed to have moved past us. I blew out a long sigh of relief.

I was a little jealous of Geoff, who was driving in weather that was barely annoying. He had almost none of the challenging driving I'd experienced.

US 59 bypassed and circled around Lufkin and continued north. The terrain was reasonably flat and once we were through the town, Geoff drove between seventy and eighty. We went through a mixture of woods, farms, and ranches. Quite a few trees had fallen on either side of the road, but the worst had passed. I thought about the weird situation in Dybbuk and was glad that it was behind us. In my life, I'd never been solicited by hookers, let alone teenage ones. Another reason to be happy we put some miles on the car.

A text from Keisha popped up on my screen. I let her know that I probably wouldn't be at the hospital until the next day, Sunday. I felt awful about that, but at least I was on my way, even if it was taking a lot longer than expected. I'd see her soon and couldn't wait to hold her.

I spent a few minutes examining the map and measuring distances with my index fingers. "Hey, Diane," I said, turning all the way around to look at her. "If we go north on US 259, we'll be on some kind of a highway all the way to Texarkana. We can also just stay on US 59 and pinball our way through this desolate expanse on two and four-lane roads to Texarkana. I think we should stay on the best roads. Let's get over to a real Interstate as fast as we can."

She pulled out her phone and spent a moment exercising it. "US 59."

"What?" I said.

"Stay on 59. Ms. Google says that's the shortest route."

"That makes no sense. If we take that—"

"I know what you're going to say, the Interstate is a better road, blah, blah, but I've been impressed with these roads. Route 59 is some sort of a US highway, so that must mean something. Let's follow that all the way to Texarkana. It's a half-hour shorter."

"Seriously, we've been lucky," I said. "I'm not sure how long our luck is going to hold out."

We approached the intersection. US 259 was straight ahead, and US 59 veered off to the right.

"Which way am I going?" said Geoff. "I need to know in the next five seconds. You tell me and I'll go that way." He paused as he sped past a road sign for the off-ramp. "Five."

"Go right. US 59," said Diane. "It's shorter."

"Four."

"The distance shouldn't matter. Take the better road. Go straight ahead on 259."

"Three."

"Go right, young man."

"Two."

"Seriously, that's a mistake."

"One."

"But . . ." was all I said. Ever the good associate, Geoff turned on his blinker and veered right onto the ramp for US 59.

"Done." Geoff took the car up to eighty as he exited the ramp.

It was 1:45 P.M. I leaned over and looked at the trip odometer. We'd left Houston five and a half hours earlier and only covered 160 miles. Crap.

I was really hoping US 59 would be a bumpy one-lane dirt road—all the way to Texarkana. Then I would have really given it to Diane. Instead, it was a good five-lane highway. There wasn't much traffic and we continued driving through a mix of woods and farms. Geoff was driving between seventy-five and eighty mph, and we were starting to make up for some lost time.

Geoff had to slow through Appleby, Texas, which was made up of a few houses, a church or two, and garages. We had plenty of gas and didn't stop. He sped up again north of the town.

The sky never cleared up. In fact, it had been days since we'd seen the sun. It was weirdly colored. To the north, it was unnaturally black, like it was midnight instead of two in the afternoon. The rest of the sky was a brown-gray-yellow mix. The clouds were moving fast, like they were trying to keep up with us as we drove at nearly eighty miles an hour toward the black sky.

"This is weird," I said to Geoff, pointing at the sky. "Ever seen anything like this?"

"Never," he said. "It looks made up. Like a movie set. I'm expecting to see flying monkeys."

I tapped the radio, turning off the satellite radio and Diane's beloved Lionel Richey, and switched to the A.M. band. There were almost no stations out there. After searching for twenty seconds or so, I found a station out of Lufkin. It was staticky. We caught the end of the announcer's statement.

"... So stay indoors. If you have a storm cellar, you should go there now. Don't delay. I repeat, the National Weather Service has upgraded the tornado watch and is now issuing an immediate tornado warning for areas north of Lufkin—the I-20 corridor from Tyler, to Marshall, to Shreveport, Louisiana, and then south to US 84."

I pulled out my paper map. "Shit. We're driving straight into it."

"Ugh," Diane said from behind me.

I glanced at her in the rear-view mirror. She was shaking her head.

"Really, boys, you guys are pussies. What are the chances? This is a tornado *warning*. That means the conditions are right for a tornado, not that there *is* one. A tornado watch or advisory is a bigger deal. Even if there is a tornado, what are they? Maybe a quarter-mile wide and they might touch down for a mile or so. You may not have noticed, but there's a hell of a lot of land out here. If we're even lucky enough to see one on the horizon, I'm sure it'll be off in the distance."

I shook my head and wanted to call her an idiot. "And you got your meteorology degree, when? You have that completely backward. A tornado *warning* is the biggest deal. They're saying that there *is* a tornado and we're driving right into it. I have no idea what we're supposed to do if it hits us. I mean, we don't have a handy storm cellar, but it might be a good idea for us to figure it out."

"What do you want to do? Google it?" She said, not hiding the mocking laugh in her voice.

Just then, we watched a truck speeding toward us, heading south. It looked like a bright orange armored personnel carrier. It was festooned with radar, a turret, antennas, and an array of gizmos attached to the roof. A brightly painted logo on the side proclaimed, *Texas A & M Storm Tracker*. Through the windshield, I glimpsed four people. The driver was concentrating on the road, but the others were looking in all directions. They were gone in a flash.

We looked at each other.

"Okay, is it good or bad if the armored storm tracker truck is charging south and we're heading north?" Geoff said.

I spent the next ten seconds Googling on my phone. "Okay, Google says we should pull off the road, duck down below the windows, keep our seat belts fastened, and cover our heads with a blanket. If we see a tornado coming, we should drive away from the funnel cloud moving at a ninety-degree angle from its path."

Just then, a load of hail hit the car. As fast as it hit us, the hail ended. I looked at Geoff, who took his eyes off the road for an instant to glance at me.

"Well, Josh-the-weather-dude," Diane said. "You don't sound like somebody who wants to get to Cincinnati in a hurry. All of that driving at a ninety-degree angle and pulling over to kiss our asses goodbye will slow us down."

"Uh, guys," said Geoff.

"I just want to get there in one piece," I said, mostly under my breath.

"You're slowing us down and we need to make up time." Her voice was sharp.

"Guys. Diane, Josh. Stop. Just stop!"

"What?" Diane demanded. Then, even she was silent.

I'd never seen a tornado in the wild. Like everyone, I've seen pictures, in movies and on TV, images of funnel clouds and the devastation they caused. One thing's for certain, you didn't need a graduate degree in meteorology to know that we were looking at a goddamn tornado.

It was headed straight toward us.

CHAPTER 18

JOSH

Tenaha, Texas, 179 miles from Houston; 605 miles to Nashville.

Looming straight ahead, the tornado was barreling down US 59. It looked huge, probably a quarter mile across. It reached thousands of feet up into the clouds and carried with it trees, all kinds of garbage, and I'm pretty sure I saw a cow. A whole damned cow. Leaves and branches whipped at the car as Geoff slowed to a stop.

"Everyone!" I shouted. "Open your windows a crack. If we don't, the air pressure from the tornado will blow them out."

As soon as we all cracked our windows, we were nearly deafened by the roar. People say it's like a freight train and that's actually what it sounded like. Except that the freight train is coming straight at you and you're standing in the middle of the tracks.

Frozen.

Mesmerized.

About to be pulverized.

I figured we had maybe ten seconds to do something. I had no idea what.

Geoff gripped the wheel like he was holding on for his life. "What should we do?" We all looked around. There were woods on our left and a farm field to the right. No roads or driveways anywhere.

"Google said to drive at a right angle from its path," I said. "We can't get through those trees, and if we try to go across the field, we could be stuck in the mud, completely exposed."

I called over my shoulder, not trying to hide my sarcasm, "So what do you suggest now, Diane?"

When she didn't reply, I checked the mirror again. She'd disappeared. I pulled off my seatbelt and got on my knees on the seat and turned around. Diane was lying on the floor in a fetal position, holding her knees. Her body was shaking. I felt a moment of sympathy for her and put my hand on her shoulder. It was quaking. *You are such an asshole, Diane. I'm never listening to you again, bitch.* "Hang in there, Diane. We'll be okay."

We were down to maybe five seconds until the tornado hit us. The car was being pelted with branches, rocks, and debris.

I turned to Geoff, "Can you turn this around? Maybe we can outrun it?"

"No time, but if we stay here, we're sitting ducks. "Did you see that cow? That could be us. What should we do?"

By now, the wind whipped hard against the car, shit of all kinds was pelting us from all directions.

"I don't know, I don't know. But we've got to get out of here."

Three seconds to go until we were hit by the wall of the tornado.

"Down there," yelled Geoff over the rising noise as the tornado approached, now just hundreds of feet away. He pointed to the side of the road. A ten-foot berm was built up just ahead, between the field and the roadway. To carry the highway over a small dip in the terrain. "It's not much cover, but it's better than nothing."

I understood his idea but couldn't see how we could get down the steep incline without rolling over. "How are you going to get there?"

Geoff looked at me and grinned. He looked crazy-mad. "Hang on. We're going full Dukes of Hazzard."

"Wait! What?" Was all I could say as I rushed to reattach my seatbelt. Geoff hit the accelerator and we rocketed into the teeth of the tornado.

A moment later, the funnel was less than two hundred feet away, and I felt as if we might take to the air at any moment. Geoff abruptly veered toward the field. The car didn't so much jump as flop onto the grass embankment, landing hard. We came to an abrupt stop at the bottom, and I crashed into the webbing of my seatbelt. The rear of the car fishtailed so we were parallel with the highway. We were still facing the tornado but now at least ten feet below US 59.

The freight train roar was intense and a huge amount of debris continued to whip the windshield. It was like being inside a car wash with those scrubbers slapping the windows. The only difference was these were made out of rocks and branches.

Suddenly, a rock came out of nowhere and cracked the windshield. I didn't think it would hold.

"Get in the back," I yelled. "Hang on!"

I undid my seatbelt and scrambled over the seat. Diane was still on the floor, and I put my arms around her. She threw her arms around my neck and held me tightly. I felt Geoff flop onto the back seat and then wrap his arms around my waist.

The freight train noise morphed into the noise of a jet engine. The sound it would make if you were close enough to be sucked in. It was the loudest, most awful noise I'd ever heard. The car rocked and seemed to levitate. I wasn't sure if we were in the air or if the tornado merely lifted the car body a few inches off its springs. After several long seconds, we could feel and hear the car settle, then levitate again. It sounded and felt like two train engines smashing into each other at top speed.

I held onto Diane more tightly. Her face was on my neck and her arms gripped me ferociously. She was shivering and making little noises, like someone having a nightmare. I stroked her hair to try to calm her down.

We were in the middle of it for maybe thirty seconds. The longest thirty seconds of my life. Then, the noise began to subside. It was as though the freight train had finally rushed past us. The car was still rocking, and debris was still pelting the roof and hood, but the worst was over. None of us moved.

Another twenty seconds passed. I began to loosen my grip on Diane, and she moved her hands to my shoulders. She turned her head and her lips brushed against my cheek. Then, after a moment, another brush before her mouth found mine. She kissed me lightly on the lips once, twice. A thank you kiss. I hoped.

Then, her lips rested on mine, and I felt her tongue gently trying to find its way into my mouth. *What . . . the . . . hell?* I kept my lips pressed tightly together. Her tongue brushed my lips and I felt very weird. Her hands stroked the back of my head, my ears. Very sensually.

As we pulled our faces away, I could see in the dim light behind the seat that she was smiling at me in a way I'd never seen before. Was this a mere thank-you kiss for jumping on top of her in the tornado? I knew better. This was much more. *Crap. Diane was trying to make out with me on the floor of the limo. Unbelievable.*

I felt Geoff move behind me and get up. I pulled myself onto the seat and helped Diane get onto the seat next to me.

"Shit," said Geoff. "If that wasn't the most intense experience I've ever had in my life . . . ?"

"Dude, you saved us," I said, my voice flat.

"Un-fucking believable," said Diane. At that moment, I realized my right arm was around her shoulders and I was holding her left hand with mine. Our thumbs were dancing with each other's.

CHAPTER 19

JOSH

Tenaha, Texas, 179 miles from Houston; 605 miles to Nashville.

The door on Diane's side was stuck. Fortunately, Geoff was able to open his side, and he pulled himself out of the car. He gave me his hand and hoisted me out. Before I could turn around to help Diane, he shot me a quick look. He widened his eyes, shook his head, and mouthed the word, *"No!"* I understood immediately.

I turned around and took Diane's hand. When she stood, she held onto my hand for several long seconds.

The car was covered with leaves, mud, stones, the remains of a crow, and other debris, along with many pockmarks and a big scrape on the driver's side. Remarkably though, it didn't appear to have suffered any major damage. I hoped Abdul's cousin knew a good body shop. Of course, we were stuck on the side of an embankment with two wheels in a muddy field.

The tornado was gone. The sky was still black over the field to our south where it lifted off the ground, but it had vanished into the black clouds. For about five hundred feet behind us, you could see its path of destruction through the field before it just ended. I guessed that was where it lifted back into the sky.

The devastation around us was surreal. The tornado had come out of the woods maybe a thousand feet ahead of us and you could see the trail where the trees had been ripped from their roots. It was as though a giant had taken matchsticks and heaped them in a pile. Oddly, there were untouched trees that looked perfectly normal, right next to the shattered ones where the tornado had touched down. The funnel had meandered down Route 59, taking out everything in its wake, before heading into the field.

"Holy shit," said Geoff. "I don't believe it. We were just hit by a tornado."

We stood there, in a circle. Without thinking, I put my arms around Geoff and Diane. As we stood still in a group hug, Diane's hand found its way to the back of my head. She ran her fingers through my hair. I jerked my head trying to shake her off.

Finally, I said, "Do you think we can drive out of here?"

Geoff pried open the driver's door, which emitted a metallic groan. "At least it opens."

He climbed in, pulled the door shut, and mumbled something. Probably a prayer. Maybe it worked, because miraculously, the car started up on the second try. Diane and I stepped back as Geoff slowly tapped the gas. The car moved forward, maybe two inches before the right wheel started spinning. It kicked up mud but could not find purchase. Diane and I moved around to the back of the car and started pushing, trying to rock it. The big car moved a little, but that wasn't enough.

Geoff looked back at us and called, "Stand back, I'm going to try something." We moved away and Geoff put the car into reverse. It moved back a couple of inches before the mud started to spray. He put it into drive and the car rocked a little. Not enough. He tried that a couple of times, but it was stuck.

I leaned into Geoff's window and said, "There's got to be a garage with a tow truck in that last town. Let me see if I can call someone and get them out here. Maybe AAA."

"You do that," said Geoff, "I'll give it another try."

I climbed up onto the road and looked to the north. Nothing moving. Just debris and tree parts scattered all around. I turned around and looked south and was shocked to see a tow truck slowly driving toward us. Unbelievable. A freakin' orange and purple tow truck. Surreal. I waved my arms madly and he pulled over. I took one look at the driver and thought, *oh crap*. It was Paulie with the eyepatch from Dybbuk.

"Hey, am I glad to see you," I said in my most pleasant-sounding voice. "We ended up in the ditch, thanks to that tornado."

Paulie looked me over with his one good eye, his eyebrows furrowing, then said, "Ah know you, Goldie Goldberg, or is it Joshie Josh? Don't matter. You need a winch?"

I wasn't sure if he was an antisemite with the Goldie line or just trying to be funny, but the Joshie Josh part took me aback. I thought about those girls in the diner. I said, "I think that's all we need. The car started up; we just can't rock it out of the ditch."

"That's why I'm here. Whenever ah hear there's been a tornado touched down anywhere nearby, I take my wrecker and go looking for folks in trouble. The next garage is twenty miles away. So, it's good for business."

"Business? So, I suppose there's a charge? You're not like some kind of Good Samaritan?"

"Hell yeah, I am. I'm here, ain't I? I'm happy to pull you fellas out of the ditch and get you on the road. I'll even bang out a dent or two if you need that to drive. I only expect a tip. Two hundred and fifty ought to do it. Cash. In advance. That's a good deal, considering there ain't no competition. It'll be hours until anyone else comes through here."

"Cash?" He nodded. "Do you take Venmo?"

He made a face. "Do I look like I take Venmo? Cash, dollars, $250 of them. No checks or credit cards."

I put my hand in my pocket and pulled out my small wad of bills. Generally, I don't carry much cash and I only had $75. "I don't have it. Hang on. Let me check with my friends."

I explained the situation to Geoff and Diane. Diane's eyes narrowed, but Geoff pulled out a wad of cash. He smiled as he peeled two one-hundred-dollar bills from his bankroll. "I'm old school. I always like to have cash for emergencies."

I handed $250 to Paulie as he sat in his truck, and he counted it out and then jammed it into his pocket. He hopped out and hurried over the side of the embankment. I couldn't help but notice he wore a holster with a gun in it. Some kind of semi-automatic. *Welcome to Texas.*

He took about twenty seconds assessing our situation, then climbed back up the berm to his wrecker. He moved the truck into position and extended the cable and hook, giving himself a lot of play. He slid down the embankment and leaned into the front window. He said to Geoff, "Put 'er in neutral and git out."

Then he attached the hook somewhere under the front of the car and looked at me. "Goldberg, hold this here. Be sure to get your fingers out of the way when it gets taut, or you might lose a few." He cackled.

Paulie went back to the wrecker and started working the levers on the back that controlled the winch. The line tightened and I yanked my hand away. Geoff, Diane, and I stood to the side and watched. The tow truck emitted a grinding noise, and I wondered if it was up to the job. A moment later, the front of the big Town Car slowly began to rise. Ever so slowly, as Paulie worked the controls, the front of the car was part way up the embankment.

"Hang on," he said. "Here's the fun part. I've got to drive the bastard the rest of the way out." He got into the tow truck and very slowly inched the truck forward, pulling the car with him up the embankment. After a slow five minutes, the rear two wheels of the car were sitting on the shoulder. The front two wheels were winched up behind the truck.

"Thanks, Paulie," I said. "Put it down and we'll see if it can drive. If so, we're good to go. If not, we may need a little more assistance."

Paulie stood in front of us. He crossed his arms and looked at Geoff and then me with his one eye. His eyebrows narrowed and any smile left his face. "You know, my niece and her friend back in town said a white dude and a colored boy tried to pick them up. Solicited them. Can you believe that? I mean, them being minors and all? Some guys are sick like that, wantin' to diddle an underage chil'."

"What are you talking about?" I asked.

"Yeah, my niece's name's Alice. You met her at the cash register in my garage. Her friend is Nancy. They're sixteen-year-olds. Look it, too. Young. No mistaking them for twenty-one, for sure. They were taking a little break from high school." He cackled as though he thought of something funny. "They said they went to the diner on Main Street for a milkshake and these two old men solicited them. A white dude and a colored boy. They said something about wantin' a four-way, blow jobs, up the ass, that kind of thing. Ain't that the damndest thing you've ever heard of? I don't know what kind of penalty there is in Philadelphia for that, probably just a slap on the wrist in the big city, but here in Texas that's ten years in the pen, hard labor. Y'all can meet lots of good buddies there, too."

"This is bullshit," I said.

"Yeah, she said the white boy was named Joshie Josh, something like that, and the colored boy was named Snoop Dogg. My niece said she recollected that the white boy had been in the store and bought some gas. I remembered y'all too. Like they say on the TV, I kept the receipts." Cackle, cackle. "I suppose I should just tow your car back to Dybbuk and let the sheriff figure it out."

"You're freakin' kidding me," I said. "This is bullshit."

He cackled again and laid his hand on his sidearm.

Diane stepped forward. She leaned way into Paulie's personal space, within inches of his face. She poked him sharply in the chest with her finger. "What the fuck is your deal, asshole? This is bullshit and you know it. This is nothing more than a shake-down. I was there and nothing happened. *Nobody* did any of this shit."

Paulie stepped back. "Well ma'am, they said someone's mama was there. You look pretty hot for a mama, to me. I'm not looking to make any trouble for y'all. Maybe it was just a misunderstandin'. I suppose we could work something out."

"Did your niece and her friend report this to the police?" Diane demanded.

"Nah, they just come a runnin' to their ol' Uncle Paulie."

Diane turned around and held her hands wide, stepping forward and pushing Geoff and me away. "This is all about that bullshit at the diner, right? When you boys stopped laughing about this, you said *they* were soliciting *you*. Right? There's no way in fucking hell anything you said could be misinterpreted. Right?"

"That's exactly right," I said. "We did nothing except sit there. They came over to us. I thought it was hilarious, maybe a joke. The whole thing was a set up."

"It's bullshit," said Geoff.

"Let me deal with this asshole." Diane said. Her eyes flashed with anger.

Diane and Paulie talked for several minutes. I couldn't hear exactly what she was saying, but it was clear she was angry. This was Diane in her classic angry-lawyer-dragon-lady mode. I'd seen it before. When she was like that, you did not want to be on the receiving end.

After several minutes, she returned. "Do you guys have any more cash?"

Geoff pulled out two more hundred-dollar bills. I had nothing. She sent me to the backseat to get her backpack, the one she took on the airplane. A small, black leather number. She rooted around in it and pulled out $150. She took the money and her backpack and went back to Paulie. I noticed she held her backpack between them the whole time with her hand inside.

After several more minutes of animated discussion with Paulie, she handed him a fifty-dollar bill. He went to the back of the truck and lowered the Town Car. She motioned with her free hand and Geoff got into the driver's seat. He backed up and then drove around the tow truck and a few hundred yards up Route 59. Then he backed up to us. As he got out of the car, he held up his thumb.

Diane handed the rest of the money to Paulie. I watched him count it. Then, he held out his hand to shake Diane's. She gave him a withering look that might have stopped the tornado. He laughed his laugh and climbed into the cab. He made a U-turn and started to head south, then stopped when he was even with us and rolled down his window.

"Y'all have a pleasant trip." He narrowed his eye. "You want some free advice? Y'all stay away from them tornadoes and you rascals stay away from them young girls." He cackled again and continued driving.

We got back into the car and Geoff began to drive. The debris, mud, and whatever else that was still on the car plopped onto the road. Geoff had to drive around downed branches and tree limbs. After about a half mile, we were back on a clear road.

"What exactly did you tell him?" I asked.

"I told him I'd give him all the money we had, $350, to settle up the whole mess and forget about that insane made-up story of his or I'd shoot him with the gun I had in my backpack."

"What?"

"Yeah, I told him I'd pull the trigger and he'd never have enough time to pull his gun. If he lived it would be three against one and I'd tell the cops he was trying to rob us and pulled his piece on us, so I shot him in self-defense. It would be hard for him to get his story across, though, being dead and all. You know, I think they give you a medal here in Texas when you shoot someone in self-defense."

Geoff and I both looked at her. "You carry a gun in your backpack?" Geoff said. "What about the airport? How—"

"No, I'm not an idiot, you moron. But he didn't know that. This is Texas. He *assumed* I was armed. He was happy to take the money."

We drove in silence through Tenaha and continued north toward Texarkana.

CHAPTER 20

JOSH

Arkansas, North of Texarkana, 310 miles from Houston; 469 miles to Nashville.

I'd been driving for over an hour. We were finally off the US route and on Interstate 30, north of Texarkana. We'd driven over three hundred miles from Houston, and it was taking about twice as long as expected. It was now after 4 P.M. and getting dark.

"At this rate, we'll be lucky to get to your sister's house by 6 A.M." I looked at Geoff, who was playing with his iPhone.

"I assume you'll want to stop for dinner," said Geoff.

I shook my head. "You never miss a meal, dude." I looked at Geoff. His Adams apple jutted out and his face was chiseled. I guessed he wore extra slim shirts and a size 40 suit. Geoff carried almost no body fat. "You know, you seriously must have like zero BMI. How do you do it? I don't think you exercise any more than I do."

Geoff didn't look up from his phone. "I'm blessed with a fast metabolism. Have you ever met my dad? He's sixty years old and plays golf once or twice a week. That's all he does for exercise and that's not exactly a fat-burner. He's skinnier than I am."

"You sound like a couple of girls," Diane said from the backseat. We looked over our shoulders at her. She was smiling broadly. "The next thing I know you'll be talking about your shoes."

"As a matter of fact, these babies are from Johnston Murphy," Geoff said, not missing a beat. "Size twelve. I was thinking about upgrading to Salvatore Ferragamo. What do you think?" He held up a foot.

"Nice. Very stylish. I prefer the rugged look. Brushed leather. You know, something you can wear on the trail *and* into the office. I get all of my shoes from L.L. Bean. I was thinking about upgrading to Cole Haan." I took my foot off the gas for a moment and extended my leg so I could show off my loafer.

"Have I told you guys lately that you're morons?" Diane asked as we laughed.

"Don't worry, Diane," I said. "We're not going to ask where you do your shopping. I expect they wouldn't let us hold your shopping bags in that store."

"I just want to know if you have your own reserved parking space out at King of Prussia Mall," Geoff chimed in.

"Ugh. Morons." Diane sat back and picked up her papers. It occurred to me that she was the only one making a profit on this trip. By the time we got to Cincinnati, she'd easily have billed eight or ten thousand dollars' worth of time.

We'd been driving in and out of downpours. The wind had picked up again, and was blowing at a feisty thirty or forty mph. The traffic had also thickened. I expected to see more trucks on the interstate, and I was right. Thankfully, the trucks were not sailing all over the highway, just weaving within their lanes. I had to keep my eyes on them though and made a point of passing very quickly when I had the chance.

"Look at that." I pointed at black clouds that were looming in the south. "The storm seems to be chasing us. Every time we escape it for a bit, the clouds find us."

"Maybe the gods are angry," Geoff said, looking up from his phone.

"Why would they be angry with us?" I asked.

"You know, for messing with the environment. We've fixed and improved everything we could get our hands on, and have we made it any better? I suspect the gods don't think so. Me, for building shopping centers and McMansions in the middle of grade A farmland. You, for representing those chemical and oil and gas companies . . ."

". . . And me?" Diane chimed in.

"And you . . . and you for being the generalissimo of the entire operation," Geoff said. "If the gods are angry with Josh and me for being peons, doing the dirty work, they must be angry at you too, for commanding the operation."

That stopped the conversation. It appeared Geoff was realizing he didn't need to kowtow to Diane anymore. Maybe that tornado had more of an impact than I realized. We suffered a few moments of awkward silence until I switched the radio from Diane's beloved Barry Manilow to A.M. and turned the dial until I found a news station in Texarkana. The announcer was in the middle of a weather report.

"Those twisters did one heck of a job along the I-20 corridor a few hours ago. We've seen reports that as many as five tornadoes touched down. People along there are still assessing the damage. Folks, I've got good news for y'all and bad news. We've been told that we no longer have weather conditions likely to support tornadoes, right now, anyway. The bad news is the National Weather Service is sayin' to be on the lookout for downpours and hail. The hail may be as large as golf balls . . ."

I held up my hand and held my forefinger and thumb apart about as big as a golf ball. "Crap. I really don't want to see hail this big. What's next? Frogs? Locusts? Sharks? So far, the storm has been biblical."

"And, before you start lecturing us again, Mr. Vice President, it's just weather," Diane said from the backseat. "Ma Nature. An individual storm tells us *nothing* about climate. I've read that over and over. Even your sky-is-falling professors say it. You should know that."

"The only thing I'll agree with you on is that it's nearly impossible to say that an individual storm is caused by climate change. When you look at the total of storms in a season and you realize that there are more and bigger storms, or that millions of acres of land are burning in California, Florida, Europe, Africa, and elsewhere, when the temperature every year is warmer than the last, then I think it's fair to say that you're looking at the effects of climate change. That's what the climate scientists are saying. This storm we've been in, it's epic. It's all people will talk about until the next one comes around next year. It's unusually strong, weirdly late in the season. I have a feeling the climate scientists would say this is evidence of climate change. In fact, that's exactly what Professor Bastogne said yesterday."

"I'm trying to keep an open mind about all of this," Geoff said. "After all, *I* was the one who saved all of our lives, did the Dukes of Hazzard thing, and drove us off the cliff when the tornado came."

I looked at him and glanced in the rearview mirror and saw that Diane was looking at Geoff, too. "So, is this going to be your fish story?" I asked. "You know, the one where you catch a minnow and tell everyone that it was the size of a whale?"

"I have a feeling we're going to hear this story for a long time to come," Diane said.

"Maybe, Diane, maybe not. You're both ingrates. I made this monster fly. The least you can do is humor me. I may tell the story that way, especially if you two are not around. Anyway, I have to say I really never thought about climate change all that much but I'm coming around to your point of view." He pointed at me like his hand was a gun, then aimed down his pointer finger and flicked his thumb. "Sorry, Diane. I know nothing at all about meteorology or climatology. I just know what I've experienced. This is F'd up. We didn't have weather like this when I was a kid or even ten years ago. It's not just Mother Nature."

Diane shrugged. "Whatever. You're just a real estate lawyer. What do you know? How to lease a shopping center? Asking you about climate change would be like asking a urologist about brain surgery."

Geoff grabbed his chest. "Ouch, the pain. The indignity I have to suffer with you people. Just remember, generally speaking it's the real estate people who you need when a client is doing a deal over contaminated property. It almost never works the other way around. You'd better be nice to us."

I was doing seventy-five on the Interstate, passing slow-moving cars and trucks and hoping I was making up a little bit of time. Then, the heavy bank of clouds from the south finally closed in over the Town Car. Trucks and cars approaching us on the highway were running their lights and wipers. A moment later, drizzle splashed against the windshield, followed by heavy drops of rain. Obese raindrops splatted on the windshield, like June bugs on a summer night. Within seconds, the sky went from gray to black with swirls of wind, like miniature tornadoes, buffeting us. Leaves and debris did a St. Vitus dance on the highway. As the winds picked up, the tall dead grass and small trees on the side of the highway bent sideways.

"Crap," I said. "Here it comes again."

A moment later, the rain intensified and pelted the car with heavy, angry drops. Mixed in with those drops were small ice crystals. Hail. *Graupel*. Within seconds, the crystals were the size of marbles, pounding us as thunder rumbled. The highway was quickly covered in icy pellets.

I watched a car approaching us on the other side of the highway. The driver lost control on the icy surface and spun onto the median. I glanced into the rearview and saw the car come to rest in a ditch.

"Effin' weather. Bro, can you get off the road?" Geoff asked.

A highway overpass was in front of us, maybe a quarter mile away. I stepped on the gas and headed toward it. By the time we got there, other cars and trucks were riding out the hailstorm under a bridge. Four cars occupied the entire shoulder hiding from the hail, taking up all of the space protected from the storm. I pulled ahead of the first one and backed up on the shoulder as insane truckers and cars whizzed by at 70 mph. Then, I turned the wheel and backed between the paved edge of the shoulder and the abutment for the overpass next to a car that sat on the shoulder. I was careful to make sure that the hood of the Town Car was protected from the hail by the bridge. Almost immediately, a red pickup truck pulled in behind me.

"Damn, this weather," Geoff said.

"I'm more worried about the morons on the highway," Diane said. "Look."

There was no more room on the shoulder or the edge of the shoulder for any more cars. Every space had been taken. Some cars and trucks had stopped in the right travel lane of the highway under the bridge, however, hoping to evade the hail. The problem was they were still on the roadway in the right lane and other cars were traveling way too fast, not expecting anyone to be stopped in the travel lane. Tires screeched and horns honked as cars skidded around the scrum of cars hiding from the hail.

Inches in front of us, the hail hit the ground like some cartoon of golf balls pummeling the earth. It came down in waves of hail stones. The hood of the car next to us on the shoulder couldn't get entirely out of the storm and hail was bouncing off its hood and windshield. The ground was covered with ice; in places it was several inches thick. It turned into an icy glaze on the relatively warm highway.

As frightening as it was watching the hail pummel the road, the behavior of the other drivers was even scarier. There were three full lanes of cars shielding under the overpass. We were off the shoulder and closest to the bridge abutment. Next to us was a line of cars on the shoulder. Next to them was a line of cars in the right-hand travel lane.

If everyone had been driving sanely, perhaps that wouldn't have been so bad. Drivers heading north on the interstate could have slowed down to ten mph in the left lane and gently eased their way around the people who sought refuge under the bridge. Instead, we watched in horror as cars and trucks came up behind the cars in the right lane, tires squealing and horns blaring as they careened around them. It was only a matter of time until someone didn't make it.

Like five seconds.

I heard the squeal of truck breaks and the sound a truck makes as he tries to power down using his transmission—Jake brakes. The trucker began honking his horn about fifty feet from the overpass. Then, he fishtailed and slammed into a pickup truck idling in the right lane. This was only fifty feet from us. I watched as the pickup was pushed into the car sitting in front of him.

"Holy shit." My profound commentary.

"What do we do?" Geoff asked. "Maybe someone's hurt?"

"I think we'll stay here," Diane said. "Seriously. Maybe consider driving away. Those morons are going entirely too fast. If we get out of the car, we could be crushed in the next accident. Think about your obligations to the firm, your clients." She paused for a moment. "Your families."

Some people did get out of their cars and went to the trucks and cars in the accident. It appeared that everyone was okay, but it was obvious the crashing was not over. Suddenly, a pickup truck moving very fast on the Interstate leaned on his horn and started swerving around the accident. Sparks lit up the underpass as the metal on the side of his truck scraped against the abutment. It looked like a pinball game, except that it was awful, real, and possibly deadly. He hit the far wall of the underpass and then bashed into the side of a truck in the right lane, then back into the far wall.

"Crap," Geoff said. "That looks bad."

"Yeah, and now the underpass is completely filled," I said. "There's nowhere to go. Anyone driving in the storm isn't going to know that the road is completely blocked until they reach the underpass. I can't watch this anymore."

"Good. Just step on the gas and get the hell out of here," Diane said. "We have clear sailing ahead of us except for the hail."

I looked at Diane and shook my head. I opened my door and looked around. A few people were sitting in their cars, shielding themselves from the storm and mayhem. Others were huddled against the wall of the overpass. A few were helping the drivers in the accident. I popped open the trunk and looked in. I thought I'd seen flares and Abdul had left us about a half dozen of them. I grabbed three and slammed the trunk closed.

As I began to jog to the other side of the overpass, I could feel Geoff next to me. "You're an idiot, bro, but I can't let you do this on your own."

As we exited the underpass, we were pelted by cold, icy rain. The hail had largely stopped, but the rain was coming furiously. My clothes were soaked in a matter of seconds.

When we got to the end of the line of cars, maybe twenty cars and trucks were lined up trying to enter the overpass. "Here," I said, handing a flare to Geoff. "Come on. You know how these work?"

"Basically. Scrape them on the ground?"

"Yeah, and keep them away from anything you value. They burn hot as hell. Also, if you smell gas, run the other way." We jogged down to the end of the line of cars and lit up the flares. "Let's get a couple hundred feet down here so we can slow these idiots down before they smash into the cars and create a bigger pile up."

Cars were still speeding toward the underpass and Geoff and I, on either side of the highway, waved the flares around like mad men. With my free hand, I made a patting motion to slow them down. The cars began to slow and come to a stop. One driver stopped and rolled down his window. He said, "Hey buddy, what's going on?"

"Big pile up at the underpass. There's nowhere to go. Everyone, big rigs, pickups, cars, you name it, are going too fast and the cars are piling up."

"You got any more of those flares?" He asked.

"In fact, I do. We'd appreciate the help."

He introduced himself as Herman. He weighed maybe 250 pounds and stood well over six feet tall. There was no time for pleasantries and the three of us continued jogging down the road to try to slow down the traffic. Ninety-eight percent of the drivers slowed and stopped, but at least two gave us the finger and tried to pull around.

"Assholes," Herman yelled.

I immediately liked him.

About thirty seconds later, an Arkansas State Police car, emergency lights blazing, screamed to a stop in front of us. The trooper leaned out of his window and yelled, "You want to tell me what happened?"

I told him.

As we were talking, four more State Police cars and two ambulances pulled up. Just behind them were fire trucks.

"Hey boys, you did real good," the trooper said from inside his car. "I think we've got it from here. Why don't you get back to your cars? That's a lot safer. I don't want to be putting you inside those ambulances."

I laid my flare on the shoulder and Geoff and Herman did the same. Geoff and I shook hands with Herman and slowly jogged in the rain toward our car. We watched as some of the police cars maneuvered around the traffic. By the time we got back to our Town Car, two ambulances and three fire trucks were coming toward us on our side of the roadway. They began positioning in front of us. Geoff and I got back into the car. I was soaked and turned up the heat.

Geoff and I were laughing at our accomplishment. I held up my hand and Geoff smacked it before grabbing hold.

Diane shook her head. "Merit badges, boys. I'm going to make sure you each get a merit badge. Did you have fun playing in the rain and shit?"

I pulled out slowly, so as not to go over any fire hoses or other apparatus or run over any emergency responders. About thirty seconds later, the commotion was in my rearview. Every now and again, a fire truck or other emergency vehicle came screaming south on the shoulder of the northbound lane, going the wrong way but keeping on the edge of the roadway. Two minutes later and the whole thing was behind us.

I looked at the clock on the dashboard. It was dark and almost six P.M. That was two hours from the last time I'd checked, and we hadn't driven five miles. I shook my head. I began to wonder if I'd see Keisha in time.

CHAPTER 21

KEISHA

It was after 6 P.M. Keisha was bored, and her butt was getting sore from her forced bed rest. She pushed off the covers and, wearing only her hospital gown which barely covered her thighs, did the stretching exercises the nurses had recommended, including the one where she planted her feet on the mattress and lifted her torso into the air, held that position for a few seconds, then settled back onto the bed. That helped, but only temporarily. A few seconds after she did five hip-raises, the achiness returned, and she did five more.

She finished three sets of hip raises, then lowered her butt onto the bed in time to see Anthony watching her. He was standing at the door, in his scrubs, holding two to-go cups of coffee. He wore a big smile and had angled his head, as if to get a better view. He looked good in his blue scrubs. Nevertheless, she made an angry face at him.

"So how long have you been standing there ogling me?"

"No, it was more like admiring. Maybe remembering. You used to do that in bed when we were together." He smiled and closed his eyes.

"Anthony! Don't you dare close your eyes like you're remembering. Stop it."

"Sorry, I'm sorry, Boo. I had a flood of memories, good memories, and all kinds of things just came back to me. When I'm with you the doctor filter goes away, we're ten years younger, and I feel like I can say anything. I promise, I won't let that happen again. Unless . . ." He smiled at her.

"Unless what?" Keisha frowned at him.

"Can you still bend your legs back to your head?"

"Ugh. Are you kidding me? I'm eight months pregnant and this is what you're thinking about?" She covered her eyes with her hands.

"Thirty-three weeks, actually. Sorry, they were all good memories. I have an excellent memory. I remember all kinds of things. Good things."

"I'll be sure to tell Josh when he gets here. I'm guessing he'll be happy to know that."

Anthony handed her the cup of coffee. "A decaf latte, three Sweet 'n Lows. What you drink after 4 P.M. Right?"

She nodded and took the cup which she set on her tray. Then, she pulled the sheet up to her neck and sat up. She watched him as he struck a pose looking out the window into the parking lot.

It had snowed about five inches and the snow was blowing in the mighty wind. In the streetlights, the snow made snow devils, spinning in mini-tornado-like formations before settling to the ground only to be picked up in the next gust of wind. The cars in the lot were covered. Only one car was moving, and it tracked slowly across the winter landscape, its wipers struggling to push away the snow. The driver seemed to find a spot, but the snow covered the lines, so it was impossible to tell if it was a real parking spot or an opening between two cars. That was the most exciting thing going on outside except for the constant wind and snow.

"The weather guy said the snow is the back side of the storm," Keisha said. "It's the humid air from the south combining with cold air coming down from Canada. As I understand it, it's kind of a nor'easter, except in the Midwest, not on the east coast. It might snow for a couple of more hours. One to two inches an hour."

"I didn't know you paid so much attention to the weather report," Anthony said, not looking from the window.

"I had the TV turned on low all day and they kept breaking in. I only pay attention every now and then, wondering how this will affect Josh. The weather comes on every fifteen minutes. I can't miss it."

"How much are we getting?"

"Maybe eight inches. They don't know. I think they're spit-balling."

"Not to get you worried, but it might make more sense for Josh to take a southern route to Philly and then come here in a few days, maybe a week, after the storm has passed. That way he can miss the hurricane and the roads will be clear of snow."

"So, suddenly you're concerned about Josh? You've never even met him."

"In fact, I do want to meet the man who stole you away from me," he said with a huge smile.

Keisha rubbed her eyes. "I didn't even meet him until years after we broke up. He didn't steal me away from you. As I recall, I walked in on you humping that bimbo from medical school. In our bed. That's why we broke up."

"*Fatima*. Her name was Fatima. You know, I never properly apologized to you." Anthony sat on the side of the bed and took her hand. "Boo, I was stupid. Incredibly stupid. I wasn't thinking. It was wrong. It was all me, not you. I'm sorry. I apologize for everything I did to hurt you. To breach your trust."

"Anthony? It *was* wrong and I appreciate the apology, but I don't really care anymore. Aside from the fact all of that happened eight years ago, I'm over you. Unless you haven't noticed, I'm engaged and pregnant. I'm not sure what little game you're playing with me, but I'm getting tired of this flirtation. It's nice to see you and I'm happy you're doing well, or seem to be. But I really don't care about some woman you once slept with."

"Four times. Twice before that morning, the morning you walked in on us, and one more time after that. I want to be totally honest with you. I'm so sorry."

Keisha flicked away his hand and shook her head. "*Four* times? So, you think that by telling me you slept with this Fatima four times, that somehow makes us closer? Somehow this makes up for the tremendous hurt you caused? For the breach of trust? You're a smart man. You're a medical doctor, a gynecologist for cripes' sake, but you're lacking in the common sense department. You may be filling in some history for me, but it's not going to change anything." She scanned his face. "Why are you doing this?"

"Fatima and the other women were stupid flings. They meant nothing to me—"

"*Other women*? While we were together? I *really* don't want to know."

"Look, I was young and stupid. Really stupid. Full of myself. I loved you, Boo. I still do. I've never married because I'm always comparing anyone I'm with to you. No one else comes close. I wish we could go back eight years and I could have another chance."

Keisha looked at the snow whirling a few feet away outside her window. Her brain was swirling like the snow. She couldn't figure out Anthony's play. Why was he doing this? Was it just a game to see if he could somehow win her over? It was too much, and she didn't need this. "Anthony, I really mean this." She took his hand and squeezed it. "You have to get over me. What we had was a long time ago. If I'd known about Fatima and the others, it would have ended the same way, just sooner. We'd have been over. Done. No amount of apologizing will change that. I'll never feel the way I once felt, eight or ten years ago. It's over. I'm going to be married to another man. Having his baby."

Anthony sighed and his shoulders drooped. "I believe you. I believe you love Josh. I hear you. One thing I know, because I lived it. I know how you made me feel. I know you told me about how I made *you* feel. I could see it. You seemed so happy when we were together. I could feel the spasms in your body when we made love. Can you honestly say this guy makes you feel the way I did? The heights I brought you to?" He lowered his voice and moved his mouth within inches of her ear. "Your endless, multiple orgasms, Boo? Those hip raises you were doing a few minutes ago weren't just stretching exercises back then. You were in such ecstasy you wanted to burst out of your skin. Tell me he does that for you."

Keisha tried to block the flood of images that invaded her head. Over the years, she tried not to think much about Anthony, especially since she was with Josh. Mostly. She backed away from Anthony and pushed him off the bed.

"Get off my bed. In fact, get out of here. This is ridiculous. Listen to me. We were done eight years ago. If I'd known you were cheating on me, we would have been done before that. I've moved on. I'm engaged. I'm having an effin' baby. It's not my job to help you get closure."

Anthony stood. "I'm sorry. I'm sorry I dredged this up, Boo. You're right. I did incredibly stupid things and completely breached your trust. No amount of truth-telling or apologizing now will make a difference. I did want you to know how I felt about you then and how I still feel about you. It's not fair for me to have done that. I'll go now."

He put his hand on the door handle.

Keisha held up her hand. "Anthony. I don't hate you anymore. I hated you eight years ago and for a long time after that. We did have something, it was incredibly special, but that was long ago."

Anthony pulled at the door and was just about to leave when he turned and faced Keisha. "Just one observation, Keisha, you just told me a number of times that you're pregnant, which as a board-certified gynecologist I recognized immediately, and you told me a number of times that you're engaged, which as your former boyfriend I need to respect. One thing you didn't say to me, you haven't said to me, is that you're happy. That this guy makes you feel better than the way I once made you feel. I want to do that again for you. I really do."

Anthony turned quickly and closed the door behind him. The room was quiet, except for the sound of the wind blowing the snow against the window. Keisha laid in the bed and didn't move. Without realizing it, large, warm tears were dripping down her face.

CHAPTER 22

JOSH

Little Rock, Arkansas, 434 miles from Houston, 349 miles to Nashville.

We settled into a booth at an Olive Garden restaurant just off Interstate 30. The place wasn't crowded, and I assumed that was because it was 7:30 P.M. and we'd missed the dinner rush. If we were in Philly, the restaurants would be receiving the first of their serious dinner crowds. This was a typical Olive Garden restaurant, just like all the rest, and we watched young waiters and waitresses scurrying by carrying giant bowls of salad sopping with dressing and baskets of Italian-like bread. I dashed off a quick text to Keisha, telling her we'd stopped for dinner, and I planned to see her sometime the next day.

"I can't believe you picked an Olive Garden," said Diane. "This place sucks."

"Well, that's one of the rules of driving, the driver gets his choice," I said. "I hope you noticed; I did drive right past a Cracker Barrel. I'm pretty sure that would not have pleased your sophisticated palate."

"Yup, you're right."

"I felt the need to relax a bit and would have stopped at a McDonald's just for fuel, but this seemed slightly nicer. Besides, I like it."

Our waiter, a kid who might've been 16 years old, stopped at our table. He was wearing a black shirt and black pants. He was pleasant-looking enough, probably had a girlfriend who let him get to second-base from time-to-time. He had some serious acne and short hair. "Hey folks, would you like our delicious salad and baked Italian rolls? We have a soup and salad combo. It's really very economical. Also, you get bread and soup or salad if you order a meal."

"What about drinks?" Geoff asked.

The waiter gave us a full-on Arkansas awe-shucks smile and said, "I can bring you water or soft drinks. If you want hard liquor, like wine or beer, I'll have to get my manager. I'm too young to serve it."

I could see Geoff beginning to formulate a cocktail order. "That's okay," I said. "We'll stick with coffee and soft drinks. We still have something like three hundred miles to go and my brother here is driving next." I smiled. The kid looked from Geoff to me and back again.

"Or, and hear me out on this," Geoff said, "you and I could get a couple of serious adult beverages and Diane could drive since we've been driving the entire way, twelve hours of crappy weather, hurricanes, and tornadoes."

Diane made a face and shrugged her shoulders.

"Whatever," she said.

We gave the kid our full orders. Geoff and I both ordered coffee, Diane, a Diet Coke.

"I need to apologize guys," I said. "Honestly, I figured we'd be in Nashville by now. I thought the weather would slow us down a bit, not that we'd get the weather from the front porch of hell. Crap. We've been driving for twelve hours to get a little over four hundred miles. At least we'll have a few stories out of this."

Geoff looked out the plate glass window at the rain. "The winds have died down; all we have to deal with now is rain from here to Nashville. That's a cakewalk compared to what we've already been through. If we can push the speed limit, we should be there by around two in the morning. I'll call my sister and let her know you'll be catching naps at her house."

I looked at Diane, "Seriously, do you think you can drive? I'm exhausted."

"I suppose I could. I'm pretty tired right now, so maybe one of you guys can start us off."

"Any luck with the airlines?" Geoff asked.

"Little Rock, Memphis, and Nashville, the airlines are all saying the same thing. Many of the flights are canceled. Even if they didn't get the full-on hurricane at the airport, the in-bound flights couldn't get there. Half of the ones that aren't canceled are delayed and probably will be canceled, and the others are booked full." She looked at me. "You're stuck with me to Cincinnati. I booked myself a flight on American on Sunday afternoon. Hopefully, they won't cancel it."

I was thinking about saying something snappy like, *Oh goody, we get to be in the car for four more hours together, just you and me.* Unlike Geoff, I wasn't quitting on Monday, so I held my tongue.

"That's okay, guys," Geoff said. "I should be able to drive. I think I can make it all the way to Nashville. That's only five hours."

Geoff excused himself and headed to the men's room. A minute later, so did Diane. While they were gone, our teenaged waiter delivered the soup and salad. I was hungry and dug into my bowl of soup without waiting for the others to return. It was lukewarm and overly salty. Nevertheless, it was the first real food I'd had in many hours. I grabbed one of the faux Italian rolls. The outside of the bread was slathered with oily butter, so I didn't add any more. I was about halfway through my soup when Diane returned.

"Did you see Geoff?" I asked.

"Nope. He wasn't in the ladies' room, and I didn't see him walking around."

"That's weird. He's been gone a long time. I have to use the men's room anyway. I'll be right back."

I found the men's room and pushed open the door. No one was in there, but I could see that one of the stalls was occupied.

"Geoff, dude, are you okay?"

Nothing. No response.

"Excuse me, whoever's in the stall. Geoff?"

Still no response.

I angled my head and looked through the small crack between the door and the jamb. I could see Geoff, seated on the toilet, pants up. He was leaning against the wall.

"Geoff! Bro! What the hell?"

I pushed on the door, but it was locked. There was a thin indentation in the lock, perhaps a place where a screwdriver or special tool would fit. I found a dime in my pocket and worked the lock. The door popped open. Geoff was bent over. It didn't look like he was breathing. I shook him. "Geoff! Come on man!"

His eyes slowly opened, and he looked at me blankly. In a thick voice, he said, "Suitcase. Outside pocket. Narcan."

He passed out again. I pulled the door shut and thought for a moment. It would make the most sense to call 9-1-1. I decided to give him Narcan to try to revive him, then would call 9-1-1 if that didn't work. I ran out the front door to the car into the rain, popped the trunk, and found the Narcan in a small box in a plastic baggie in the outside pocket of Geoff's suitcase. As I ran back into the restaurant, I wondered why anyone would happen to have Narcan in their suitcase. I was afraid I knew the answer. I jogged past the short line of people waiting for seats and back into the men's room. An older man wearing a blue sport coat was peeing into a urinal and glanced at me. I pushed open the door to the stall, shut it behind me, and spun the lock.

My hands were shaking. I wasn't sure Geoff was breathing. I wished I'd had maybe two minutes to look up the instructions on YouTube but didn't have the time. I ripped the Y-shaped dispenser from the box and glanced at the box. It had minimal instructions in tiny writing on the side. I pushed Geoff's head back and shoved the nozzle into his nose. I pressed the plunger, heard the soft whoosh, and waited. The box contained only one Narcan dispenser and I prayed this would work.

"Come on, come on, come on. This better work . . ."

It seemed like it took forever, but Geoff's eyes popped open. His head weaved unsteadily. He took a deep breath.

"Is everything okay in there?" Older southern man's voice on the other side of the door. The guy who'd been peeing, probably.

"Yes, yes, my friend wasn't feeling well. He's okay now though."

"Well, I'm going to tell the manager. Y'all can figure it out."

I heard the door to the men's room open and close.

"Nosy bastard," Geoff muttered.

"What the fuck, Geoff. What's going on?"

He looked at me for a moment while his eyes focused. "Honestly? I was snorting some meth. Amphetamines. That was supposed to keep me alert for the drive to Nashville. It was too strong. They must've mixed it with something. Fentanyl. I don't know."

"Are you okay? I think we should get you to a hospital."

Geoff's eyelids shot up and he stared at me with wide, bloodshot eyes. His expression became fierce. "Absolutely not. That's the last thing I need. Look, I was just doing it so I could drive. It's not like I'm addicted or anything."

I shook my head. "Yeah bro, you are."

He looked at me and didn't respond.

I helped him up and he washed his face at the sink. I gripped the back of his shirt, in case he passed out again. I took the box and dispenser and threw them into the open waste can. As an afterthought, I crumpled a few paper towels and covered the evidence. As we were leaving the men's room, a middle-aged guy with a black shirt and black necktie hurried in. He wore a green name tag that said, "Steve-Manager."

"You the guys that were having trouble in the stall?" He had a husky southern voice.

I looked at Geoff and said, "No. Not us. We came in maybe thirty seconds ago. There *were* two guys just leaving when we came in."

Geoff and I went through the door and the manager continued inside where I could see him looking into the stalls a moment before the door closed.

Food had been delivered to our table and Diane had eaten some of her soup and salad.

"What the hell? Where have you guys been? It's been like fifteen minutes."

I could see to the men's room door. The manager came out and looked up and down the rows of booths and tables.

"We have to go," I said. "I'll explain later."

"No, no," Geoff said as he began to take his seat. "That's okay. I need something to eat. I want to stay here and take it easy for a while."

The manager stopped at a table a couple of rows over and was talking to four older people. I vaguely recognized the one man, from his hair and blue blazer, as the guy in the bathroom.

"Do. *Not*. Sit. Down," I said, enunciating every word. "We have to go."

I got Geoff to give me one of his hundred-dollar bills. That was plenty to cover the cost of the dinner and give the waiter a hefty tip. I threw it on the table.

"Seriously, let's go."

I stood close to Geoff to make sure he didn't stumble and guided him to the car. Just as I was about to get him into the back seat, he leaned over. I thought he was maneuvering into the car, instead he vomited, missing my shoes by inches. I waited until he was done, then shoved him into the car, and slammed the door.

Diane stood next to the front passenger door. "Do you want to explain this to me?"

"Not now. Get the fuck in the car, Diane. I'll explain it to you later. Just get in the car."

Diane blinked at me, but opened the passenger door and got in.

I backed up and we pulled out of the lot. In the rearview, I could see the manager standing at the front door with Mr. Blue sports coat watching us drive off. I wondered if he was able to see our license plate. I pulled onto the highway and took the car up to eighty mph. After ten minutes of silence, I slowed to seventy-five and explained to Diane what happened to Geoff in the men's room. I didn't slow down again until we crossed the Mississippi River into Tennessee.

CHAPTER 23

JOSH

Nashville, Tennessee, 272 miles to Cincinnati, Ohio.

I'd been dozing in the passenger seat for about an hour. Geoff was asleep in the back seat, on his back, snoring and making a noise like some kind of giant hog. After I'd driven for several more hours, Diane had finally taken over near Jackson, Tennessee. I was so tired. Exhausted. I couldn't fall asleep, though, and half-slept while she drove.

Geoff had given me his sister's address when we started out in Houston, and we followed Waze into the city. His sister didn't live in one of Nashville's cute neighborhoods. She wasn't near the downtown, Grand Ole' Opry, or Music Row. Instead, she lived in a ranch house near the airport. I woke up when Diane slowly began cruising a street of tract homes. One after another, they were modest houses and looked identical.

"Are we there yet?" I asked as I rubbed my eyes.

"Close. I think it's the next block."

Most of the houses were dark. A light was on in one house up ahead on the right.

"Want to bet that's it?" I said, pointing.

"You *are* a clever lad." She pulled into an open spot and put the transmission into park. "That was some drive. Nice of you guys to save me for the most exhausting stretch."

I looked at her. "You're joking, right?"

She reached over and squeezed my knee. "Lighten up."

I looked into the back seat. Geoff was sprawled along the seat. I leaned toward Diane and said quietly, "Shit, he's lucky he didn't kill himself."

"He said that was his one and only. Do you believe him?"

I made a face and shook my head. I opened my door and ventured out into the drizzle. The rain had poured down when we were in western Tennessee but slowed considerably as we approached Nashville. I threw my windbreaker over my head and opened the door to the back seat. I was surprised when Geoff awoke easily.

"Dude. Geoff. Come on, get up. We're at your sister's house."

Geoff sat up quickly and cleared his throat. He smiled that broad smile of his and said, "See, I told you it was an easy drive from Memphis to Nashville. It went by quickly, don't you think?"

I watched him climb out of the car, impressed that he seemed fine. Geoff wasn't just my good friend; he was like my brother. I was sure that we would have a conversation about this when we were back in Philly. I didn't buy the once and done bullshit. No one just happens to have meth in their pocket and a Narcan inhaler in their suitcase. Plus, his drinking.

Geoff grabbed his suitcase, and we approached the front door. He lightly tapped twice and the door opened.

I said that Geoff was a good-looking man. The Black woman who came to the door was smoking hot. I mean, movie star good looks. Her hair was curly and hung past her shoulders. She wore a low-cut black tank top with spaghetti straps and jeans, no makeup or jewelry. The resemblance to her brother was obvious. Geoff and his sister ought to have been models. She smiled at Geoff and held out her arms.

"Geoffy, it's been too long."

"Sissy."

They hugged long and hard and Diane and I glanced at each other and smiled.

"Jayda, this is my friend, Josh." We shook hands. "And this is Diane." They shook hands, too.

I wondered if Geoff said it that way on purpose or if Diane caught the slight.

When I shook Jayda's hand, I immediately noticed her scent. Some kind of perfume—vanilla. Subtle. It was perfect for her. You wanted to follow it to its source.

We sat in a small living room and drank bottled water. There were toys in one corner and decent-looking furniture around the room. A medium-sized TV hung on the wall.

"It's a little cramped. I had the baby last year so that makes two kids, a one-year-old and a three-year-old. This place has three bedrooms. At least we have a den downstairs which is really where most of the kids' stuff and play area is."

I thought about that. Jayda and her husband had one room, her kids had one or two rooms, I assumed that Geoff would sleep in one of the kid's bedrooms or on a sofa. That didn't leave much room for Diane and me. I looked at Diane and knew she was thinking the same thing.

"I can give you two the sofa-bed in the den. Is that okay? It's full-sized and reasonably comfortable." Jayda asked, smiling as she looked from Diane to me.

Diane and I smiled at each other. "That's not a great option; we're not together," I said, trying not to laugh.

Diane said, "If that's the best you can do though, Josh and I are grownups, and we'll figure it out."

Jayda laughed and said, "Whoops. My bad. It'll take a little juggling, but I haven't seen Geoffy since before the baby was born; I'm so happy he's here." She yawned and stretched. "You must be exhausted. I know I am. Before you know it, the kids will be getting up."

I looked at Diane and, again, we were thinking the same thing. "Actually, it's only four hours to Cincinnati," I said. "The weather here isn't terrible right now, but if we leave now, we can get to Cincinnati in time for an early breakfast. Diane has a flight out of Cincinnati in the afternoon, so getting an early start will make our trip easier."

Jayda didn't look upset about us leaving. Maybe relieved. "Are you sure? I can make a soft spot on the floor with sofa cushions."

"No, really, I think we want to push on." I said. Diane nodded in agreement.

We stood, and the four of us said goodbye. I pulled Geoff into the small dining room and locked eyes with him. "Look, man, we need to talk. This bullshit in the men's room, the drinking, it's too much."

"You're my brother," Geoff said quietly. "I'm okay. Really. On Monday, I give notice to the firm, and in two weeks, I'll be at a new job. Once this place is behind me, I'll be fine."

I wasn't so sure.

"I'll text you from Cincinnati," I said.

"Good. Look, one more thing." He lowered his voice even more. "Diane. Be careful."

I looked at him. "I can handle myself."

He gripped my arm. Hard. "I'm serious, bro. Watch it."

He walked me to the door, and I pulled him in for a bro-hug, except that it was more than that. A brotherly hug. "Thanks for coming with me, take care of yourself," I whispered.

He nodded, then Diane and I covered our heads with our jackets and stepped into the cold, misty rain. I waved back at Geoff and Jayda. Probably the best-looking brother and sister I've ever known.

Diane rounded the car and opened the driver's door.

"Hey, Diane, I'm feeling okay. Let me drive for a while."

"No, you look exhausted. I've got this. I'll tell you what, you grab some sleep, and in a couple of hours, you can take over for the drive into Cincinnati."

I was exhausted, and for once in her life, Diane was behaving humanely. Almost as if she was thinking of someone other than herself. The last thing I saw before I nodded off was a sign for I-65. Under it, the sign read, *Bowling Green,* and under that, *Louisville.* If the weather cooperated, we'd be in Cincinnati by 7 A.M.

CHAPTER 24

JOSH

Somerset, Kentucky, 158 miles to Cincinnati, Ohio; 687 miles to Philadelphia, Pennsylvania.

I woke up, feeling stiff from leaning against the door. My phone said it was 4:50 A.M. Diane was staring straight ahead as she drove. The headlights illuminated the highway and small glimpses of the land just off the pavement. Clouds loomed overhead and it seemed particularly dark. There were few cars on the road. I could see from the speedometer that she was doing about seventy. A mix of farms and woods on the side of the road flew by. The terrain was mostly flat, with some rolling hills. We should have been most of the way to Louisville. Instead, I saw a road sign that pointed the way to Somerset, Kentucky. That didn't mean anything to me. Then, I noticed a highway sign that read, *Cumberland Parkway*. We were no longer on the Interstate.

I looked at Diane. "Where are we?"

"Kentucky."

"I can see that. Is Somerset on the way to Cincinnati?"

She didn't respond right away. Finally, she said, "Not exactly. Just after you drifted off, I checked the weather report for Cincinnati. Some kind of crazy storm has blanketed Ohio and northern Kentucky with snow. If we go the route you picked, we'd hit snow way before we got to Louisville. The traffic looks snarled the closer you get to Cincinnati. There was some kind of crazy accident and the interstate is closed down. I checked and a lot of the flights out of the Cincinnati airport are delayed or canceled."

"So . . . is this some alternate route to Cincinnati that avoids the snow and traffic?"

"Not exactly. I think there's a good chance we'd get stuck in the snow or traffic and never make it to Cincinnati or the airport today. Since you were sleeping, I made a command decision to drive directly to Philly. I have to be in Philly tomorrow morning for my meeting with Lindstrom. Also, you want to be with Keisha sooner, rather than later, so if we go to Philly, you can hop a flight from Philly to Cincinnati as soon as the airport opens. That's a win-win." She glanced at me and smiled. Her face was ghostly in the greenish light from the dashboard.

I shook my head to clear out the remaining cobwebs. "Wait a minute. You're driving us to Philly? How far is that?"

"From here?" She picked up her iPhone from the dashboard and glanced at it. Six-hundred eighty-seven miles. We should be there in about ten hours."

It was nearly pitch black all around us. Even though it was very early in the morning, the sky was a deep indigo. No streaks of sunlight had yet invaded the night. It was the darkness you see just before the sky begins to brighten. The color suited my mood as I pondered my next move. We drove for another minute or so. We sped past a sign for a roadside motel. The motel's shape, the drive-up-to-your-room kind, was barely visible in the gloom. Then, abutting the Parkway, I watched us sail past a trailer park, the trailer homes and RVs barely visible in the dim light.

Finally, I said coldly, "Stop the car. Stop the car and get out." The frustration and anger fought in my chest, both ready to explode. "I'm going to drive the rest of the way. We're going to Cincinnati. I don't care how much fucking snow there is. I don't care about your fucking meeting with a Norwegian billionaire. *I* made all of the arrangements for this trip—*I* rented the car, and we drove through a goddamned hurricane and tornado to get to Cincinnati. *Not* Philly. We've come this far, so I can be at the hospital with Keisha and our baby if it comes. I'm not driving to Philly."

Without slowing down, Diane looked at me for a long time, too long at seventy mph. "Josh, Josh, calm down." Her right hand found my knee and rubbed it. "My meeting tomorrow is a potential decades-long engagement. Lindstrom has facilities in Philly, Pittsburgh, Chicago, and all across the US. Cities where we have offices. The firm will take in millions in legal fees over that time. It will keep you, me, and the rest of the department busy for thousands of billable hours a year. It's a game changer. We'll go from being in the middle of the pack to the top for environmental law departments, not just in Philly but in the Northeast. We can't screw this up. We need to do this." She kept rubbing my knee, then patted it, then stroked my thigh. As if to calm me down or excite me, I didn't know. It wasn't working.

"I said stop the car."

Diane ignored me and sped up. Now, we were going close to eighty mph and she continued to accelerate. Eighty-five. Ninety.

"Stop the car, please, Diane."

She pressed her lips together and shook her head. We went faster. Ninety-three miles per hour.

Is there a word stronger than furious? Maybe enraged? Maddened? Insane? I was insane with anger and felt my breathing come in pants. My mouth was dry. Maybe that was adrenaline kicking in. All of the bullshit I'd put up with. For the last twenty-four hours. For the last eight years. For what?

I looked around and noticed we were on a straightaway. There were no cars or trucks in either lane going in our direction. I knew what I was about to do was foolhardy, but one of my friends had done it to me as a joke when I was sixteen years old in my dad's old Buick. I was fairly certain I could get away with it. Pretty sure, but not entirely confident. I didn't care.

I leaned toward Diane as if I might kiss her on the cheek, then quickly turned the key and pulled it out of the ignition. The Town Car sputtered, shuddered, and immediately slowed.

"What the fuck have you done?" Diane said, gripping the steering wheel as tightly as she could. The power steering had locked up when I pulled the key. The car bucked as it slowed. Diane's knuckles were white as she squeezed the wheel. Her eyes were wide with fear. I leaned toward her and put my hand on the wheel. Without the power steering, it was stiff, and with all my strength I helped angle the car to the right, so it would drift onto the shoulder.

"You're going to have to lean on the brake with all you've got," I said. "It's got power brakes and there's no more power going to them. If you don't put all of your weight into it, we'll go off the road."

"Goldberg, you're a fucking idiot." She gasped as her body stiffened. She was laying everything she had onto the brake pedal.

Sweat ran down the side of Diane's face as she continued to wrestle with the steering wheel. Together, we were able to maneuver the car toward the shoulder. It was a long and slow landing. I leaned over and pressed the button for the four-way emergency lights. After maybe a thousand feet, the car drifted to a stop on the shoulder.

Diane looked at me. She gave me the full-on dragon-lady death stare. "You moron. You could have killed us. It's a good thing there were no other cars on the road."

I ignored her. "We're driving to Cincinnati. Get out of the car. I'm driving the rest of the way. You're going to have to take your chances with a flight from Cincinnati to Philly. I'm not screwing around. I mean it."

She sat in her seat, not moving. Looking at me. It looked like she was willing me to die. I stared back. After maybe five minutes, she slowly and reluctantly opened the door. I stepped into the cold night air. The temperature was in the low thirties, and I wasn't dressed for it. Mist formed in front of my face as I breathed. We passed each other in front of the car. She looked like she was ready to hit me, and I actually tensed my body getting ready for a gut-punch from her. We stopped and stood in front of the headlights and just looked at each other for several seconds. I was completely shocked when she reached out, put her arms around me, and laid her head on my shoulder. A moment later she was weeping.

"What? What's going on?" That was the most profound thing I could think of to say.

"You just don't get it. You're a good guy, a good lawyer, but the business of the law escapes you. I could teach you that, I'd love to teach you that, if you'd let me. It would be so good for you. For us. Don't you get it? This client, this potential client, it's the biggest opportunity I've ever had. *We've* ever had. If we land him, it will make me the number one billing partner in the firm. Don't you understand how that benefits me? The department? Ultimately you?"

She was speaking in a voice I'd never heard from her. Almost girl-like.

She pulled her head from my shoulder and was inches from my face. Kissing distance. I half-expected her to move her lips toward mine and braced myself. "I'll tell you what. If we drive to Philly, right now, I'll split the origination with you seventy-five – twenty-five. Get it? That could be millions of origination for you over the coming years. It's that important to me. There's so much more we could accomplish together. If you'd only let me." She kissed my cheeks lightly with soft kisses.

I know it sounds weird, but I actually felt sorry for her and hugged her more tightly. "I know you don't get this, but Keisha needs me, and I need her. For all I know, she's having our baby right now. I really don't know her condition. I'm concerned the baby will come early. Something else is going on, too, and I need to be there. We're going to Cincinnati. I promise, I'll get you to the airport and every airline flies from Cincinnati to Philly. One of them will have a seat and you'll get there. I'm sure of it. I have to get to the hospital to be with Keisha. It's just the way it is. I'm sorry, but I don't want what you want."

Her mouth was near my ear. "What is it you really want, Josh?" She was whispering and her breath tickled my ear.

I didn't think. The words spilled out. "I don't want this. The firm. It means so much to you and the others. I have no problem with that, but it took me this long to realize I don't want it for me. I want a family. I want Keisha and our baby. I want to do work that is meaningful and does some good. I'll survive just fine on less money, and I can be happier doing good. That's what I really want."

She looked at me from inches away, like she was looking at some alien object she didn't know or recognize. Breaking off the embrace was actually more awkward than embracing. Her hands were on my neck. Then, she slid her hands down my arms. It was a light, sensual touch. Loving. Like the next thing that might happen would be much more than a mere hug or kiss on the cheek.

When she reached my hand, she swiped at the key and snatched it from me. She paused and held it in front of her. She looked like she was in disbelief that she had it.

I reacted quickly and grabbed her arm and hand. We struggled for the key.

She bit down until her teeth sunk through my shirt into my forearm. Hard.

Finally, I tore the key out of her hand.

"Give me that key, give it to me, Goldberg." She was shouting. I wondered if they could hear us at the trailer park.

"No way."

"Give . . . me . . . the . . . fucking . . . key.

I now had the key in my right hand and with my left hand, I held Diane at arm's length. She was slapping at my arm. Spit was flying from her mouth as she continued to yell.

I looked at the woods next to the highway. Then, with all the strength I could muster, I did my best to impersonate Mariano Rivera and gave it my best relief pitcher heater.

I threw the key into the woods.

CHAPTER 25

JOSH

Somerset, Kentucky, 158 miles to Cincinnati, Ohio; 687 miles to Philadelphia, Pennsylvania.

The key arched through the air and disappeared in the blackness. I heard it hit a tree and ricochet in the woods with a metallic clink. Diane and I stood in the cold, dark, damp and glow of the headlights. Neither of us uttered a word. There were no cars on the road and the only sound was from some early bird chirp-chirp-chirping in the night. Other than that, complete silence.

Finally, the cold got to me, and I climbed into the driver's side and sat behind the wheel. I watched Diane in the glow of the headlights as she walked to the shoulder and peered into the gloom. She was no doubt wondering if it would be at all possible to find the key, how long it would take, whether she could get an Uber out here on the highway in rural Kentucky, and whether she could murder me with her bare hands. Probably not in that order.

As I sat there, I thought about Diane and the firm. Basically, they had been good to me. As advertised. They had made me the kind of lawyer I'd become. On the whole, the people were good, smart as hell, high achievers, and ambitious. The firm did what it said it would do: it made me a great lawyer and gave me opportunities I'd never imagined.

I appreciated them. They gave me a platform to build a practice and interesting cases to work on. They paid me handsomely. They generously doled out the perks from a firm credit card, to bonuses, to box seats at Phillies and Eagles games. They only demanded three things: I had to work hard; I was expected to be honest with them in all things; and I owed them complete loyalty.

The firm culture had seduced me. Changed me. I needed to make money to pay off those damned student loans and have a place to live, but the whole thing just made me feel . . . dirty. None of this was what I wanted for myself on the day I started college or the day I started law school. It was like I was sucked into the gaping maw of some alien creature. Instead of consuming me, it transformed me into something else when it shit me out. Made me something I didn't expect or want to be. I wasn't happy about it.

My feelings about Diane were unequivocal. I hated her. She used people. Manipulated them. And she did it well. I saw it in the way she handled clients and other lawyers. Don't get me wrong, she's a terrific lawyer. One of the best. But she's a user. I'd seen associates come and go. One day they would be working sixteen-hour days for Diane and have the office next to mine; the next it would be empty. Diane would say, "they didn't work out." That kind of crap. I never understood how it was that I'd survived nearly eight years of working with her. She could be so sweet and then a switch would flip, and she would tear the guts out of you. I'd known people who had relationships like that. Their relationship could be very hot at times, but one thing was certain, it didn't end well.

Diane hugged herself in the cold, damp Kentucky air. I couldn't see her face, but I could imagine her expression. After maybe five minutes, she climbed into the passenger seat and slammed the door. Hard.

"You're a fucking idiot, Goldberg. Now I'm going to miss my meeting and you're going to miss being with Keisha. I offered you so much. I wasn't even done negotiating. Something beautiful could have happened. Now, nothing. We're both losers. You're an asshole. Un-fucking-believable." She crossed her arms and looked straight ahead. I thought I saw a tear form in her eye, which she quickly rubbed out with the heel of her hand.

I said nothing in response. I sat with my hands on the steering wheel, looking at her. She was wrong. She looked broken. I'd finally won.

For now.

"You just don't get it, do you?" I said. "You really don't understand how important it is for me to be with Keisha. Be there for her when the baby is born. My grandma said to me, 'You don't live to eat; you eat to live.' That's what this is about. We don't live to work; we work to live. I want to be a successful lawyer, a partner even. But some things are more important to me than that. I'm sorry you don't understand."

"You're right," she said. "I don't get it. I want to win. I want to win more than I want anything else. Do I want a relationship, a man by my side? Sure. But that's just not the most important thing to me. Almost all of my friends have kids. I get it. For them, it's a big deal. Not for me. We have—had—a chance to be the number one environmental law firm in the east. Now we'll just be an also-ran."

Her expression revealed a mixture of sadness, hurt, and anger. I'd worked with her for years and it dawned on me that we may as well have been speaking in different languages to each other for all of that time. Neither of us understanding. I felt sorry for her.

She stared deeply into my eyes. Without breaking off the look, I put my right hand into my pants pocket and dug around. Then, I pulled out the second set of keys Abdul had given me under the portico at the Four Seasons and inserted the key into the ignition. I watched Diane as her jaw literally dropped.

"You motherfucker," she said quietly. She pulled her arm back and hit me in the right shoulder. Hard. I ignored her.

It took me a few moments to figure out how to undo what I'd done on the highway. The car was still in drive, but I'd turned off the ignition at ninety mph. After I turned off the radio and heat and fooled with the ignition and gear shift, I was able to get it back into park and restart the engine. Damn, that Town Car was a solid machine. It purred.

I commanded Siri to find the best route to Cincinnati and learned that Interstate 75 was only about half an hour east. From there, it was a straight shot north to Cincinnati. I asked Siri and learned that with light traffic and with no bad weather we would make it to Cincinnati in under three hours. When I asked her for a weather forecast, Siri reported that a significant amount of snow was falling as far south as Lexington and into Ohio. I hoped that the highway department was doing its job. If they were, we'd be in Cincinnati by 8 A.M., nine at the latest.

I looked at Diane. She was staring straight ahead. She'd pursed her lips as though she was restraining herself from talking. I could only imagine what evil was running through her mind. I didn't really want to know, and I didn't need to talk with her. I needed to get to the hospital to be with Keisha.

CHAPTER 26

JOSH

Georgetown, Kentucky, 65 miles to Cincinnati-Northern Kentucky International Airport.

I'd been driving for nearly three hours on Interstate 75. This was supposedly a straight shot to the Cincinnati Airport which, to my continuing surprise, was actually located south of Cincinnati, in Kentucky. So close. Unfortunately, we'd hit rotten weather around Richmond, Kentucky just an hour north of where we entered the Interstate.

Snow and sleet were coming down furiously. We danced in a slow conga line of cars, crawling north, trying to avoid the mounds of white slush piling along the highway. By the time we reached Lexington, we were going maybe twenty miles per hour. The wipers were having trouble with the wet snow. The only good news was that the truly crappy weather had made most everyone drive carefully. Those insane enough to drive too fast sent billows of snow and slop onto the windshield of anyone unfortunate enough to be nearby. We circled around Lexington at five or ten mph.

Although we hadn't spoken since the incident on the Parkway, I had turned on Diane's favorite radio station, the one with the moldy oldies. Maybe I was trying to appease her. Maybe I actually liked some of her music. In any event, it seemed the least I could do for her.

As we got to Lexington, I switched to A.M. and searched for an all-news station, finally locating one. The station reported that Cincinnati had already received nearly a foot of snow. Lexington, over six inches. Not surprisingly, the highway department was barely keeping up. The snow was piled on the shoulder in great heaps. The trees had mostly lost their leaves by then, and the ones that hadn't yet done so were bent to the ground. What really concerned me, though, was the traffic report that a major accident sixty miles south of Cincinnati had virtually shut down the Interstate in both directions.

I looked at Diane, who was awake and maintaining her stony silence. From time to time, she furiously worked her phone, texting with who-knows.

"Diane . . . Diane. Can you help us out? Is there an alternate route, so we can get around the logjam on Seventy-Five?"

She looked at me, rolled her eyes, and gave me her you-are-a-dumb-ass look. "Yes, we take that Parkway I was on before some moron threw the key into the woods. Then we hit the Interstate that takes us directly to Philadelphia."

"Let's not go over this now, please. Is there an alternative route to Cincinnati?"

She worked her phone and finally said, "There's a little tiny road up ahead called US 62. It shoots off through some farmland to US 27, which gets you pretty close to the airport. I know how much you like those little bitty back roads. I'm just guessing here but I suspect they're going to be snowed in, especially as we drive further north. There *is* another alternative, according to Waze. We could turn around and go back to I-64, then head west and hook up with I-71. That also goes near the airport. That route forms a giant triangle, and it would take us at least 175 miles out of our way. Also, those roads probably have as much snow as this one does."

I looked at the clock on the dashboard. It was after 7 A.M. We'd been traveling for nearly twenty-four hours and the only rest I had was the little bit of sleep I snuck in a few hours earlier while Diane hijacked our car. I was exhausted and really didn't want to give Diane the opportunity to drive again. I didn't have any more sets of keys, so if she tried to drive us straight to Philly, throwing another set into the woods wouldn't be an option.

"You said US 62?" She nodded. "That's just up ahead. Let's get off this highway and give it a try." I tried to sound chipper but could tell Diane wasn't buying it.

The exit was only about a mile away, but it still took nearly ten minutes to get there. As I drove off the highway, it was clear I wasn't the only one with the brilliant idea of taking the back roads to Cincinnati. To make matters worse, the highway department had made nearly no effort to plow this route. The traffic was moving at about thirty mph until we slowed to twenty and finally stopped in a long line of cars. Ominously, no one was coming toward us. We were surrounded by fields and farms. I could see the red and blue lights of a police car up ahead reflecting in the snow. A couple of cars pulled out of the line of traffic and made awkward U-turns to head back toward the Interstate. I inched forward. A cop in full-length winter gear holding a flashlight with a bright red light approached my window and I rolled it down.

"Hey buddy, turn it around. Some idiot in an SUV managed to spin his car and caused a chain reaction accident up ahead. Took out two semis. Both lanes are closed, and I doubt we're going to be able to open it for hours."

"What about I-75? I heard on the radio that it was closed down too."

"It is, but I suspect that will reopen in three or four hours. My suggestion? If you can find a place to hole up for a while that would be best. I suspect the Interstate will reopen by around ten or eleven. As long as no one plays the fool, traffic should move at a decent speed considering the weather."

I looked at Diane and she lifted her chin triumphantly. I wasn't sure why. As we drove back toward the Interstate, I saw a motel—the Roadside Rest. I'd never heard of that chain before. It was one of those drive-up-to-your-room places.

I looked at Diane and shook my head. "I can't go on. I need to shut my eyes for a few hours."

"Suits me. I hate driving in the snow, and I'm exhausted too."

I pulled into the parking lot and noticed right away that cars were parked in front of every room.

I got out of the car and stepped into the driving sleet. All I was wearing were my Houston clothes and by the time I got to the front door, I was soaked right through to my skin.

The office was steamy and smelled of Pine-Sol. Inside, a gray-haired woman wearing a gray cardigan sweater was perched on a café chair behind the counter. She shook her head as I came into the lobby.

"Do you have two rooms?" I asked in my sweetest voice. "They don't have to be great. I'd even rent them by the hour." I smiled.

She frowned at me. "By the hour? We're not that kind of place."

"No, no, I just mean we need to get a few hours of sleep before we push on as soon as we can. You can rent them out again as soon as we leave."

"Sorry, we're booked up. A lot of people pulled in here when the storm hit and we're full."

"I'm so exhausted. Don't you have anything?"

She made a face. "Well, we have one room, but the guests checked out a little while ago and it's not made up yet."

"How much?"

"Today it's $150."

Probably twice the regular price. It didn't matter. I said, "If you can get it ready, I'll take it. If you get it cleaned up in the next five minutes, I'll pay you a fifty-dollar tip."

She disappeared through the door. While I waited for her to return, two more cars pulled in next to the Town Car. Five minutes later, I paid her $200 using my credit card and she gave me the key.

"By the way, does that room happen to have twin beds or two queen-size beds?"

"Sorry, just one king-size bed."

"Great." Sheesh. Wonderful.

I got back in the car, pulled the car keys from my pocket, and drove to the room.

"You're going to love this," I said. "This is the very last room in the whole joint. I don't think there's another motel room for a hundred miles around. There's just one bed. I'll sleep in a chair or on the floor. You take the bed."

Diane looked at me and shook her head. "Don't be an idiot, Josh. Nothing's going to happen. We'll both take the bed. You stay on one side, and I'll stay on the other."

I knew that wouldn't work. No way.

We shuffled through about eight inches of snow and slush and pushed our way into the room. I thought about getting out my luggage but realized the only thing I had was the suit and soiled shirts I'd worn in Houston. The jeans I was wearing were the only extra slacks I'd brought. It didn't matter. I'd get under a blanket or a sheet and that would be that.

The room was Spartan. Fake pine paneling from the 1970s. It had a king-size bed with a thin blanket, an ancient color TV, a noisy forced-air heater, and worn orange shag carpet. There were no chairs. I found an extra blanket and pillow in the closet. I arranged the blanket on the floor and said to Diane, "You take the bed, I'll sleep down here."

I went into the bathroom and peed, then I took off my jeans, shirt, and socks, which were soaked. I threw them over the shower rod and hoped they might dry out while we were stuck in the motel. I dried myself off with a thin towel.

I remembered to take the car keys from my jean's pocket with me and hid them in my hand as I came out of the bathroom wearing just my shorts and a grimace. Diane gave me a quick up and down glance as we passed, and I tried not to notice her looking at my body. Don't ask me why, but I held in my stomach as she looked at me. Dumb ass. Then, when Diane went into the bathroom, I stuck the car keys under the radiator. Unless she was watching, she wouldn't know where I'd hidden them. I knew I was being wildly over-cautious, but I really didn't trust her.

Diane came out of the bathroom five minutes later. She'd taken off her jeans and blouse. Now, all she was wearing were her underpants and bra. Both were black. I tried not to notice her well-defined abs and smallish boobs barely hidden behind the black lace. I guessed she'd picked up her tan a few weekends earlier on a trip to the Virgin Islands. On any other day, with any other female friend, I probably would've made a smart-assed comment and we would have laughed. I said nothing, laid back, and pulled the blanket over me. As I was lying on the floor, I tapped my phone and sent Keisha a quick text.

> **Funny story. Stuck in a snowstorm about 60 miles south of the airport. The highways are closed due to storms and accidents, and I've been up for 24 hours. Diane and I found a motel and are camping out for a few hours catching some sleep. Don't worry, we're wearing all of our clothes and I'm pretty sure nothing is going to happen. LOL. She's in the bed and I'm on the floor. We'll get up at 11 and hopefully the Interstate will be reopened. If all goes well, I'll see you in a few hours. I love you.**

I set my phone to wake me at 11 A.M.

"Diane." She didn't respond. "Diane, please. I'm going to get you to the airport in time for your flight. I promise. I'm just too exhausted. I need to crash for a couple of hours."

She leaned over the side of the bed and looked at me. Her bra strap was off her shoulder. "Oh, Josh. You just don't get it, do you?"

She reached down and stroked my shoulder with a fingertip. I took her hand. "Friends?" she asked.

"Friends," I said. She squeezed my hand and I let go quickly.

I'm sure she said more, but I was asleep within seconds.

CHAPTER 27

KEISHA

Keisha slept badly. Normally, she slept soundly, after she put away all of the day's issues that had invaded her mind. Before she was pregnant, she was asleep by eleven—unless she was fooling around with Josh—and up at six, when she went for a run. The hospital bed was uncomfortable, and the rubber-covered mattress made noise every time she moved. Plus, the baby had shifted and now was resting on her bladder. She was lucky to sleep for thirty minutes at a time.

Anthony strongly discouraged her from getting out of bed, but the nurses said it would be okay for her to go to the bathroom two or three times a day. She waited as long as she could and at about 6 A.M., she pulled the intravenous stand and wires from the monitors with her to the bathroom and peed. On her way back, she looked out the window. The snow had finally stopped falling, but she could see it was thick and heavy. According to the TV weather report, Northern Kentucky had received a total of fourteen inches. In November. At least the storm had moved past Cincinnati. The sound of the heavy equipment and plows rearranging the snow was constant and annoying.

Josh was on her mind. He'd texted her when he left Geoff's sister's house, so she knew he was on his way and getting closer. She hadn't heard from him in hours and figured he must be driving, otherwise, he would have texted her again by now. She wanted to see him. Badly.

Her nighttime thoughts were invaded both by memories of her long-ago relationship with Anthony and his recent reappearance. In the middle of the night, she found herself thinking about the mostly good times she had with him.

Despite his despicable, traitorous behavior, he'd been a loving and fun boyfriend. Very different from Josh. Anthony was adventurous and spontaneous. She remembered coming home from work once and finding red rose petals leading from the front door of their apartment to the bedroom. She hadn't even realized that it was their three-month anniversary. He was waiting for her in bed with champagne and chocolate-covered strawberries. All he was wearing were tiny black underpants. Anthony was like a high waterfall that sparkled in the sunlight as the water danced from rock to rock, cascaded a thousand feet, then disappeared into a deep gorge. If you fell into that waterfall, you would be in a world of hurt.

Josh was like a wide river. A slow-moving stream. Steady and constant. If you were a boat on that river, it would get you where you wanted to go. He had no sense of romance. Josh was the guy who was always there, loving and affectionate, without the fireworks. As busy as he was at work, he always went with her to see her ob-gyn in Philly. He was a rock. Keisha knew there would never be a chance she'd walk in on him in bed with another woman.

Fireworks. That was Anthony. He had talked about that with her the night before. He was right. Anthony was the most talented lover she'd ever had. He'd brought her to heights of ecstasy, and she'd never experienced anything like that before—or since. It wasn't that Josh was a bad lover; he was good in his own way. It was just that Anthony had been so damned good. But she was older now and things were different. Starting a family and getting married were important now. Keisha didn't need a few dazzling seconds of fireworks; she needed a solid relationship that would last forever.

Keisha wondered what the hell Anthony was doing. It wasn't like he'd reached out to her in the past eight years. It was just happenstance that she ended up in the same hospital where he worked as a gynecologist. If she hadn't passed out at the airport and been brought to this hospital, she may never have seen him again. Ever. Maybe the gods were playing with her.

Even so, she wondered—had he really compared all of his relationships to the one he had with her? Was he telling the truth when he said he'd never married because no one measured up to her? As flattering as it was, she knew she couldn't trust him. So much of what he said was pure bullshit.

The door opened and for half a second, Keisha hoped it might be Josh. It was the PA. Loretta. Maybe in her late 20s, she was attractive, white, and local, with a strong Kentucky twang in her voice. Slim, she wore her blonde hair pulled back in a ponytail and unflattering scrubs.

"How are you feeling, hon? Your color looks good. You look perky," Loretta said.

Keisha smiled. "In my whole life, I've never been called *perky*. You do know how to make an eight-month pregnant woman happy."

"We aim to please." They both laughed.

Loretta checked her blood pressure and pulse, then took her temperature. She lifted the sheet from Keisha's feet and felt her ankles. "How are those compression socks working out?" The night before, the nurse had removed the inflatable pneumatic stockings and replaced them with compression socks.

"Better. Not as annoying as those inflatable things. I have enough going on right now to keep me awake without them inflating and deflating every minute."

Loretta looked around and closed the door. "You knew Anthony, I mean Dr. Sudor, from way back, right?"

Keisha wondered where this was going. "Yes, he was in medical school, and I was just getting started as a teacher back in Philly."

"Were you close?"

"Close? You could say that. I mean, we lived together for a while."

"But that's over, right?"

Keisha paused. Now, she really was curious where this was heading. "Yes. We haven't even talked to each other for eight years. I'm engaged and, of course, there's this." She patted her belly. "What are you getting at, Loretta?"

"I wouldn't say Anthony is my boyfriend. We go out after work and occasionally date. A couple of movies, a concert, dinners. That kind of thing."

"Uh-huh."

Loretta glanced furtively at the door. "I mean, the hospital discourages this, but doctors and nurses have been doing it forever. He's spent the night at my place a few times. I don't think it's serious. I mean, I'd like that, but right now it's just occasional. Do people still say *friends with benefits*?" She smiled.

"Maybe. But what I had with Anthony was years ago."

"I thought that. He hasn't said anything particular, but I just know there's something more. The thing is he talks about you. A lot. How you won some big teacher of the year award in Pennsylvania. He brags on you, the way a close friend or someone closer might act. Also . . ."

Another glance at the door. "He's in here a lot. I mean, you're not the first pregnant patient we've had who needs bed rest. Usually, the doctor will stop by once, *maybe* twice a day. They leave the attention-giving to the nurses and PAs. But he's here four or five times every day. Brings you coffee. I don't mean to . . ."

Keisha reached out and grabbed Loretta's hand. "You're very kind. You don't need to worry about me. I'm with another guy, Josh." She pointed at the window. "He's been driving up from Houston through that for the past twenty-four hours just to be here with me. He's the dad of this little pumpkin." She patted her stomach. The two women looked deeply into each other's eyes for several seconds.

"Just a word about Anthony," Keisha said. "From one woman to another. I know he's a great doctor. Let me just say that as a boyfriend, he's not very reliable. He could hurt you if your expectations are too high. I'm not saying you shouldn't have your fun, but don't get your hopes up."

There was a tap at the door, and it opened before anyone could respond. Anthony.

"Well, my favorite patient and my favorite PA. What secrets you could tell each other." He let out a hearty laugh and said, "Time for a quick exam."

"I just checked," said Loretta. "All of her vitals are fine. Well within normal limits."

Anthony pushed aside the sheets and felt her belly. "Hmm." He put his hands under her gown and continued examining her. "Loretta, would you do an internal exam for us?"

Loretta slipped on examination gloves and tapped Keisha's knees. Obligingly, she moved them apart. Anthony stood near Keisha's head, stroking his chin. Loretta seemed to take a few seconds longer than she had in the previous exams.

"Interesting . . ." Loretta said, "You're going to feel a little pressure. Take a deep breath. Okay." She snapped off the gloves and replaced the sheet over her feet. "You're a little dilated. Maybe a centimeter."

Anthony nodded. "That's not unusual and it doesn't mean you're going to have the baby today or tomorrow. This is why we have you on bed rest. We'll monitor that and it's entirely possible you won't have the baby for several more weeks. I'm not at a point yet where I'd put a timeframe on delivery. If I had to guess though, I'd say you're going to deliver sooner rather than later."

Keisha took it in, then said, "But I could have the baby . . . soon?"

"It depends on what you mean by soon. Probably not today and not tomorrow, but soon."

He looked at Loretta. "I'd like to talk with my patient, in private."

Loretta frowned and bit her lip. "Of course, *Doctor*." She left the room and pulled the door shut.

Anthony waited until the door was closed and then sat on the bed and took Keisha's hand. "You'll be fine, Boo. Don't worry. Everything's fine. It's possible the baby will be a little premature, but we have a great NICU in this hospital. Also, we have three neonatologists here on staff and they're all top-notch."

"You really think the baby will be born soon? Or is that something you say to cover your ass? Did you really mean it?"

Again, the hearty laugh. "A little of both. I think the baby will be born on the early side. It's just too soon to say how early."

Anthony stood and looked out the window at the snow. "Is your boyfriend still coming? Maybe he decided to avoid the weather and head straight home. Any word from him?"

"He's not my *boyfriend*. He's my *fiancé*. I heard from him a few hours ago when he was in Nashville. He's on his way."

Anthony sat on the bed again. "You know, I meant what I said before. I'm ready for a real relationship. Marriage. With you. I wasn't kidding. I'd love to raise this baby with you."

Keisha took that in, then nodded. "What about Loretta?"

Anthony sat back and blinked. "What about her?"

"Don't you think she'll be disappointed if we run off and get married? I mean, she might have expectations considering . . ."

Anthony smiled a broad smile. "I've dated a lot of women since we were together . . ."

"And by dated you mean . . ."

"Yes, of course that. We're grown-ups. I make a point of not deceiving anyone or leading them on. She knows the nature of our relationship. It's mutual. In my life, I've only ever told one woman I loved her. That was you. I swear it." He held her gaze.

"Anthony, this is very flattering. I'm a big fat pregnant lady and you're a good-looking doctor. I appreciate the offer, but I've already accepted another."

"Except that you're not married." He reached over and held up her left hand. "I don't see a ring on this hand. You've never been clear about this, but at least one of you, maybe both of you, can't commit. Have you ever asked yourself why? It's not that big a deal to go down to City Hall and get married. You could do it during a lunch break. Part of me wonders whether you may have been waiting for me to come back into your life."

Keisha looked at him and let his words settle for a moment. "You're kidding, right? You think this is all about you?"

Anthony's phone rang. He looked at it and put it to his ear. "Okay, I'll be right there."

"Look, a woman just came into the emergency department in labor. I'll be back in a bit."

He got up and strode to the door. As he was about to go, he turned his head and said, "You know, you haven't actually said 'no' to me. I mean you've said a lot of other stuff, but I haven't heard the word 'no.' I'm hanging onto that."

Before Keisha could respond, he was gone. She waited until his footsteps disappeared down the hall, then she said out loud, "Yes."

She listened to her own voice, then said, "No."

She lay in bed, bombarded by the monitors and general noise from the hallway. After a few minutes, her phone chimed, and she looked at it. A text from Josh. She read it and then read it again. She focused on a few words:

Diane and I found a motel and are camping out for a few hours and catching some sleep. Don't worry, we're wearing all of our clothes and I'm pretty sure nothing is going to happen. LOL

Keisha took a deep breath. She was in the hospital while Josh and Diane were in a motel. In bed or on the floor. It didn't matter. He never ever said 'LOL.' In fact, he'd told her how much he hated that abbreviation. She didn't care how tired he was. What the hell was he doing in a motel with Diane?

CHAPTER 28

JOSH

Georgetown, Kentucky, 65 miles to Cincinnati-Northern Kentucky International Airport.

I wouldn't say I slept soundly on the motel room floor, but I did sleep hard. My subconscious was active, but a bomb could have gone off in the parking lot and I wouldn't have heard it.

Finally, a dream came to me. A good one—I was with Keisha. She was lying next to me and stroking my hair, face, and chest. Kissing me gently on my ear and on my cheek. She wasn't pregnant; her stomach was flat. It was a beautiful and warm dream. I put my arms around Keisha and drew her in close. Her hands stroked me tenderly and her lips found mine. We kissed long and deeply. Not the kiss-madly-rip-off-your-clothes-and-have-wild-sex kind of kissing. It was the no-rush-we-can-kiss-all-night-and-then-have-sex kind.

Our hands ran up and down each other's body, tenderly stroking every part. They were gentle, loving touches. It was vivid.

As I touched her, however, something felt wrong, unsettled. I'd been with Keisha for over two years and thought I knew every inch of her body. She just felt different: her hips bonier, stomach tauter, breasts smaller. Her reaction to my touches was not quite right, not what I expected. Her smell was off. Keisha wears a particular perfume: Jimmy Choo's, like the shoes. She does this thing where she sprays the perfume in the air and walks through it so it's not too strong. That's her scent, unique, citrusy. Her perfume is not all that common, and I'd know her from her smell alone. In my dream, she smelled different, some other perfume. Her taste was different too. We've kissed a lot over the years and she's a great kisser. I know her taste, her tongue action, and how she kisses. That was off, too. Her kisses were more insistent, probing me deeply. What a weird dream.

I awakened slowly, not wanting the erotic dream to go away. As the dream evaporated and the room took shape, I realized I was lying on the floor of the Roadside Rest Motel. A thin blanket was wrapped around me, and Keisha vanished. Instead of Keisha, lying next to me was Diane.

Diane.

I was on my back. Diane was leaning over me, kissing my face. Her bare breasts grazed my chest. My hands were around her. One of her hands was inside my underwear. Stroking me. With every exhalation, she groaned quietly.

Suddenly, reality came to me as though a bucket of slushy Kentucky snow had been dumped over my head. I awakened with a start and pushed her away from me.

"What the . . . What the hell?" I said.

"Baby, let's do this. Come on, I want it; you want it." She leaned over me again and ran her hand along my side. She began to slip her hand inside my underwear again.

I put my hands on her arms and held her back. "Are you kidding me? What are you doing?"

There was enough light slipping between the curtains that I could see her breasts. Her bra was gone, and her legs were tangled up with mine. I was very aroused.

I backed away from her until my back was against the heater. I sat up and pulled my legs to my chest and shook my head. "What the fuck, Diane?"

She smiled and wiggled next to me. "Come on, baby, let's finish what we started." Her hand was on my stomach. She kissed my shoulder.

"*I* didn't start anything. I was asleep, dead to the world. Alone on the floor. What time is it? Why are you doing this?"

Diane sat up and crossed her legs. I glanced and saw that she was still wearing her black underpants, so at least *that* had not happened. I hoped. She sat maybe a foot or two away from me with her back against the bed. Her breasts were staring me in the face. "I thought you wanted this. I laid awake for about an hour after you fell asleep and then asked you if I could join you down here. You didn't respond, but you didn't say no, either." She smiled at me and angled her head. "We made out for the longest time, baby. It was wonderful. You seemed to be enjoying yourself." Her eyes drifted to below my waist.

"I didn't respond because I was asleep! I dreamed you were Keisha. I didn't want this. I'm with Keisha."

"Josh, let's talk about that—"

"No! I really don't want to talk about it. Also, could you please cover up?"

She placed her hands over her breasts in a move that was more caressing than covering up. Then she smiled and turned. She felt around on the bed until she found her bra and put it on slowly. It was a sexy damn bra and maybe in some corner of her mind she felt she'd covered up, but not really. It was black and very sheer.

"You're a good guy. You happen to be a great lawyer. You have skills that I don't have, and I have skills that you lack. If you put us together, we'd be an unstoppable team. Don't you get it? Also, baby, unless you haven't figured it out, I really have the hots for you. We should be together."

Diane reached out and put a hand on my knee, rubbing up my thigh. I took her hand and pulled it off.

"I can't believe we're having this conversation," I said. "We're colleagues. You're my boss. I'm ten years younger than you. Keisha is having our baby. *My* baby. I'm with Keisha. You and I are *not* together, and I don't want to be with you. I don't know how to say it any more simply and directly than that."

"I don't know, we kissed in the back of the car, you held me when we got out, and you seemed pretty hot for me for the past half hour."

"I was asleep! I was dreaming I was with Keisha. I slept on the goddamn floor so this wouldn't happen."

I was trying to figure out how to end this mess without telling Diane to go to hell. She was, after all, my boss. There was no way I could report her to the managing partner or anyone. She was one of the chosen ones at the firm. Somehow, I knew this would come back on me. Who would believe that Diane took advantage of me in a motel room? No one. If I reported this to management, she'd say *I* was the predator who tried to have sex with her. I'd be totally screwed. I'd lose my job. Maybe my law license. Be ostracized. Maybe arrested.

My mind raced as I tried to figure this out. All I knew was I wanted to end this because it could destroy everything I'd ever worked for. Disengaging had to be her idea.

"Look, Diane, this wouldn't work," I said as gently as I could. I made a calculated guess and reached for her hands. We sat on the floor holding hands in our underwear. "I work for you. I'm with Keisha and we have a baby coming soon. I like you, I *really* do. You're very attractive. Hot. Part of me would love to . . . Maybe if we'd gotten together a few years ago, before I was with Keisha, before she was carrying my baby, maybe something would have happened. But that ship has sailed."

Diane dropped my hand and gave me one of her patented looks, raising her chin as if to say *you're an idiot*. "You think this has never happened before? You think I didn't sleep with a partner or two along the way? I'm not proud of that, but I was never one of those *me too* people. I wanted to make partner as badly as you do and didn't want to be on the front page of the New York Times for setting the firm on fire. I know this sounds awful and I won't win any awards for it, but whatever happened, happened. When it was over, the partner was still smiling and my road to an early partnership was secure."

We looked at each other for a long moment. Then, she smiled a wicked smile. "You know, your buddy Geoff wasn't so high and mighty."

"Geoff? You slept with Geoff?"

Again, the chin and the thin smile.

I thought about Geoff and Imani. They seemed to have a good marriage. Five kids. They even talked about adopting. What the hell?

"You know that trip to Atlanta last year?" she said. "We were meeting with clients. A big real estate deal with environmental issues. We were there for two nights. Let's just say that Geoff didn't argue with me, and we both enjoyed ourselves."

I shook my head. "Enough. You've already told me more than I ever want to know. He's never breathed a word of this to me."

"I meant what I said, Josh. I'm not talking about a fling with you, I'm talking about a relationship. Long-term. As long as you want. I could do so much for you. The firm *loves* me." She dragged out the word *loves*. "Honestly, they just *like* you. I could make things happen for you. A full equity partnership, for one. This year, not in three or four years, or maybe never. There's so much we can accomplish together, and I'm not just talking about mind-blowing sex. New clients, massive billings, fantastic trips. You'd have the life most lawyers only dream about. With me."

In that moment, I thought I wanted none of that. I was happy with Keisha, really happy. I wanted a long relationship with *her*, not anyone else. I was looking forward to having a family with her and couldn't wait to be a dad. I liked working at the firm, but if I didn't work there, I'd work somewhere else. Where I worked didn't mean a whole lot to me anymore. Unlike Geoff, I wouldn't feel any less of a person if I never made partner. There were things I could be doing—should be doing—that I couldn't do at the firm. Represent the right people for one. Take on the issues that matter. Do good.

I really, really wanted to end this conversation and get this trip over with. But Diane seemed to be enjoying it. She was a world-class negotiator and manipulator. I suspected in her mind, the longer we talked, the more likely it was that we'd finish what she'd started. She leaned forward, landed her hands on my arms, and stroked them lightly.

"Come on, baby. Let's do this." Her mouth was inches from mine. It would have been so easy. Life-changing.

I quickly kissed her on the forehead and stood up. I was still generously aroused, so I quickly wrapped the blanket around me and headed for the bathroom.

"We'd better get dressed," I said from the bathroom door. "We don't have many more miles to go, but I have a feeling it's going to be some hard sledding."

I went into the bathroom and locked the door. I looked at myself in the mirror. I had dark eyes and a crease across my face from the blanket. I didn't have a clue about how to fix this.

CHAPTER 29

JOSH

Georgetown, Kentucky, 65 miles to Cincinnati-Northern Kentucky International Airport.

My clothes were cold and clammy, but with Diane in the room, I wasn't going to wait around for them to dry off while wearing nothing but my underwear. I waited for her in the car with the heat turned up while she took her time getting dressed. We found a McDonald's near the on-ramp and got coffee. Large and black for both of us. Other than discussing our drinks, we said almost nothing to each other. We were back on the road before ten.

The snow had stopped, and the Interstate was open. Traffic was moving, albeit slowly. I'm not sure if it was Diane's unusual wake-up call, or being so close to seeing Keisha, but I was wide awake. For nearly two hours, the traffic was heavy, and we never got over forty mph. All around was a winter wonderland. The highway department had done a decent job clearing off two lanes, but the shoulder hadn't been touched. Every thousand feet or so we passed a lump of snow in the shoulder like a boil not quite ready to pop, buried evidence of an abandoned car. I was grateful when I finally saw a highway sign for Cincinnati/Northern Kentucky International Airport. Just five miles and I'd be done with Diane. For now.

I took the exit and within a few hundred feet, traffic slowed considerably. We went from thirty mph to walking speed. It was maddening. A large sign over the highway announced the exit for the airport as just two miles away. That's where the traffic came to a complete stop. Up ahead, I could see one of those overhead electronic road signs. I pulled out of the stalled line of cars into the left lane and slowly approached the sign. It read:

Airport Access Road Closed for Snow Removal
Noon to 1 P.M.—Expect Delays

I looked at the clock; it was 12:15. Traffic was at a stand-still. Frustrated and anxious drivers sat in every car. Quickly, rounding the numbers and making a lot of assumptions, I figured if the road reopened at 1 P.M., it probably would take us another hour to reach the terminal, which would be around 2 P.M. Two hours to travel a couple of miles. I looked at Diane and said, "What time is your flight?"

"5:15."

I thought for half a second. "You have plenty of time. The last thing I want to do is sit in a line of cars going nowhere."

"Wait. What?"

I spoke to my phone and commanded Siri to give me a route to St. Elizabeth-Florence Hospital. A moment later, she complied, and I drove straight ahead. If we didn't have any more delays, we'd be there in ten minutes.

"Where are we going? Josh, what the hell are you doing?" Diane said.

"Even when this opens up, there's going to be another massive traffic jam at the airport."

"This had better be a back route to the airport."

Up ahead, a road sign pointed the way to the hospital. I put on my signal and pointed at the sign. "Not exactly. We're going thataway."

"Wait a minute." Diane said. "I'm not interested in visiting your girlfriend."

"That's fine with me." I was looking straight ahead. "You can sit in the car and wait. I'll come back at around 2:30 and drive you to the airport. The roads should be clear enough by then. I'm taking the keys, so it might get a little chilly sitting out here in the snow by yourself."

"Are you kidding?"

I turned to look at her. "Do I look like I'm kidding?"

The access road for the hospital and much of the parking lot was surprisingly clear of snow. I realized that if any roads were going to be cleared first, it would be the access to a hospital.

As I pulled into the parking lot, it was obvious which cars belonged to people who had been at the hospital throughout the storm. They had foot-high piles of snow on them. Doctors, nurses, staff, patients, families, they'd been here for days. Maybe half the cars in the lot were covered with snow. I pulled into an open parking space that had been plowed, put the car into park, and took the key.

"I'll be back in two hours," I said as I got out of the car.

"Seriously, you're going to leave me in the car for two fucking hours?"

"Depending upon what's happening inside, it might be longer than that. You can wait in the hospital or consider Uber."

Diane shot me her dragon-lady death stare, which I ignored, and slammed the door on her. A moment later, I heard her get out of the car. I turned around and locked the car with the key fob. Together, we walked around the piles of snow to the hospital entrance.

Inside, it was hospital-warm. Short-shirtsleeves-warm, which felt good since I was still damp in places. I got Keisha's room information from a registration desk clerk and looked at Diane. "What are you going to do?"

She paused for a moment. "I'd love to visit the woman carrying the child of the man for whom I had such high hopes."

As we began making our way through the lobby, I realized how excited I was that I was finally going to be with my fiancé who was about to have my child.

And I was in the company of the woman with whom, three hours earlier, I was mostly naked on the floor of a motel.

Who had seriously tried to seduce me.

Lovely.

You can't make this stuff up.

CHAPTER 30

KEISHA

Keisha was lying in the hospital bed considering the flowers that had been delivered a few minutes earlier. A dozen red roses in a vase. Pretty. No card to tell who sent them. She wondered if Josh had felt guilty for shacking up with Diane and sent them as a peace offering. She loved flowers and especially roses. It was so unlike Josh to send her flowers. He was frugal. She hoped he had no real reason to feel guilty. If he did, flowers would never be enough to make her happy.

She began doing some of the stretching exercises the nurses had prescribed for her. She made sure Anthony wasn't around, then planted her feet firmly and raised her hips five times. Of all the exercises they gave her, these actually helped her the most. The last thing she needed, though, was for Anthony to drop by and remind her of their past escapades together. She had plenty of flashbacks to those magnificent nights and days without the constant reminders from the man she once loved.

Other than being stiff and sore from lying in bed, she didn't feel bad. In fact, she felt remarkably good. She wondered whether this was the calm before the storm. She was willing to do what she needed to do to give her baby the best chance possible. If she had to stay in bed for a month, then that's what she would do.

There was a tap on the door and a moment after Keisha said to come in, Loretta pushed her way into the room with a cart carrying a monitor on it. "Hey, hon, I have to do another sonogram. Dr. Sudor is still giving you the full princess treatment."

Keisha made a face and shook her head.

Five minutes later, Loretta finished the test and wiped the contact gel off Keisha's belly with a rough towel. "Everything looks fine. I'll get the report down to Dr. Sudor."

"Thanks." Keisha paused and watched her arrange the equipment. "Loretta, do you remember what I said about Anthony? He's a great guy, or at least the version of him I knew eight years ago was. But please, don't forget what I said about the thing he's most interested in."

She didn't answer for a moment. "You mean himself? I won't forget. I can't. I guess I already knew that."

"You know, I barely thought of him for almost ten years and then just happened to land in this hospital where the guy who once was the love of my life is my doctor. Meanwhile, the guy whose baby I'm having is driving up here to be with me. It's crazy."

"Why are you telling me this?" Loretta asked. She pulled a chair close to the bed and sat.

"I don't know exactly. I feel I can trust you. You know, I've always had a guy. High school, college, after college, one after another, like a series of railroad cars. You know what I mean?"

"Not exactly," Loretta said. "I can go for months without even going on a date, let alone having a boyfriend. So, no, I don't know what it's like to have guys lining up to go out. Maybe that's why I'm so happy with Anthony." She hesitated again. "Do you feel like you can't handle being on your own?"

"Honestly, I've always felt that if I don't have a boyfriend, I'm adrift. Trust me, I've envied people like you who can make it without needing someone else."

"That's funny. There have been times when I've envied people like you who always have someone. I do have to admit, while some mornings I wake up and wish there was a man next to me, there are many mornings I really like not having to interact with anyone. The bathroom is all mine. Sometimes, I like the peace and quiet of my place at night when I get to decide what I want to do or wear."

"Are you happy?" Keisha asked.

"Mostly. I value my independence and I'm glad I know I can make it on my own. I wouldn't mind having a man in my life, a permanent relationship, but I don't need that right now." Loretta thought for a moment. "Are you happy?"

"I think so. I mean, I love Josh, but if seeing Anthony again has reminded me of anything, it's not that I want to be with him, but I wonder if I really want to be with Josh . . . or anyone."

Loretta sat up straight and looked shocked. "Wow."

"Yeah, wow," Keisha said. "I can't believe I just said that."

Neither woman said anything for many seconds.

"You do remember you're about to have a baby." Loretta lightly patted Keisha's stomach. "Josh's baby. You're going to need some help."

"I know that. For me, it's temporary insanity. It's probably just the hormones talking and I'm sure we'll be together. The funny thing is, everyone thinks Josh is the one with commitment issues. He's got some of those for sure, but believe it or not, it's me. I'm confident Josh will be there for me, our baby, every step of the way. No matter what."

Loretta glanced at her watch and abruptly took Keisha's hand. "I'm sorry, Keisha. I've enjoyed this and I appreciate your honesty, but I've got to go. I'm sure every other pregnant woman here is beating on her call-button. I'll stop back again as soon as I can. I'd love to talk with you more."

Loretta pushed the sonogram cart away from the bed, then leaned over and hugged Keisha briefly. After she left, Keisha pulled out her phone to see if she received any messages from Josh. She looked again at the last one she had from him: "Diane and I found a motel . . ."

She read it over and wiped a tear from her eye.

CHAPTER 31

KEISHA

There was a light tap at the door, and it opened immediately. Anthony strode in wearing a big smile and a long, white lab coat over blue scrubs. He pushed the door shut behind him until it was mostly closed. "How's my Boo doing today?"

"I'm feeling pretty good, *Doctor* Sudor." She smiled at him.

"Nice flowers," he said, smiling back and dipping his head toward her tray to sniff them. "Red roses. Sweetheart roses, your favorite, as I recall. Generally sent when someone is trying to send a message of love to their sweetie, I believe."

"Yes, I think that's right."

"Do they remind you of anything?"

Keisha looked at him. "Oh, they're from *you*. I thought . . . Never mind. Um, I don't know, summer? Longwood Gardens?"

"How about that time you came home from work and the hallway was covered with red rose pedals? All the way to the bedroom."

"Yes. Our third-month anniversary. I never forgot."

"I never forgot either, Boo. The rose petals, the champagne, the awesome delights that happened next and next and next."

They looked at each other. Finally, Keisha said, "That PA, your friend Loretta, was in here a little while ago and did a sonogram."

Anthony angled his head. "I'd say she's more my support staff, my colleague . . ."

"Oh? Is that what we're calling that today? Support staff *with benefits*? I know all about you two. Don't worry about it. You and I are not together and it's not like you're a monk or have to be true to anyone. Now, about that sonogram."

He furrowed his brow and seemed to be thinking, then said, "Normal. I may want to get another EKG for you. I'm not only worried about the baby; I'm worried about you too, Boo." He rested his hand on her thigh and rubbed it.

Keisha smiled. "You mean as my doctor? You worry about my delicate condition?"

"That too."

"Seriously, Anthony, you haven't even seen me in eight years, and you've been flirting with me from the moment I opened my eyes. I'm pretty sure you weren't thinking about me all the time over the last eight years. In fact, I'm going to bet you're not thinking about me when you're in bed with Loretta."

Anthony looked very serious. "You may not know how this works for some people, and you may be surprised to hear it, but I *especially* think of you when I'm with Loretta, or with anyone else for that matter. I'm always with you, Boo. You're always with me. Always have been."

Anthony sat on the bed and took Keisha's hand. "I apologized yesterday, and I need to apologize again so I'm sure you heard me. What I did back then, eight years ago, was incredibly stupid, despicable. I let my ego and my hormones take control of me. I did what I did because I could, even though I knew I shouldn't have. I ruined the one thing that really mattered to me, that ever mattered to me, my relationship with you. Maybe you don't believe me and maybe you think it's bullshit, but it's true. I loved you then and I love you now. No one, and I mean *no one*, compares to you. I'm not exactly a church-going guy, but I'm praising the Lord that he put us together again. I'm a much better man when I'm with you."

Keisha wanted to speak but she couldn't. Tears ran down her face. With her free hand, she grabbed a tissue from a small box next to the flower vase and wiped her eyes and nose. "Don't think I'm crying because of you. This is just my hormones talking. I don't know why I'm crying."

"I don't think so. I think you *do* want to be with me, too. You feel some crazy sense of loyalty to Josh because of the baby. Boo, you're not married to him." He held up her left hand and turned it. "See, no ring. You're free to come and go as you please. That says an awful lot."

"Unless you haven't noticed, Anthony, I'm about to have Josh's baby. No matter what, I'm together with him forever for that."

"Of course. I never said I wanted to exclude Josh from caring for his child. If we were together, he'd be welcome in our home anytime to change diapers and feed the baby." Anthony smiled a broad smile. "Especially to change poopy diapers."

Keisha smiled, then shook her head and closed her eyes. "Wait a minute, why are we having this conversation? You're talking as though we're together or will be getting together. That's not happening."

"I get it, Boo. It's a bit sudden. Very sudden. I think it was meant to be. You want a commitment. You want to be sure there's something more than just a bed at my house. You want the real thing. Keeping it one hundred."

Anthony slipped from the side of the bed onto the floor with his left knee touching the floor. He rested his elbow on his right knee. The traditional pose. He grasped her hand. "Keisha, I've thought about you every day for the past eight years. Will you make me the happiest man alive and marry me? I promise you; I've changed. I'll be devoted to you and the baby. I'll make a home that's happy for all of us. Make me happy, make us happy, and say yes."

Keisha pushed herself up in the bed and shook her head in disbelief. Anthony felt around in his white coat pocket and a moment later produced an engagement ring. The small diamond sparkled in the hospital light.

"I went home last night and got this ring for you. I've been saving it. You remember my Grandma? She *loved* you. She actually slapped me on the face when I told her we broke up. I didn't tell her why, but she knew it was my fault. When she died six years ago, she left me this ring, and her lawyer gave me a note from her saying to give it to my one true love. To you. I've kept it hidden in my dresser drawer ever since." He tried to slip it on her finger.

Keisha withdrew her hand before he proceeded too far and held her hand to her chest. "Just hold on. Wait a minute. I mean, I'm so confused.

I loved you so deeply back then, but that was a long time ago. My life is in Philly now, not here. I'm with Josh. I love him. I'm about to have his baby."

"But you're still not saying no," Anthony said, as he got off the floor and sat next to her on the bed again.

"I'm not . . . It's just too much."

Anthony took both of her hands in his and lightly squeezed them. Tears streamed down Keisha's face as Anthony leaned over and kissed her on her cheeks. She closed her eyes and didn't turn away from his next kiss on her lips. Gentle, soft, warm. He very gently brushed her ear with a fingertip. It was so intimate and loving. The same way he'd done it eight years ago. Chills raced up and down her spine.

She put her arms around him and hugged him tightly. Anthony's mouth was on hers and he continued to kiss her mouth, cheeks, and chin. Finally, he pulled his head back and smiled.

She opened her eyes and saw Josh standing in the doorway, looking as though he'd been punched in the face. Standing next to him was his boss, Diane, wearing the widest smile.

CHAPTER 32

JOSH

Florence, Kentucky, St. Elizabeth-Florence Hospital.

I rushed past the nurse's station on the third floor and found Keisha's door partially closed. I pushed my way through it. Keisha was in bed and a man in a long white lab coat and scrubs was standing over her. At first, I thought he was conducting some medical test. Then, I realized he wasn't. Their lips were fully locked, and they were embracing each other. For a moment, I tried to convince myself this was nothing more than an ill-timed 'see you later' kiss. But this was no casual peck on the cheek.

Her eyes were closed as she kissed the man. Her arms held him tightly. From the white coat and the stethoscope around his neck, it appeared he was a doctor. For a moment, I considered backing out of the room and knocking loudly. Then I thought, *What the hell? This is my fiancé*. In the end, I didn't have to make that decision, as Keisha's eyes fluttered open and she saw me. Immediately, her mouth disengaged from the doctor's, and she pushed him away.

"What the hell?" I said. "What's going on?"

"Josh, you're here. You made it."

The doctor stepped back and straightened his coat. He was in his early thirties and looked vaguely familiar, although I was sure I'd never met him before.

"So, this is Josh," he said with a broad smile. "We finally meet. I'm Anthony Sudor, Keisha's doctor."

He held out his hand, and I let it hang without offering mine in return.

"Well, I sure as hell hope that was some sort of medical procedure you were performing on my fiancé."

Keisha put her hand over her eyes and said, "Oh, Josh. I wish I could explain. This is Anthony, we were together, lived together, eight years ago. We talked about him, remember? You've seen some pictures of him."

"What the hell, Keisha? I've just driven almost thirty-six hours through the worst weather known to man and I find you sucking his tongue. This had better be good." I crossed my arms and leaned against the wall. "I'm waiting."

Keisha didn't say anything for a moment.

Finally, the doctor said, "There's no easy way to say this, Josh, but I'm back in Keisha's life. It was just good fortune that brought us together again. After all these years, I've let Keisha know my feelings for her have never changed. Her feelings for me seem to be as strong as mine, too. You may not want to hear this, but I've asked her to marry me, and I think she's going to say yes."

"What the fuck?" I said. "Anthony, aren't you the guy Keisha was living with who she walked in on humping another medical student? I've talked with Keisha about you, and she's told me the biggest mistake of her life was getting involved with you. Are you that screw-around-on-Keisha Anthony or some other dude?"

"That's a little harsh, friend," Anthony said. His face betrayed no emotions. "There was a lot going on back then and you don't know the context."

"Context? What exactly was the context of you having your dick inside another medical student? I know I wasn't smart enough to go to medical school, so maybe you can explain that to me in layman's terms?"

"Josh, Josh, calm down," Keisha said. "Nothing's happened." Keisha had sat up fully in the bed and she held out her hand to me. I didn't take it.

I looked at Diane, and she seemed to be completely amused by the situation. She stood in the back against the wall, taking it all in with a grin from ear to ear.

"We drove over one thousand miles, almost nonstop in a freakin' hurricane, to get here to be with you. Then I have to walk in on this?"

Keisha didn't say anything for a moment, then said, "And that motel that you and Diane stayed in together? Am I supposed to believe that nothing happened during your little sleepover?"

I was shouting. "That's right. Nothing happened. We needed a break from driving through the blizzard and the motel only had one room. Nothing happened."

Keisha looked at Diane and said, "Nothing happened? Is that what occurred, Diane? Nothing?"

I looked at Diane and wondered how she might spin this. "Josh slept on the floor. I was on the bed. He was a good boy and didn't do anything. You can believe him." Diane smirked.

I looked at Anthony and said, "Get the hell out of here. I don't want you in the same room as my fiancé and my baby. Leave!"

Anthony made himself tall and balled up his fists. "This is *my* hospital. You can't order me around in my hospital," he growled, his nostrils flaring.

Anthony was bigger than me, at least six feet tall with broad shoulders. I have no idea how or why I thought of this, maybe I saw it on some TV show or movie. I took a step toward him and lightly tugged on the lapels of his jacket, like I was fixing them. Then, I smoothed down the lapels. He looked at me like I was crazy. Then, I suddenly yanked back my right fist and drove it into his stomach. A solid sucker punch.

Anthony bent over gasping, and I stepped back. He was back up and hit me across the head with his forearm. I was able to block it mostly, but a moment later he made a perfect wrestling move and had me in a headlock. I used my elbows and pummeled him in the guts and chest as hard as I could.

I barely heard the screams from Keisha and Diane. "Stop it! Stop it! Please, just stop."

With one arm, Anthony had the crook of his elbow around my throat choking me, and with his other he restrained my arms so I couldn't elbow him. A young woman in scrubs, blond, pushed her way into the room and screamed at us.

"Dr. Sudor, I'm calling security!"

He pushed me away. Panting hard, in a deep voice he said, "Stop. Josh, stop." He held up his hands. "Maybe I deserved that, but just stop man, this is a hospital."

I'd fallen against Diane, and she grabbed me around my chest, holding me back and embracing me from behind. She forcefully restrained my arms. I was so angry. For a change, I wasn't angry at her. I looked at her and for a moment was surprised to read sympathy in her eyes. Maybe hopefulness. I don't know what it was.

"Are we done?" Anthony said.

I nodded. "For now."

Diane loosened her grip but still held me. Anthony gave me another questioning look. I nodded again and said, "Okay, I'm done."

Diane finally let go and rubbed her hands up and down my arms.

Anthony looked at the woman who'd walked into the room and said, "Loretta, cancel security. We're okay here. It was just a little misunderstanding."

"Are you sure, Dr. Sudor?"

"I'm sure. You can go. We're good."

She left the door wide open as she left. I could see her lurking just outside the room, cell phone in hand.

I crossed my arms and forced myself to breathe before I asked quietly, "Keisha, would you please tell me what's going on here?"

Keisha had pulled up her knees and hugged them. Tears streamed down her face. "I haven't seen or talked to Anthony in eight years. I had no idea he was a doctor here. We had a lot of time to talk over the past couple of days and he *did* ask me to marry him."

I looked at Anthony and did my very best to imitate Diane's death stare. I really did try to kill him. "And you said?"

"I *didn't* say yes."

"You didn't say no, either," Anthony said, barely suppressing a smile.

I could feel the blood beginning to boil again. "Last I checked," I said looking at Keisha, "You and I were engaged and the baby you're carrying is ours. I thought we were going home and heading straight to City Hall before the baby was born. I'm not sure why your doctor friend even felt he had an opening to ask you or why you didn't turn him down flat, when he did."

Keisha's face was wet with tears. Part of me wanted to reach out and hold her, comfort her. Part of me didn't want to see her again.

"It's complicated." Keisha rubbed her eyes with the back of her wrists, inhaled, and said, "But I've had enough time to think about it now, and I've reached a decision."

We all looked at her.

CHAPTER 33

JOSH

Florence, Kentucky, St. Elizabeth-Florence Hospital.

The wind blew a pale curtain of snow just beyond the insulated glass of Keisha's hospital window. Trees swayed slightly in the draught. This was not the violent wind of a few hours earlier but was now little more than a heavy breeze. The sound of trucks removing snow seeped through the window and the low murmur of a busy hospital were the only sounds in the room. Everyone's attention was on Keisha.

Diane had assumed a position against a wall where she could watch everything, like she was the audience watching some Greek tragedy play out. Loretta had positioned herself in the doorway. This was high drama. No one wanted to miss it.

"And?" I said.

Keisha reached toward Anthony, who took her hand. She squeezed it firmly, working her thumb on his fingers. "I love Anthony. I've loved you for a long time." She looked up at him. "You really hurt me eight years ago, and some of what you told me yesterday hurt me again. I appreciate your honesty, though, even if it came so late in the game. None of that diminished my love for you, a love I've never felt for any other man."

Anthony looked at her and smiled. He threw his head back and a triumphant smile formed on his face.

"But I'm sorry, I can't marry you. It's been too long and it's too complicated. I will always feel love for you, but you and I are the past. Josh and the baby are my life now."

Anthony's smile evaporated.

Keisha pulled him close and kissed him on the cheek. All the triumph in his face was gone. It was replaced by a contorted expression. He let go of her hand and stood back, his shoulders drooping.

Keisha turned and held out her hand to me. I took it, feeling victorious. We were finally going to do this. Get married and have our own little family.

"Josh, I love you so very deeply. I've never been with a man who I love and trust the way I love and trust you. You give me love, warmth, and loyalty. You'll be a great father to our baby. I know that. I can't wait to raise our child with you." She smiled at me, and I realized it was the same sad smile she wore when she looked at Anthony a moment earlier.

"At the same time, being totally honest, something's missing. As much as I love you, I don't think I'm *in* love with you. I've *never* been in love with you. The warmth I've always felt has never turned into a fire, and I need that. I'll probably kick myself for saying this, but I can't marry you either. It wouldn't be right for either of us."

It was my turn to feel the gut punch.

I looked around the room. Everyone seemed to have tears in their eyes. Even Diane was wet-eyed. Maybe it was an icicle melting.

"We'll just have to figure this out," Keisha said. I barely heard her speak.

We all stood still, saying nothing. Then, for the first time in a week, the sun came out. Its rays penetrated the window and hit the vase of flowers, which seemed to catch on fire.

CHAPTER 34

JOSH

Philadelphia, two months later.

It was 6 A.M. and the house on Wharton Street was dark and quiet. Keisha's light snores made their way down the stairs from the bedroom and reached me on the first floor. She was grabbing a few hours of the well-earned sleep of an exhausted mother. The sound made it seem like the house was breathing. Breathe in. Breathe out.

I held our little boy in my arms, swaddled in his blanket, and rocked him gently. He was a truly beautiful child. So peaceful. All potential. God-willing, he'd easily live to see the twenty-second century.

"So, that's why your mommy and daddy never got married, little man. I love her and she loves me, but marriage and living together don't seem to be in the cards. Don't worry about it, though. I'm here for you and so is Mommy. We'll both always be here for you."

The tiny baby had finished his bottle of Keisha's milk a while earlier and was now asleep. I lovingly rocked little Booker Jake Goldberg Jones. His name was a mouthful, but Keisha named him after one of her grandfathers and one of mine. She wanted him to have my last name, so she added it as an extra middle name.

I live around the corner on Eighth Street in a small apartment and spend many hours a day in what used to be our home. Our relationship is pretty much the same as it was before, except that I go to my apartment at night to sleep. Keisha's alone at home with the baby until I arrive in the morning with a couple of cups of coffee and bagels from the corner store. It's not ideal, not what I imagined, but it works.

Fortunately, my firm has a great paternity leave policy. Fathers get the same paid time off as mothers, which is ironic since women had to fight for decades for maternity leave. Then, a couple of years later in a nod toward equality, men got it with hardly a peep. As a result, I have a total of three months paid leave. After the thing with Diane, I knew I could never go back to the firm. I haven't told them yet. Why screw up this paternity leave situation? I'll tell them next month when I need to.

I've been talking with a good friend of mine, Mike Jacobs, who lives in Harrisburg. He's pretty sure he's going to quit his job as a lawyer with the state Department of Environmental Protection. As soon as my paternity leave is over, I'll quit the firm, and Mike and I are talking about forming a partnership: Jacobs & Goldberg or maybe Goldberg & Jacobs. We're going to practice environmental law and do it the correct way, representing the right kind of people and doing good. We'll set up in Philly and Harrisburg and plan to add Pittsburgh as soon as we find someone we'd enjoy practicing with. Then, we'll be a statewide environmental law firm, the first in Pennsylvania, practicing entirely out of our kitchens and bedrooms. Maybe we'll be able to afford real offices someday. Then again, maybe we won't want them.

There was a light tap at the front door, and I opened it quietly without bothering to look. It was Geoff, wearing his winter running gear and carrying two steaming cups of coffee.

"Here," he said and handed me the coffee as he stepped inside. "Let me hold that little guy."

He and Imani have five kids, so he's a real pro at this. Watching him hold Booker was like watching Derrick Henry of the Tennessee Titans carrying the football for a touchdown. Five kids will do that to you. Me? Not so much. I'm more like a tryout for a team of eight-year-olds in the Pop Warner league.

"Have you finished your run?"

"Yeah, I did three miles in the snow and ice this morning." Geoff and his family live about four blocks from the house and almost every morning he comes by with my second cup of the day.

"How's the rehab going?" Two days after he flew back from Nashville, he entered rehab, detoxed, then began an outpatient program for addiction treatment.

"Good," Geoff rocked Booker back and forth in a sophisticated dance move. "I'm sticking to a schedule—up at five, run, coffee with you and Booker, go to my new job, support meeting at 6 P.M., then family." He took a sip of coffee.

"Sounds busy."

"Yeah, but it's good. No time to get in trouble. I've been clean and sober for eight weeks." He rocked Booker with one hand and swigged coffee with the other. "How are you doing?" He'd lowered his voice to a whisper and nodded toward the stairs and Keisha's room. "Everything okay?"

"Alright, I guess. Keisha and I get along fine. It's almost like nothing's changed, except that I go to my apartment at night. We're friendly and Keisha's loving, even a little affectionate with me at times, but there's a line we don't cross. I doubt we'll ever be together again the way I'd like to be with her."

"You sure about that?"

"Hope springs eternal."

Geoff handed Booker back to me, then looked at the way I was holding him and repositioned my son in the crook of my arm. "Keep his head up, bra. Straighter. He's depending on you."

Like I said, he's the expert.

As Geoff started to head back to the front door, he asked, "How's Diane doing? Still mad at me for leaving?"

I smiled. "Brad Allen says she's been out of the office a lot lately. It turns out Niles Lindstrom, that Norwegian billionaire, was divorced and the two of them seem to be a match. He's twenty years older than her, but I don't think that matters. She got the chemical company business *and* the billionaire. A match made by the gods."

Geoff shook his head. "I'm sure they're perfect for each other."

I followed him to the door, and he nodded and left. I watched him walk down Wharton Street toward his house on the other side of Pat's Steaks.

I laid Booker in the little bassinet we kept him in when he was downstairs. I looked out the window toward the Italian Market, just a few steps away. It was already active with vendors and shoppers. Rocky probably ran right down this street in the movie. I always loved that old movie, a story about self-respect as much as anything else. Integrity. Hanging on. Never giving up, no matter how much you've been beaten down.

I have no regrets about any of my choices. I'd be happier if my situation with Keisha had turned out differently, but you have to let go of the things that aren't yours to keep. Sometimes you have to realize you have no alternative but to move on. I expect that before too long Keisha will find a guy and I'll find a woman. When that happens, it happens. For now, this is working out.

I'll always be there for my little boy.

EPILOGUE

ATLANTIC OCEAN

It was the end of the second day after the Weatherbird had crash-landed in the ocean. Somehow, Major Windy Logan and her co-pilot, Lieutenant Jazzy Turner, had managed a reasonably soft landing in a wild hurricane into a rolling sea with both starboard engines out.

From his cramped spot in the cargo area right behind the cockpit, Thor, the master sergeant, deployed a giant yellow life raft and everyone quickly scrambled into it. Less than three minutes later, the captain and her crew watched mutely as the crippled Lockheed disappeared beneath the waves. Whatever rescue beacon was on the Weatherbird was now fifteen thousand feet underwater. It would never be found.

First Lieutenant Mr. Spock Yang had broken an arm and Jazzy was still reeling from a concussion, but they had enough medical equipment and supplies on the raft to take care of themselves for now. Their greater challenge was not being swamped or capsized. Although the storm had passed by, the ocean continued rolling in big swells.

Within a few hours on the raft, everyone in the crew had vomited at least once. Some were worse off than others—Thor seemed to heave continually. More than discomfort or a mere nuisance, seassickness threatened dehydration, and the supply of fresh water was limited.

By the morning of the second day, though, the swells began to calm. Windy would have liked an IV bag full of saline for Thor, but she made sure he got more water than the others.

After crash-landing, the ocean and sky were almost the same color—gunmetal gray. As the raft continued to rise and fall, it was hard to see the horizon, making their ordeal even more unbearable. On the morning of the second day, the sea took on a bluish gray color as it calmed. The sky was a lighter shade of blue. Windy thought about her husband, Fred. Thinking about him holding her in his arms soothed her some. She thought about Maddy too, and promised herself that when she returned home, she was going to put in for some leave and take her daughter somewhere, just the two of them, so they could reconnect.

Later that morning, they watched as sharks began circling the raft, even bumping into it. Eventually, the damned fish seemed to lose interest and disappeared under the surface. Even so, everyone knew they'd be close by. It was bad enough being stuck on a life raft in the middle of the ocean. No one wanted to think about what might happen if the sharks decided they wanted a quick lunch.

It had been nearly two full days since the crash-landing. The raft contained emergency supplies of food, but apparently, the Air Force's expectation was that no one would be stuck on a raft for more than a few hours. Windy rationed the food and water, apportioning it so it would last three days. She wasn't sure what to do after that. The raft's radio beacon had not survived the crash-landing. All they could do was hope that a rescue team would locate them. They nibbled on their rations, told stories, and waited. And waited.

Late on the second day, the sun was setting low on the horizon. The storm clouds had moved off to the west, toward North America, but a thin layer of cirrus clouds replaced the blue sky they'd experienced for a few hours. A new storm appeared to be coming in. Spock estimated it was three to six hours away. As the sun began to set, the sky turned into a brilliant palette of orange and red.

Jazzy heard the noise first. Far in the distance. A droning sound. It was a Navy C-2 prop plane flying three or four miles south of them. The C-2 was the kind of plane deployed on an aircraft carrier. It was too far south to see them. Nevertheless, everyone waved their arms and lit smoke flares, and they shot a flare into the sky. Despite that, the plane flew on and disappeared over the horizon without slowing.

When the C-2 was out of sight, everyone sat again on the flimsy benches and no one said a thing. The only sound was the breeze and water lapping against the raft.

After many minutes, Windy said, "Hang in there, guys. At least it looks like they're still searching for us. Hopefully flying a grid pattern and coming back around."

"Yeah," Spock said. "Hopefully."

The sky continued to darken.

About twenty minutes later, they heard again the droning of a plane, this time closer. It was the Navy C-2 coming toward them, flying at maybe 5,000 feet. It flew several thousand feet south of them without slowing. Again, the crew went wild, waving and shooting off smoke flares and the flare gun.

The plane appeared to be flying away, until suddenly it banked, turned, and flew directly over them. The crew continued waving wildly as the plane flew by. Perhaps a quarter mile in the distance, it banked sharply and made another turn.

This time, it flew directly over them, even lower than before. The pilot tipped his wings, confirming he'd seen them. A small parachute appeared, descended toward them, then splashed into the ocean and floated a hundred feet away. They rowed the raft to it and pulled up emergency provisions including food, medical supplies, and a radio.

As soon as they opened the pack, Windy got on the radio. "This is Major Stacy Logan. Do you read me?"

"Lima Charlie, Major. Lieutenant Billy Hernandez here. It's good to hear from you, Major. Where've you been? The *George H.W. Bush* battle group has been looking for you for two days." He laughed. "I've got two rescue choppers and a fast cutter on their way. I'm going to circle around and keep you company until they get here."

"Roger that. We had ourselves a bad date with a bit of weather, Lieutenant."

"The weather dudes are saying that little storm developed into the biggest one ever recorded. None like it. Climate change and all of that. And that bastard is chewing its way right through the Midwest and it's still not done."

"Well, I hope it hasn't done too much damage."

"Other than to you?"

"Roger that."

"Hang on a sec. Just checking on the status of the choppers, Major," Hernandez said, then paused. "The rescue choppers are twenty minutes out. There's a couple of gallons of Gatorade in the rescue pack and plenty for you to eat. Let me know if you want me to drop anything else. Sit back and relax. The Navy has you covered."

"Hoo-ah! Roger that, Hernandez."

Windy threw her arms around the crew, and they all hugged. Hernandez tipped the wings of the plane as he flew in circles around them.

"Click your heels together, Jazzy. We're going home," She knuckled a tear. "We're going home."

ACKNOWLEDGMENTS

During my legal career, I was fortunate to have been associated with three law firms and knew literally hundreds if not thousands of lawyers. While some of the book's characters are lawyers and a mythical law firm is described, the characters are not intended to represent any particular lawyer and the law firm in the story is not representative of any firm. Like the rest of the story, the lawyers and law firm have been drawn wholly from my imagination. Any similarities are purely coincidental.

Special thanks go to a number of people who helped to make this book more accurate and a better read: Sherry Bennington (Lt. Colonel, U.S. Air Force, ret.), Marcia Buckingham (NASA, ret., flying and airplanes), and the members of the International Thriller Writers Critique Group "Epsilon": Dani M. Brown, N.J. Croft, Janet McClintock, Tina O'Hailey, Patricia Rosemoor, and, especially, Gregory Wilson Taylor (who gave the manuscript a significant edit). Thanks, also, to my beta readers for their helpful comments: Greta Pucci, Irwin Richman, and Eva Siegel. The story is much better as a result of everyone's efforts. My apologies if I left anyone out.

Special thanks are due to the people at Sunbury Press, Inc., who have worked hard to help produce the best possible book. Thanks to Lawrence Knorr and special thanks to my Sunbury editor, Taylor Berger-Knorr.

Thanks also to my "alpha" reader who offered helpful comments on every chapter, not to mention who provided aid and comfort to the author, my wife Gail.

Any mistakes, errors, or omissions are entirely mine.

You may have seen some references to *The Odyssey* by Homer. This was intentional and there are more than twenty. Here's an easy start... Paulie, the one-eyed tow truck driver, parallels *Polyphemus* the Cyclops. Another easy one—Dr. Anthony *Sudor* is Keisha's *suitor*. How many can you find?

If you enjoyed this book, I'd appreciate your five-star review on Amazon, Goodreads, and/or BarnesandNoble.com. These reviews only have to be two or three sentences long, but really do make a difference.

ABOUT THE AUTHOR

JOEL BURCAT is an award-winning author of three environmental legal thrillers: *Drink to Every Beast* (about illegal dumping of toxic waste), *Amid Rage* (about a coal mine permit battle), and *Strange Fire* (about a fracking dispute). He has received a number of awards, including the Gold Medal for environmental fiction from Readers' Favorite for *Strange Fire*, and as a Finalist in the Next Generation Indie Book Awards for *Amid Rage*. His latest novel, *Reap the Wind*, is an action/adventure thriller that is being published by Sunbury Press in February 2024. He has written numerous short stories.

Burcat's books are infused with realism developed over a forty plus year career as an environmental lawyer. Burcat worked in government as an Assistant Attorney General and in a private law practice. He was selected as the 2019 Lawyer of the Year in Environmental Litigation (for Central Pa.) by Best Lawyers in America. Among his numerous professional writings, he has edited two significant non-fiction books on environmental and energy law. He has retired from the practice of law and works full-time as a novelist.

He is an active member of the International Thriller Writers and PennWriters.